Also by John Lawe

Pure Evil

Deadly Consequences

Right To Kill

The Geocache Murders

by

John Lawe

The Kinler Mystery Series

The Geocache Murders

This is the first trade paperback edition July 2017.

Cover design by Design Point, Inc.

Cover photo by Sipris / CC BY 2.0

ISBN 13: 978-0-9972467-1-1 (sc)
ISBN 13: 978-0-9972467-2-8 (e)

Library of Congress Control Number: 2017912886
John Lawe, Mehama, OR

Printed in the United States of America

Available through Amazon.com, Kindle and other retail outlets.

Acknowledgements

I wish to acknowledge the contributions and encouragement I received from my Oregon Christian Writers' critique group. I am thankful to Linda Nathan, Logos Word Designs, LLC, for editing services and Design Point, Inc. for the cover design.

Chapter 1

"So, he didn't say why he wanted to see you?" Anna leaned back in her Adirondack chair.

"Nope." Matt sipped from his coffee and slid the mug back onto the table between their chairs. "Trudeau's always been secretive. We'll both find out when he gets here." A breeze rustled the boughs high above the porch as he caught the fragrance of the wood fire.

Smoke from the chimney drifted out over the canyon. Two weeks in their new house, Matt relished this first dry day to enjoy his outdoor cathedral. Pillars of old growth fir, sunlight filtered through the canopy of boughs, and a view across the canyon. Maybe he should pull the plug on his private eye business and spend all his time at home.

After an arsonist destroyed their first house, Anna redesigned this new one and supervised the construction. Months camped out with friends passed like years for him, but his wife loved every minute of every day.

"It's a shame Trudeau had to retire." She closed her eyes. "Sheriff's Office had been his life— has no family."

"After his stroke—no way they'd keep him as a detective." He studied the giant, cumulus clouds as they drifted above the ridge on the other side of the canyon. "Never be happy doing anything else."

Their border terriers scampered up the stairs as they returned from a romp. Sam filled Matt's lap and Eddy chose Anna's. "They're much happier in their own place." She stroked Eddy's ear.

"Me too." Matt reached across the table and squeezed her shoulder. "And you make this a happy place."

"That's nice." She offered her hand. "We've been blessed."

"True." He raised the carafe. "Can I warm your coffee?"

"I've had enough for now. I think I better go inside and fix a little lunch for you two. He'll probably be hungry by the time he gets here."

"I'm sure he'd like that." Matt poured himself a refill. "With his chain smoking, maybe we'll bring our food out here."

"He'd better have a jacket." She dislodged Eddy as she stood. "Not too warm out here." The dogs followed in her wake.

"Hey—typical spring day in the Pacific Northwest." Matt held the warm handmade mug against his chest as he leaned back. Eyes closed, he savored the coffee aroma.

As a senior detective at the Sheriff's Office, Pasqual Trudeau had become a legend in the state's law enforcement community and one of Matt's trusted allies. Trudeau, a straight shooter, had no time for bureaucratic nonsense. Often at odds with management, his success as an investigator had protected him from administrators with personal vendettas. Matt doubted he'd find another ally in law enforcement like Trudeau.

He opened his eyes at the sound of tires on gravel. An old white Ford pickup wasn't what he'd expected. Matt smiled as he recalled the old unwashed county car Trudeau had used. Another change his friend faced. He'd need to help the seasoned detective adapt to his life after the stroke.

Parked beside Matt's truck, Trudeau labored to steady himself on his good leg as he juggled a cane and shoulder bag. Matt leaned on the front porch rail and fought the urge to rush down and help his friend. But in a previous conversation, Trudeau had expressed his resentment toward those who doted over him. The challenge for Matt: learn the fine line between doting and acts of kindness.

"Welcome to my hideout." Matt felt a twinge of sadness as he watched his friend climb the stairs, one labored step at a time. The stroke had robbed Trudeau of the full use of his left leg, but he managed with the cane. "Anna's fixing us some lunch."

Trudeau paused and flashed his tobacco-stained teeth in a smile. "I'll be hungry after this climb." He waited a moment before he resumed. The strap on the soft-sided briefcase hung across his chest. The weight on the strap bore down and rumpled the shoulder of his jacket.

Matt greeted his friend at the top of the stairs. "Let me take the bag and you can use Anna's chair." The weight surprised him. "What you got in here—a bowling ball?"

Trudeau smiled. "Nah—a little project I brought to discuss with you." The smaller man settled into the chair.

Matt dropped the bag beside the chair, grabbed a spare mug for his guest, and poured. "Thought you were retired. What are you doing with a project?"

"Ha—Why should I slow down? You didn't stop after you retired from the FBI." Trudeau removed his glasses and grabbed a napkin from the table to wipe sweat from his face.

"I heard that." Anna joined them. "I think both of you should slow down."

Matt blocked the dogs from Trudeau's lap. "Stay down. Off."

"Sorry. I should've left them inside," Anna said.

"They're okay. I like dogs."

"Ignore them and they won't pester you," Matt said.

"I've always enjoyed it up here." Trudeau scanned the canyon view. "On the way up, I realized this is my first visit since the firebomb." He twisted in the chair to view the front of the house. "A lot like before, but no second floor."

"Anna decided one story would be better for when we reach the golden years."

"Still got those to climb." Trudeau nodded at the front steps.

"Yeah. But the way the house is built into the slope, our back door gives us a ground level entrance," Anna said.

"I let my designer figure all this out." Matt placed his arm around her shoulders. "We like the all cedar, post and beam look."

"As long as I included your river rock fireplace and chimney." She smiled and poked him in the ribs. "I came out to tell you guys I have some lunch ready."

"Guess we should go inside." Matt eyed the shoulder bag. "Be easier to spread out."

"Warmer too." Anna spun and re-entered the house.

"Do you need a smoke first?" Matt asked.

"Quit. I'm smoke free." Trudeau pushed himself out of the chair. "Doctor's orders."

"Ha—first time I've known you to take orders." Matt grabbed the heavy bag. "How—cold turkey?"

"Nah." He slapped his upper right arm. "Got one of them patches."

"Good for you. I've heard it's not easy when you've smoked a long time."

"Most of my life. I enjoyed it, but maybe not the best habit to have." He shrugged.

"Let's have some lunch and we can discuss your project." Matt hung the bag's strap on his shoulder. "What's in here?"

"A cold case."

"Murder? You're retired."

Trudeau locked eyes with Matt. "Not until this killer's retired."

Matt raised his eyebrows. "Guess I'll need to hear more."

Inside the entrance, Trudeau leaned on his cane as he scanned the room. "Kept the raised ceiling. Always liked the exposed beams."

Matt closed the door. "We enjoy the look and feel—we also kept the front half open, like before." He pointed ahead to the hallway that ended at the back door. "Without the stairs in the center, we had more space for a small office and larger pantry on the left, and the bath is in the same place on the right." Matt led Trudeau to the left where Anna had the dining table set. "You take the head of the table."

"I laid out stuff so you can make your own sandwich." Anna swept her hand over the platter of cold cuts, a cheese board, trimmings, and condiments. "Our lunches are pretty light fare."

"Wonderful. Looks like a bachelor's feast." Trudeau hung his cane on the back of the chair and eased onto the seat. "Did you make the bread?"

Anna smiled as she nodded toward the back of the house. "I've got some cookies in the oven now."

"Whatever they are—smells good."

"She's always baking something," Matt said. "That's why I became a runner—burn off the calories."

"I better not hang around here much," Trudeau said. "Since I quit smoking, I've gained weight."

"You look healthier with a few more pounds," Matt said.

"This bum leg don't make me so healthy." He slapped his left thigh.

"You guys start. I'll finish my cookies." Anna moved around and behind the long granite-topped counter between the dining area and the kitchen.

Matt returned thanks before he passed bread to his guest. "Tell me about this case. Are you doing this for the Sheriff's Office?"

"No way—case went cold." Trudeau reached for the strap on his soft-sided case to hoist it into his lap. "Something happened a week or so before I had my stroke." He fished inside a pocket and passed some folded papers to Matt.

"A copy of a picture from a newspaper?" Matt gave a puzzled look.

"Baby's Grave—it's a historical site in the Ochoco National Forest. That's a copy of a published picture, but I don't know what publication it's from."

Trudeau assembled his sandwich with white bread, salami, and slices of pepper jack cheese.

"No butter, mustard, lettuce? Anything?" Matt peered over his glasses at his friend.

"Nah. I never took time before." He shrugged. "Hard to break old habits."

Matt strained to read. "Fine print under the picture … in the eighteen hundreds, a wagon train of settlers buried an unnamed baby here. Folks found the marker and made this memorial." He flipped to the second page. "What kinda poem is this? It's handwritten.

> 'Seven years. Tick, tick, tick.
> Baby, Baby way too long. Tick, tick, tick.'

"What are these blotches?" Matt asked.

"I sent the original to the lab—canine blood."

"And this is your cold case?"

"No. But there's a connection—nobody else agrees with me."

Matt fixed his sandwich and as the two men ate, he surfed the Internet with his laptop to locate the memorial in the Ochoco Forest.

"What can you tell me about your cold case?" Matt wiped his mouth with a napkin.

"Maybe I'm too close to this one, but it haunts me. If it's the last thing I do, I'll solve this murder." Trudeau pulled a folder stuffed with papers out of his case.

Matt made room on the table for them to work.

"Mari Davies was killed up near Silver Creek Falls almost ten years ago." He handed Matt a short stack of papers held together with a spring clip. "I don't get around so well. I'd like you to help me. Read those reports—think it over."

Anna arrived with fresh coffee and a plate of molasses cookies. "What happened to her?" she asked.

"She was hiking alone. Someone jumped her and strangled her. A couple of mountain bikers heard her screams and rode to help, but they were too late. They found her body sprawled on the trail. The killer was gone."

Matt raised a document from the stack. "This says they found her body north of Shellburg Falls—not Silver Creek?"

"Correct," Trudeau said. "Found near the south edge of the Silver Creek State Park. She'd hiked up through Shellburg, but access to the crime scene was easier through Silver Creek. So—created some confusion at first."

"Shellburg Falls isn't as well known," Matt said.

"These unsolved cases must haunt everyone involved—so sad," Anna said.

"How does this picture with the poem and animal blood tie in?" Matt asked.

"That's the strange part." Trudeau plucked a cookie from the plate. "Umm. Still warm." He smiled. "Mari died about ten years ago. I checked with the Sheriff over in Harney County where this monument is located. They had a white female killed near Baby's Grave three years ago."

"They solve it?" Matt asked.

"They think so, but I don't."

"If it's in a national forest, how'd the Sheriff get jurisdiction?"

"Matt, stop with the questions and listen." Trudeau slapped his sandwich on the plate. "The Sheriff had the case, all I know. Okay?"

"Sorry," Matt said.

"The Sheriff's suspect in Harney died." Trudeau fixed his eyes on Matt. "This picture means the killer wants us to know he's the one who did them both."

"Wants to get caught, bragging—or toying with investigators," Matt said.

"Toying. All these creeps think they're smarter than anyone else. It's a rare killer who provokes or taunts police. This guy is one who does."

"Fill in the blanks on why you think you're dealing with the same killer."

"Like I said, Mari happened around ten years ago." Trudeau tapped the picture of the grave. "Seven years after Mari, a dead woman is found near here—and then three years later this message shows up close to where we found Mari."

Anna tugged the pages from under Trudeau's hand and read. "This guy's a sicko. How'd you get this picture?"

"From a retired cop. He took his grandkids geocaching up at Shellburg Falls. They found a cache, opened the ammo can, and this picture was inside. Gramps figured we needed to see it."

"No accident—this guy definitely wanted someone to find that poem," Matt said.

Trudeau nodded. "Mari's body had been found within fifty feet of the site. Both she and this other victim were geocachers. Both were out alone when they were killed."

"Geocachers?" Anna flashed a puzzled expression.

Matt poured refills of coffee as he spoke. "It's a game—hobby. You get map coordinates off the Internet for a cache hidden somewhere. Then you use a GPS receiver or a phone app to find the treasure, which is usually inexpensive stuff—knick-knacks. Most have a log book inside for you to record the find. If you take a trinket, you're supposed to replace it with something else."

"Who hides these caches?" Anna asked.

"Anybody can. They just register the location on one of the geocache websites."

"Oh, I think our friends Herb and Phyllis do that."

"Think you're dealing with a serial killer?" Matt asked.

"Not sure, but that's the way I'm leaning," Trudeau said. "But with only two victims, it's too early to call."

"I'd think this would be a major case—all hands on deck."

"Not yet." Trudeau drank from his coffee. "With me out the door, Mari would go back on the shelf and Baby's Grave wouldn't be re-opened."

"Why do you say that?" Anna asked.

"Just what will happen. I'm not criticizing anyone. Mari was Eurasian. She'd survived an abusive marriage. Her former husband's in the pen for a different murder. Her father's dead, but I still talk to her mother. Probably one reason I can't let go—sweet and gentle soul." Trudeau grabbed another cookie. "She has me over for a Vietnamese meal about once a year. Good cook."

"How about Harney County? Aren't they interested?" Matt asked.

"The detective on that case figured he'd solved his murder. Closed—but nobody ever charged."

"Sounds unusual."

Trudeau nodded as he studied the dark coffee in his mug. "They had a male suspect. Physical size of a healthy eighteen-year-old, but he had the mental capacity of a twelve-year-old."

"And they were able to pin this on him?" Matt tapped the picture.

"The boy discovered the body. The detective zeroed in on him. Never got enough to charge him, but the detective hounded him for over a year until the kid hung himself. Case closed—detective's retired."

"Oh, what a tragic story—if he didn't do it," Anna said.

"And they won't re-open on this?" Matt asked.

"You'll have to read those reports," Trudeau said. "There are big differences in the murders and the crime scenes. Those and seven years apart make the link a hard sell."

"But you're convinced the same man did both," Matt said.

"Can't prove it. But I got a gut feeling."

Chapter 2

The dogs bolted from the master bedroom ahead of Anna. "You get any sleep?" She ran fingers through her hair and fluffed the dark curls as she moved across the living room.

"Not much." Matt jerked the lever to raise the back on his recliner to accept his morning kiss.

"After you'd read parts of those reports to me, I didn't sleep much either."

"I'm sorry. Should've spared you."

"No. I want to know what you're getting yourself into. Want more coffee?"

"Please. I just made a fresh pot."

"I'll get you a refill, if you'll let the boys out."

Matt yawned on his way to the front door. The dogs rushed outside and he followed as far as the porch. The early morning air chilled his face and hands as he inhaled the fragrance of the evergreen forest. A layer of fog hung over the canyon floor. His thoughts lingered on the reports he'd read. Murder happened all too often and seldom made sense to him. Mari had turned her unhappy life around only to meet her death. He shook his head at the tragic irony as he followed the dogs back into the house.

Legs curled under her, Anna waited on the couch. He stirred what remained of the fire, grabbed a chunk of fir and tossed it on the enlivened coals. Sparks shot up the chimney as the pleasant scent of the wood fire filled the room. "I'm not sure I want to get tangled up in a long drawn out murder investigation." Matt returned to his recliner.

"Oh, Matt. You have to help him."

"Maybe I can do little projects for him." Matt gripped the mug between his hands. "I don't want to spend years on a murder investigation. He's lived with this case for ten years, Anna."

"It's your call." She straightened her legs to make room for the mutts to settle beside her. "But he's disabled, Matt. He's going to need someone."

"Don't say that in front of him."

"Never." She grabbed the afghan from the back of the couch and covered her lower legs. "If you helped him, it'd be a chance to talk with him about the Lord."

"Yeah. I've tried over the years, but he's been pretty cool to the subject."

"It's hard to understand why something that makes so much sense to us is rejected by others— ridiculed and scoffed at."

"Unless God removes their blinders, that's the way it'll always be."

"Oh, I know." Anna sipped from her coffee mug. "I'm going to pray the Lord will open his mind and heart."

"I told him to haul his files over to our office today—eleven o'clock. We'll sit down and see what he has. With Allen on vacation, there'll be room to spread out."

"Good idea. Allen and Beth will be gone another week. She sent me a text from Idaho."

"I'm not sure how far Trudeau will get on this. If he doesn't realize it yet, he will. When you're out of law enforcement, a lot of information and databases are off limits. We'll only have access to information available to the general public. Makes the investigation a lot harder—and slower."

"I had the impression he had a copy of the Baby's Grave file."

"When I asked him, he was a little coy in his answer. But, if they closed the case as being solved, the records might be available through a public record request. An unsolved case—no way."

"You've read his stuff. Were the murders done by the same man?"

"There aren't a lot of similarities, but the summary he pirated from the Harney County case may not be complete." Matt leaned his head back and recited from memory. "Victims were female geocachers, death by asphyxiation and killed in remote areas."

"You're right. Not much."

"Gets thinner when you add in the differences. The first one, Mari, was mixed race, fully clothed— lots of defensive wounds and strangled with a coarse material or rope. The white woman in Harney had been assaulted and strangled with a thin wire—cut across the front of her neck. Left her naked."

"Wire? Killer must've been prepared."

"Killers who use wire want to silence the victim quick and avoid any struggle."

"Oh—gives me chills." Anna shuddered. "No wonder you didn't sleep."

"Not pleasant to think about," Matt said. "Of course, there are the other obvious differences. Murders occurred on opposite sides of the Cascade Mountains and seven years apart."

"You've about talked me out of thinking they're related."

"Me too, except for several things. There's the poem on the picture, the geocache angle and Trudeau's gut feeling."

◆◆◆

Matt drove into the parking lot, passed in front of the closed garage doors on the unused car repair bays, and parked in Allen's reserved space. Trudeau, in his truck, waited in Matt's reserved spot. Matt remembered how honored he had been when Allen allowed him the space next to the entrance. Now he wondered if he'd been tricked.

Not like they had a lot of visitors. Before Matt came along, Allen Mann had purchased this commercial property, which had been used as an auto repair business. The two white single-story buildings were arranged in a hockey stick pattern. The long rectangular one with the vacant bays, Allen used for storage. The smaller square building in front of Matt served as their office. They had no signage because they'd never settled on a name for their informal business arrangement as private investigators.

You're retired. That's a hobby—a business makes money. Anna's words flashed in his mind as he removed the ignition key. She never missed an opportunity to tease him. He loved that about her. She kept him anchored in the realistic and practical. His fond thoughts of her tugged a slight smile as he headed for the entrance.

Trudeau leaned on his cane with the heavy soft-sided bag slung on his shoulder.

"Been waiting long?" Matt asked as he unlocked the door.

"No. There's a box on the passenger seat. If you don't mind." Trudeau shuffled into the office.

The sides of the book box bulged. Matt wondered how Trudeau carried the heavy carton by himself. "You can use Allen's desk." Matt carried his bag and the carton to his desk against the back wall.

The previous owner had divided the room with a service counter. One side had been a customer lounge and the other a business office. With the counter removed, they furnished the single room with a couple of file cabinets, a work table, and two gray metal desks. All purchased from the State's surplus property warehouse. A coffeemaker, desktop computer, and the printer/copier received heavy use.

Matt scooted the long work table midway between his and Allen's desk. "We can unload your box here. There'll be room to spread everything out."

With his good leg, Trudeau propelled the wheeled desk chair over to the table. While Matt prepared the coffeemaker, the detective unpacked his files.

"This is all on the Shellburg Falls murder?" Matt asked.

"My work copies—all the stuff I worked on at home." Trudeau slapped his hand on a thick envelope. "This is what I got on the Baby's Grave case."

"I thought you didn't have that."

"Didn't, but I do now." He shoved the package toward Matt. "Day before my stroke, I asked a lady in the Harney Sheriff's Office to send me what they could. She sent an email summary because it'd take some time to get the file out of their archives. I gave her my name and personal post office box number. I used that when I didn't want things to get delayed in the mail room downtown. Glad I did—arrived this morning."

Matt flipped through the papers. "We got reports, autopsy, and crime scene photos."

"Here." Trudeau tossed another envelope in front of Matt. "Might help to tape the crime scene photos from our two cases side by side on the back wall."

After Matt poured coffee, he grabbed a roll of tape and arranged the photographs on the wall beside his desk. He paused to study one of the pictures. "Ohhh—ouch. She lost an earring in the struggle."

"Mari?" Trudeau peered over his glasses.

"Yeah. The guy must've stripped her jewelry off, earrings, necklace, watch."

"No. The earring was ripped off. You can see the tear on the ear lobe," Matt said.

"She put up a heck of a fight. You'll see the defensive wounds on her hands and arms."

"Did they get any DNA?"

"They got a partial DNA profile from scrapings under her fingernails. Unknown male contributor. But not enough to check any national database."

"Too bad." Matt flipped through several photos. "The victim at Baby's Grave doesn't have any jewelry either. Wait—here's a close up shot of one of those colored silicon wrist bands people wear." He read aloud a note on the back of the photo. "From victim's right wrist." Matt rummaged in his desk and found the magnifying glass. "Dirty, but it might've been a lavender or purple color."

"Wonder why they took the band off before they photographed the body at the crime scene?" Trudeau asked.

"Maybe they thought it'd help identify her." He examined the photo with the glass. "There's lettering on the band. I can make out L-O-V."

"Seems odd." Trudeau shot Matt a puzzled expression. "Stripped his victim, but left a dirty silicon band on her wrist. I missed that when I hurried through the papers the first time."

"He took the time to pose his victim." Matt added the picture to his display. "Arms out at forty-five degrees, legs spread."

"In that second crime scene diagram—" Trudeau propped his elbow on the table and aimed his finger at the photograph "—he positioned her with the head toward the east."

"Second crime scene?"

"You'll see. She had been killed near a geocache site off the highway near Riley. Probably near where they found her pickup. The killer moved the body and posed her near the Baby's Grave monument."

"That's why the Sheriff had jurisdiction. Homicide happened in the county and the killer dumped the body in the national forest."

"That'd make sense," Trudeau said.

"Her head pointed east? What's that mean?" Matt moved back from the display to reach for his coffee cup.

"Don't know. Maybe nothing. Just what the sketch has."

"Here's the ammo can from the geocache." Matt read the notation on the back of the photo aloud. "Lid found open." He taped the picture in place. "This shows the cache's log book inside."

"That's how they ID'd the victim," Trudeau said. "She'd made a log entry with her name, Judith Rhime."

"As I put these up—" Matt moved back to survey the two sets of photographs "—I don't find a lot of similarities. You sure it's the same guy?"

"No—not a hundred percent."

"Good thing they got a partial DNA from under Mari's fingernails," Matt said. "DNA from any suspects could be compared in her case. Get anything from Baby's Grave?"

"The lab found nothing."

"Going to take a lot of work to link the two, if they are." Matt rolled his chair to the table across from his friend.

"Something's bugging me about that wrist band." Trudeau grabbed his cell phone. "I'll call Mari's mom." He swiped, tapped and eyed the display on the wall as he waited.

"Linh, Trudeau here."

Matt drank coffee as he eavesdropped on Trudeau's conversation with Mari's mother. His interest peaked when the small talk ended.

"You don't remember the name … unhuh … some support group for abused women? Ahh." He raised his eyebrows as he glanced across the table. "She always wore one? I thought I remembered you telling me a band or bracelet was missing when we found her. Yes—has been a long time."

Matt leaned forward as he waited.

Trudeau clenched a fist and stuck his thumb in the air. "Purple? You do? Could you check? I'll wait." He pressed his hand over the phone's microphone and whispered, "Mari always wore a wristband and Linh thinks she kept the extras with other keepsakes."

After a moment, Trudeau said, "You do. Linh, this is important. Could I have one of those for some lab tests? Okay. Faded? What does it say? 'Love shouldn't hurt'." His eyes locked on Matt's. "Do the others have the same thing? Ah ha … I'm going to send my helper over to pick one of those up." He ended the call with a broad smile.

"Helper? I've been promoted," Matt said.

"Each one has the same saying pressed into the band."

"So, Mari's band may have ended up on the Harney County victim?"

"What are the odds something taken from her shows up seven years later on this Rhime woman?" Trudeau asked.

"Slim."

"Very."

Chapter 3

"I'm stuffed." Matt tossed the napkin on his dinner plate and scooted the chair back. "My head's stuffed too." He clamped his head between his hands. "Trudeau had a pile of information for me to absorb."

"Did you guys get through everything?" Anna asked.

"Only an introduction for me, but he's lived with the Shellburg case for years."

"You're certain the same guy did both now?" She refreshed his coffee.

"To quote Trudeau, 'ninety-nine percent'." He added half and half. "When I dropped by to get the wrist band, her mom asked, 'You find who killed my Mari?' I told her we would."

"She's waited ten years, Matt. You shouldn't raise her hopes."

"I had to give her some encouragement. Her eyes … pled for something to keep her going."

"Where do you go from here?" Anna collected dishes and carried them into the kitchen.

Matt gulped the last of his coffee and toted cups and utensils to the sink. "Trudeau's going to ask his replacement to have the Harney Sheriff's Office send the wrist band from their case to the State lab. Then he'll give the lab the one I just got. Thinks he can get them to test to see how much they're alike."

"It's been a good number of years." She opened the dishwasher. "Will the sheriff over there still have their evidence?"

"Three years—should still have the wrist band. I hope." He loaded the dirty dishes.

"I didn't understand what you meant when you said there may be more murders," Anna said.

"Before the stroke, Trudeau sent a request to all law enforcement agencies in Oregon, Washington and Idaho. He described the two murders and asked for information on any similar murders, solved or unsolved."

"Get any responses?"

"Not before he ended up in the hospital. But one of the detectives visited him and said they had received information on several homicides to analyze."

"And he can't get that list?"

"Nope—not officially. That's the problem he's going to have."

"You'll be doing a lot of waiting around if nobody will tell you guys anything."

"Maybe not. Trudeau has a lot of friends around and he'll get some information from his contacts. But he wants me to do the door knocking and old-fashion grunt work."

"Does this mean you'll be gone a lot?"

"Some."

"Matt, we've talked about this. I don't like you being out of town. We had too many years of that in the FBI."

"I understand, but you told me I should help. Look—if I travel, maybe you can come with me."

She sighed. "We'll have to wait and see." Anna faced the counter on the wall that separated the kitchen from the pantry and office. She lifted the mixer from a lower cupboard and placed it on the granite surface. "I need to make some brownies before Herb and Phyllis get here."

"I'll gather my bag and work papers and get them out of sight. There're a couple things I'd like to read. Call me if you need some help?"

"Go ahead."

Matt closed the office door and moved from the back hall into their living room. The wood in the fireplace had burned down. He tossed a couple of chunks on the coals. Moments later tongues of flame flickered and danced behind the glass fireplace screen. He warmed his hands as he watched the fire.

His past life as an FBI agent had created occasional tension in their relationship. Secrets he couldn't share, stress he couldn't explain, and dangers his wife didn't need to know. Anna had been his anchor. She tolerated the long hours he was away and remained rock steady in her support.

After he retired and became a licensed private investigator, he tried to select cases he could work without nights away from home. If he had to travel, the subject awakened the resentment Anna had tucked away.

To help Trudeau, the requirement to travel into the high desert of Central Oregon loomed in his future. Matt's initial reaction to the prospect had been to tell his friend he had no time for an old homicide case. But Trudeau had never turned him down and now the disabled detective needed help. His friend trusted Matt enough to ask. He couldn't say no.

Settled in the recliner and adjusted at an angle to read, Matt began the first of two reports on interviews of the eighteen-year-old suspect in the

Baby's Grave murder. The sound of Anna's cell phone intruded, but he blocked out her conversation. The report stirred a sadness in his heart for the simple boy swept up and destroyed by circumstances he didn't comprehend. *Why did the kid remove that wrist band from her arm? No wonder the detective zeroed in on him as a prime suspect.*

"Matt, they're on the way. Give me a hand?"

He stashed his reports under the table beside the recliner and hurried into the kitchen. "Brownies smell good." He gave her a light hug from behind as she worked at the sink.

Hands in soapy water, Anna placed the back of her head against his chest. "I've got to finish these— you can make a fresh coffee smell and set the table."

His wife had met Phyllis Jenkins several years ago in Lyons. Anna had a knack for meeting strangers and parting friends. Phyllis and her husband owned a llama farm near the Santiam highway.

Herb Jenkins had owned a tree felling business until he lost his left eye and forearm in an accident— an accident on Herb's part when he made the first cut to fell a tree. Collateral damage for the environmentalist, who had hammered the railroad spike into the tree.

The dogs danced at the door before Matt heard the rumble of the diesel engine. He opened the front door and waited on the porch for their guests.

The dually one-ton truck rode high off the ground. He smiled as Sam and Eddy scampered under the parked truck and circled the big knobby tires. First to climb down, Phyllis flipped her long gray ponytail back over her shoulder and flashed that perpetual smile as she waved. Herb dropped to the ground on the driver's side. Not a tall man, stout and muscled, his stride and movement were those of a woodsman. His denim trousers hung on red suspenders. The pant legs, frayed without a hem, had been shortened to hit the laced leather boots above the ankle.

Matt greeted them at the top of the stairs and Phyllis continued into the house.

"Anna tells me you have a new gig," Matt said.

"Don't know about gigs." Herb removed his Seattle Mariners' cap and pinched the bill while he brushed the palm of his only hand over his head. "I started a new felling business."

"Great. Explains your wardrobe."

"Yeah. Well, just got home from a job. I didn't have time to change." Herb glanced down at his boots.

"Hey, we're not too formal here." Matt slapped him on a shoulder. "You've been around us enough to know that."

"I did wash my hand and face." Herb smiled.

"Tell me about your work."

"Rounded up several young bucks who want to learn the business. When I hear of a job, I'll bid on it. Then call my guys and supervise everything. Don't make a lot, but gets me out in the timber again." He gazed into the fir boughs high above the house.

"Heard the doc gave you a good report," Matt said.

"Yep." He replaced his cap. "Cancer free … second year now."

"God has been kind to you." Matt placed a hand on the porch rail. "He knows how much you've been through."

Herb reached across his chest to brush a finger over the scarring around his glass eye. "I've had lots of good too. Like you said, be thankful for whatever comes my way … good or bad."

"Did I say that?"

"Close to it."

"I notice you've more gray in your hair."

Herb grinned. "Runs in the family."

"Ha, this runs in my family." Matt ran a hand over his sparse hair. "We lose it before gray sets in."

Herb joined Matt. "Canyon gets quiet as the sun goes down."

"Sometimes I think I could hear a pin drop." Matt leaned to rest his forearms on the handrail.

"You never talk much about your PI work. Anything interesting?"

"Habit I guess. Never talked out-of-school when I worked for the FBI." Matt gazed down into the darkness over the canyon floor. "A retired detective friend has asked me to help with an unsolved murder. He can't let it go."

"Happen around here?"

"Shellburg Falls on the southern edge of Silver Creek Park—about ten years ago."

"I wouldn't remember."

"Tragic. Has one unusual twist. The victim had been at a geocache site."

"Geocache! You could ask Phyllis about geocaching. She's always dragging me along on her hunts."

"Maybe I'll tag along and learn something." Matt pushed off the rail. "It's cooled down, let's go inside."

The men served themselves at the dining table and carried their dessert into the living room to join the ladies.

"You guys almost missed out—gabbing so long out there." Anna relaxed on one end of the couch, Phyllis on the other.

"Glad you saved some for us." Matt settled into his recliner as Herb headed for the easy chair near the fireplace.

"We finished our girl talk," Anna said. "What kept you?"

"Boy talk," Matt said.

"Good brownie, Mrs. K." Herb raised his plate in a salute.

"How's the coffee?" Matt smiled.

"Matt—stop it," Anna said. "Quit trying to be cute."

"Good, Mr. K." Herb smiled again as he set his plate aside and drank. "Phil, Matt's got a murder case that involves geocaching."

Phyllis uncrossed her legs and leaned forward. "Can you talk about it?"

A gulp of coffee and Matt placed his mug on the side table. "A little." He blotted his lips with a napkin. "Happened nearly ten years ago." He stuck with information that had been in the newspapers on the Shellburg murder.

"Do you think geocaching had anything to do with the murder?"

"Too soon to tell."

"It's been ten years," Phyllis said. "You'd think they'd know by now."

"Just can't be sure." Matt avoided any mention of the Harney County murder. No need to start a firestorm of rumors about a serial killer on the loose. "Herb says you guys hunt for caches."

Her freckled face brightened and the smile wrinkles returned. "We're in a small group. We go off-road on longer treks to find treasures."

"How's all that work?" Matt asked.

"We use several websites that have caches registered for locations in Oregon."

"Have you planted any?"

"Oh, yes. It's fun. We put little things in them and stuff in riddles or poems. There are log books in each cache. People who find them write their names or nicknames—different things. I like to read the entries. Other people put fun stuff on the websites too. Our group holds cookouts and we swap stories."

"A lot of people do their hunts in towns, city parks or shopping malls," Herb said.

"Our group has a bunch of caches hidden along the highway all the way to the summit in Santiam Pass," Phyllis said. "We plan to cover more of the state."

"Been up Monument Peak, to Marion Lake, Breitenbush, even on part of the Pacific Crest Trail," Herb said.

"It's especially fun for me." Phyllis said. "I usually take one or two of my llamas. Load them up to carry our lunch and drinks and they get some exercise."

"We camp out sometimes," Herb said.

"If you really want a challenge, there're some caches you can find and inside there's a clue for another cache, and another, and another," Phyllis said. "We've done a few of those."

"And all you need is one of those GPS receivers?" Anna asked.

"A good map helps because the GPS only gives you directions 'as the crow flies'. Doesn't warn you of lakes, rivers, mountains, cliffs, things like that."

"Matt, someone's here. I think I heard a car out front," Anna said.

He rose and hurried to the window. "Sheriff's patrol rig. Might be Deb." Matt moved to the door. "I'll see what's up."

On the porch, Matt waited. The interior lights in the black SUV shined on Deputy Deborah Abbott as she opened the door.

Abbott had been one of the first friendships he had formed with the department's patrol deputies. Since she worked this end of the county, her arrival didn't raise concern. After all, Deborah dated Anna's second cousin, who lived five miles away. They called him their nephew because he was much younger and nephew didn't require an explanation of the family tree. Trent lived with his grandmother, Anna's elderly aunt. A big strapping former SEAL, Trent had suffered a head injury and had battled to regain his ability to remember ordinary things.

"What brings my favorite deputy up here?"

Deborah trudged up the stairs. "Got some bad news, Matt." She stood with her thumbs on her belt. The body armor made her appear larger. "Trudeau. He's had another stroke."

"No." Matt dropped his shoulders and hung his head. He exhaled a sigh and groaned, "He doesn't need this. How is he?"

She shrugged. "Sorry, but I wanted to tell you in person." She brushed her short dark hair away and pressed on her earpiece to listen. "Not for me."

"Where is he?"

"He's alive. They took him to Salem Hospital. A neighbor found him in his truck and called 9-1-1."

"He has no family." Matt wiped a hand across his mouth and chin. "Anybody with him?"

Again, she shrugged. "I told you all I know. He's one of the good guys."

"He is."

Chapter 4

"Why are you tho quiet my little flower? You don't laugh at how I talk."

Since early childhood, Sydney Smythe had been tormented and teased about his lisp. Troubles over how he pronounced the "S" sound made him a social recluse. The onset of severe teenage acne drove him into a self-imposed ostracism. He entered adulthood with profound physical and emotional scars.

Sydney tapped the key to display the next naked image in his laptop slide show. He leaned forward with his marred face closer to the screen. "And you my lovely—you don't turn away from me now, do you?" His finger paused above the key as fantasies replayed in his demented mind.

He tapped again. "Ah, yeth. You don't mock me like all the others."

"Sydney! Who is down there with you?"

"Nobody, Mother." He cringed at the sound of her voice. The basement provided refuge from her prying eyes, but her whiny, nasal voice ruined the moment. The carpeted, windowless room dampened sounds and gave him privacy. He closed his picture file and logged off.

Swollen and painful joints from rheumatoid arthritis had disabled his mother for years. She used pills and inactivity to control her pain. A powered scooter had become her latest indulgence.

"Sydney?" Her call echoed down the stairs. "Angel's on the phone."

"Okay, Mother." He had no interest in friendships, but he stayed in touch with his former cellmate. Both gamers, they had competed on prison computers for hours as they served their time in Lompoc. Prohibited from computer use by his probation officer, Sydney could only read about the new products. He reached for the phone.

"I got a new game, Dude," Angel said.

"Hey, tell me about it." Sydney fought to keep the resentment from his voice. One day he'd be off probation. Then, he could compete with Angel and other faceless gamers. He listened and engaged in small talk until his mother interrupted.

"Sydney, I need help with dinner."

"Coming, Mother." He hung up and stowed the computer behind the bookcase. A precaution he took in case his probation officer happened to pay another surprise visit.

Almost forty, Sydney had spent five years in a federal prison for hacking into a national defense agency's computer system. He'd been told because of the nature of his crime they'd deny him the use of computers. Sydney had bristled when the probation officer included GPS receivers, but he lost his appeal for access. One more thing to hide.

He tramped up the stairs as his mother glared down from her motorized perch. "I told you I'd help, Mother. Didn't you believe me?"

"I can't believe anything you say, Sydney Smythe." She spun the scooter and propelled herself into the kitchen. "We need to do dinner before you leave for work."

He stopped at the pantry and selected two cans of bean and bacon soup. A box of crackers secured between his paunch and arm completed the menu. "If you set the table, I'll do the thoup."

"What kind?"

"Bean. Got crackers too."

"I thought you said you got tired of bean soup in prison."

"This ain't prison food—store bought." He opened the cans and dumped the contents into a sauce pan. The electric stove was older than Sydney, but half the age of their house. Brown linoleum covered the floor and mustard colored laminate topped the counters under dark prefab cabinets mounted on the wall.

"I'd like some salad or something, Sydney."

The whiney voice grated. "How 'bout I chop thome lettuce and find a bottle of dreththing, okay?" He'd endured her self-pity all of his life. Probably caused by his father's death in a car accident, but he'd been too young to remember. He didn't pity her, he despised her weakness.

Wanda Smythe, parked at the edge of the red laminate table, transferred the dishes and utensils from her lap onto the table. "I hope you can find steady work with this temp agency." She grimaced as she moved from the scooter to a chair.

"Me too, Mother." He stirred. Since his release from prison, each of his last three jobs had lasted less than a year. With ignorant bosses ordering him around, one year was more than he could endure. Prison forced him to tolerate stupid people in authority. His last employer listed "insubordination" as the reason for his termination. His boss had accused him of stealing the laptop, but had no proof. Sydney remembered how he'd laughed as he left the personnel office. Why should he care? Besides, he needed time to pursue his obsession with a trip to the coast. He had to find the right place for his western flower.

"Maybe you'll meet a nice girl this time." Wanda scooted the chair up to the table.

"Ha, ha, Mother. Why would any girl want me? I'm almoth forty." He struck a pose to show the profile of his fleshy body. "Look at me," Sydney pushed on his cheeks to make his lips pooch out and mugged her. "They all avoid me—laugh at the way I talk. I don't need 'em."

"Oh, stop being silly, Sidney." She toyed with her napkin. "You're old enough to know your looks have nothing to do with what you are inside."

If you only knew, Mother, if you only knew. "Yeah, maybe I'll find a girl, Mother." He placed bowls of soup on the table and straddled his chair. Bald on top with collar length hair on the sides, he worked the long strands of hair behind his ears with his thumbs.

"Did you call your probation officer back?"

"Yeah, she wanted to schedule a visit. Told her I'd call when I get my new work schedule."

"It'd be nice to get off probation so you can have a computer again. I know you miss your games. Maybe you could get a computer job."

"Ha. I didn't finish school—never had any formal training. Nobody'd hire me."

"You've always been clever with computers, Sydney. Your attorney told me at the trial no one had ever been able to hack into NORAD records before."

"I'd never heard of them until I thaw on TV they're tracking Thanta Clauth. I just tinkered around. A big game for me, but I didn't hurt anybody. Why would I care where their generals or employees live in Colorado?"

"That's what I said when they arrested you." Wanda sipped from her spoon. "I think the government framed you, Sydney. Some big shot got embarrassed and made you the scapegoat."

Sydney leaned back with a broad smile on his blemished face. "Remember the headlines? 'Aerospace Defense Command cracked by hacker,' Got a lot of fan mail."

"Some not so nice, Sydney." She spooned more soup.

"Well, I'd like to be able to go geocaching again."

"Then you'd have both hobbies back—the flower pictures and finding those little trinkets." She fingered the earrings hung from her pierced ears. "I've always liked these."

Sydney's mind flashed on the time he'd grabbed those. "Me too."

"What'd Angel want?"

"He got a new game. Asked me how long before I'll be able to play."

"One or two years—right?"

"Yeah."

"Does he call from Mexico?"

"Nah—lives in L.A. with his mom. They moved up to Pacoima when he was a kid."

"Mr. Barnes came by while you were on the coast."

"He's never liked me. What'd he want?"

"Same as before … ah … his little dog's missing. He thinks you did something. Did you?"

"No, Mother. Thtupid little dog's always running in the road and yapping. Wouldn't be thurprised if it got run over. Who cares?" He didn't, and he'd never tell what happened.

"I hope you didn't hurt his little dog, Sydney. Not right."

"He's always had it in for me, Mother. Remember when he said I burned down his chicken coop?"

She nodded. "Yes, I do. Long time ago."

After dinner, Wanda downed her pain pills and wheeled back to her bedroom for the night. Sydney called and got his work assignment.

He jumped in his old Nissan truck and headed for the state offices. The trip from his home near the fairgrounds took little time. He found the janitorial company's van parked near the golden arches on 12th Street.

A tall rotund man in white coveralls waited beside the commercial van. "Smythe?"

"You got it." Sydney stood chest high on the man.

"I'm Ross. My regulars start at nine. How tall are you?"

"Five-ten."

Ross ambled to the open side door on the van and pulled out a folded pair of coveralls. "This is a medium—run a little baggy, but should fit you." He tossed them to Sydney. "Slip 'em on and you can follow me in your truck. I'll give you a tour of the building you'll clean."

The foreman led him into an older neighborhood. Sydney parked in a diagonal space at the curb. He paused to survey the old homes mixed with two-story apartment houses and an office building. On the sidewalk, Ross twirled a ring of keys as he waited.

Sydney followed his foreman inside. The tour didn't take long. Ross left him with the keys and instructions. One meal period and two breaks at times of his own choosing. After he finished, the keys had to be returned before five in the morning. Ross claimed he'd check on him during the night, but with the foreman's labored breathing during the walk-through, Sydney had his doubts.

Alone, with a two-story building to himself, pleased Sydney. The previous janitor had been fired. Ross suggested Sydney had a chance to keep the job, if he performed well during his probation.

He had halls, a stairwell, restrooms and offices. Sydney decided to leave the upstairs offices until last so he could spend any spare time on the Internet. Because of his federal probation, he couldn't use his mother's connection. She talked too much. He planned to subscribe to a wireless service for his new laptop. First, he had to establish a false identity with an address different than his own. Then he'd get a credit card with his phony name.

After midnight, Ross paid a visit as Sydney ran the buffer in the second-floor hallway. The foreman reminded him where to take the keys when he finished. Ross would wait where they'd met earlier, beside McDonald's. Sydney figured the foreman ate a lot of fast food.

Work as a night janitor in this office building made a good fit for him. No co-workers and little contact with any ignorant supervisors. With all the computers around and his skills, he felt like the proverbial kid in a candy store. Passwords and covering his tracks posed little challenge for him.

Sydney finished his work before he settled at a desktop computer to spend the rest of his shift. He queried several websites for the news story he longed to find. The plan needed time to work, but, with each newspaper he checked without one mention, a pit of disappointment grew in his stomach. He'd hiked to the cache at Shellburg Falls and confirmed the picture had been removed.

He searched websites of newspapers in Portland, Salem and Bend. He tried every keyword combination he could imagine—the City of Burns, Harney, Baby's Grave, Shellburg or Silver Creek. The story he waited for didn't pop up on the screen.

His face flushed with anger as he recalled how the ignorant detective in Burns stole his murder and pinned it on some kid. *Dumber than dirt*. Sydney cursed. He'd left a clue on the woman's wrist, in plain sight. The stupid detective or some helper must've ignored the band or lost it.

In prison, he got his hands on a book titled "The Mineshaft Killer." The author used the cops' nickname for Billy in the title. He wished he could've met Billy before the execution. Sydney had memorized Billy's methods and how he'd planned each murder. The book described the crime scenes near mineshafts where Billy had posed his victims. *"The most notorious serial killer in Arizona's history."* Sydney crossed his arms and leaned back in the office chair with his memories.

The one mistake Billy had made was that his last victim escaped. Sydney realized the danger and had not allowed any escapes since his release from prison. A cold sweat swept over him as he recalled how his first victim almost got away. Her strength and quickness caught him by surprise. The rope didn't subdue her quick enough. The book in prison taught him new methods, how to plan, build his kit, and be patient for the right opportunity. The wait had become the hardest part. The pictures and souvenirs helped him remember and reimagine each of his flowers. His first had been incomplete. A great disappointment because of the fight and the mountain bikers.

The time displayed on the bottom of the screen caught his attention. He cleaned his browsing history and other trails in the computer before he shut down. Sydney secured the building and headed for his truck. He'd be more famous than Billy. He'd show the cops his brilliance and expose their incompetence. But first, he had to get their attention.

Chapter 5

Hospital visits could be grim or joyous. Tonight, Matt didn't know what to expect. He hurried to the escalator and climbed two steps at a time. When the lady at the front desk gave a room number instead of directions to intensive care he wanted to hug her. All the way in, he had pictured his friend on life support with a hospital chaplain outside his door.

After Herb and Phyllis had left, Matt grew troubled with thoughts of his friend being alone. Trudeau had never mentioned family. Anna agreed when he'd decided to check on his friend. By the time he'd left for Salem, she had gone to bed.

The only pedestrian on the sky bridge, he glanced at his watch: eleven-forty. In the elevator, he'd asked God to be merciful to his friend. When bad things happened, Matt didn't think in terms of luck, good or bad. God had His ways. Matt hoped to be content with His will.

Two nurses held a hushed conversation in front of the nursing station. Matt passed with little notice and arrived at Trudeau's room. He eased inside and stopped at the foot of the bed. Relief swept over him at the sight of his friend. Only an oxygen tube under his nose, a few sensors, and a drip bag hooked to his arm. Monitors flashed data Matt didn't pretend to understand. He'd expected worse. While Trudeau slept, Matt moved toward the window, settled into a chair, and drifted into a restless sleep.

Hours later, noise and commotion at the entrance startled Matt. Clips on the privacy screen scraped and rattled as the nurse jerked the curtain aside. "I need your vitals," she said.

Awake, Matt glanced out the window. It was daylight and the hands on the wall clock indicated five-thirty.

As the nurse worked on his right side, Trudeau rolled his head toward Matt and asked, "You been here long?"

Matt pushed out of the chair and moved to the bed across from the nurse. "Came to check on you and fell asleep." He placed a hand on Trudeau's shoulder. "Gave us a scare."

"Me too. I could tell I had a problem, but only made it as far as my truck."

"Deputy Abbott said your neighbor found you."

"Yeah, guess I fell forward on my horn. He called 9-1-1."

"There," the nurse said. "Next time you call 9-1-1, don't try to drive yourself." She dropped the side rail. "We need to get you up. Can I help you get into the bathroom?"

"I'll try." Trudeau waited as the nurse used the controller to raise the head of the bed. "Doctor told me I caught a break getting here so soon. They gave me some clot-busting stuff."

"t-P-A," the nurse said.

"That's it." Trudeau waved his right hand. "May have stopped too much damage this time."

"I hope so, Buddy. When we heard, Anna and I prayed for you."

The nurse strapped a belt around the patient and walked him into the bath.

Matt moved from the bed close to the window and called Anna. "Hey, Sleeping Beauty."

"Oh, Matt. What time is it?"

"Five-thirty. You've got a sultry voice this morning."

"Stop. I'm not awake yet." She cleared her throat. "How is he?"

After he answered, Matt lowered his voice and cupped a hand to the phone, "Anna, there's no way he can do this murder case without help."

"Maybe he should drop it."

"That won't happen," Matt said.

"I know—and you're the only one he's asked."

Matt ended the call as the nurse walked Trudeau back to the bed.

"My left arm may be weaker." Trudeau flexed and worked his fingers.

"They'll re-evaluate your condition today," the nurse said.

Later, Trudeau grumbled over his breakfast, something pureed served with clear apple juice. "Tell your wife to smuggle a few of her cookies in here."

"You've done pretty good," Matt said. "Did it seem like you couldn't swallow so well?"

"No. That paste had no flavor. I'll order steak for lunch."

"Doubt you'll get any red meat."

"Rats."

After Trudeau fell asleep, Matt slipped out to find breakfast in the snack bar. Weary from an uncomfortable, restless night, he leaned heavily against the elevator wall on the ride down. He thanked God for the merciful answer to prayer. His friend hadn't suffered the severe setback he'd feared. Matt selected a couple of muffins with a large coffee.

Seated at a small table along the windows, he watched as a trickle of cars and vans arrived and left. Inside the main lobby, visitors and patients moved about, while some waited in line for help at the reception desk.

Matt removed his glasses and placed them on the table to rub his tired, itchy eyes. "Ouch," he whispered as the first sip of coffee burned his lip. He replaced his glasses and waited for the beverage to cool. People passed between his table and the snack bar as they headed for treatment or a visit.

Among those in line for the receptionist, he spotted Linh Johnson. The small Vietnamese woman wore a gray sweatshirt jacket, dark slacks, and a pair of slip on canvas sneakers. She had her thick black hair tied back with a white scarf. In one hand, she clutched a purse and a colorful gift bag hung from her other.

After her visit with the receptionist, she approached with quick, short strides. Matt waved his hand and rose to greet her. "Mrs. Johnson. You remember me? I picked up the bracelet."

With a broad smile, the small lady stopped beside the table and gave a slight bow. "Ah. Yes. I remember. You call me Linh."

Her manner and slight accent invited compassion. "Are you here to visit Mr. Trudeau?"

She nodded.

"I just came from his room. He's sleeping." He motioned to the empty chair. "Have a seat and when I'm done we'll go up together."

She backed onto the chair and sat, erect with knees and feet tight together.

"Coffee?"

She wrinkled her nose.

"Tea?"

"Yes. Please."

After Matt returned with hot water and a packet of green tea, he settled on his chair.

Mrs. Johnson placed her purse and gift bag on the table before she prepared the tea. "Can he still find who killed my Mari?"

"The doctor has to check him over. But I think so."

She slumped back in the chair and sighed. "Really?"

"Really."

A smile formed as she leaned forward to grip the paper cup between her hands.

"I'll help him." Matt bridled his gnawing questions to avoid being too abrupt with her. With his forearms on the table, he fiddled with the cup between his hands. "Linh, we have a little time. Could you tell me about Mari?"

Her soft-spoken delivery required Matt to concentrate as she answered. She didn't dwell on Mari's troubled times as a teenager or years as a young adult. Instead, Mrs. Johnson described the more recent years when Mari had become drug free and found new friends in a support group for abused women.

She'd adjusted to her daughter's death, but her love and desire for justice remained intense. Matt understood why Trudeau couldn't abandon her cause.

"I understand the pride you have in her." Matt sipped from the hole in the lid. The coffee had cooled. "Don't mean to stir up old memories, but can I ask you something?"

She waited.

"Why did she go on that hike by herself?"

"She planned to go with friend, but friend got sick." She opened her hands. "I told her wait—she went—very independent."

"How'd she learn this treasure hunt thing?"

"She work in a sports store—sold things to hikers, campers, hunters. People she worked with took her out and she liked. She exercised at club—very strong."

"Had she been to Shellburg Falls before?"

"I think, maybe." She leaned forward and lowered her voice. "I go too."

"To the place—where—?"

She nodded. "Every year I go visit where Mari found." She bowed her head. "I didn't get to tell her goodbye."

"No, you didn't. I'm sorry."

With her head down, she dabbed at her eyes with a napkin. "When they took me to identify her, the man told me cannot touch—she evidence." She shook her head. "My Mari's not evidence."

"Detective Trudeau wasn't there?"

"No. He's my friend."

"I admire the devotion to your daughter, Linh—to her memory." He cleared his throat as he shifted in his chair. "We ... lost our only son to an accident, but we don't know exactly where the accident happened ... where he died." He fingered the lid on his cup.

"The park man, he showed me." She covered her lips with a hand as she chuckled. "Funny name on his shirt—'Duck'."

"Must be a nickname." Her delight brought a smile to his lips. "I didn't know they had employees at Shellburg."

"No. I didn't know where Mari found. I drove to Silver Creek Park and I asked Duck—very kind."

"He took you to where she was found?"

"Down a long narrow lane." She motioned with her hand and widened her eyes. "The park man—Duck, told me once—he think another man visits where Mari found."

"Really? Who?"

"I don't know. Mr. Duck never told me who."

"Does Trudeau know about this?"

"No. I never tell him. Didn't think important."

"May be nothing." No need to embarrass or alarm her, but something to follow. "Let's go wake him up."

Matt accompanied the small lady to their friend's room. The flurry of morning nursing chores had calmed. Trudeau slept on his back with the head of the bed raised.

The gift bag in Linh's hand brushed the wall. The patient's eyes snapped open and showed his delight. "Linh." He cleared his throat. "Nice of you to come."

She gave a slight bow before she approached and placed the bag on the edge of his bed. "Something for you."

"Thank you. Matt, could you?"

Matt grabbed the handles and placed the bag on the table beside the bed. He removed several pieces of colored tissue paper from around the gift and paused at the sight of a dead turtle. He remained stoic as he removed the lifelike, brown four-inch reptile, which had been preserved by a taxidermist.

Trudeau's smile didn't hide his puzzlement.

Matt eased the creature onto the table.

Linh beamed. "In Vietnam, turtle bring good luck."

"Thank you very much, Linh." Trudeau examined the turtle in his right hand. "I've needed a little luck."

Behind Matt, a woman cleared her throat. "Excuse me." She pressed a clipboard against her chest as she brushed Matt aside to address Trudeau. She gasped "Oh—my!"

Matt caught her as she backed away. "It's dead—won't hurt you."

"Oh—oh." She spun and left the room.

"Wonder how she does in ER?" Matt chuckled with Trudeau as he spotted Linh's bewildered expression. He said, "Linh, we're laughing at the lady, not your gift. She doesn't understand the turtle means good luck."

"Yes, Linh. Thank you for this." Trudeau brandished the turtle in his hand.

The smile returned to her face as she gave a slight bow.

A younger woman with a clipboard arrived at the bedside. She eyed the turtle as she spoke. "Mr. Trudeau. The evaluation of your condition has gone well. The doctor wants to discharge you tomorrow, if you have no further complications."

"It's working already, Linh," Trudeau said.

Linh nodded.

The woman positioned the clipboard to read from a form and found a pen in the pocket of her blazer. "Now. We have a list of approved rehabilitation facilities. You can choose which you prefer."

"No. I want to go to my own home," Trudeau said.

"Well, Sir. The doctor won't approve your release until you have proper care. Right now, you need rehabilitation and twenty-four-hour care. The stroke weakened your left arm and you've developed problems swallowing. The doctor ordered physical therapy. Then you'll be evaluated to determine if you can go home."

"I gagged on that awful goop you tested me with—not a swallowing problem."

"What if he had someone to give care at home?" Matt asked.

Linh moved to the foot of the bed. "I can do."

"I … ah … I will check with the doctor." The woman left the room.

"Linh. You don't need to do this. I'll be fine."

"I will help."

"Let's wait to hear from the doctor," Matt said.

As Trudeau and Linh visited, Matt moved to the window to call Anna.

During his short conversation, Linh had left and Trudeau fought to keep his eyes open.

"I'll come back later. You need to rest."

"I don't want them to stick me in some strange place."

"Won't let that happen." Matt moved beside the bed. "With all you've been through, I've been impressed. I haven't heard you complain one time."

"My life's not always been easy." The drowsiness in his eyes was gone. "Not as bad as crime victims, but tough spells. Don't do any good to wallow in self-pity. I refuse to get discouraged. The best way for me is to push the problem aside or work through it. Just ignore what troubles me."

"Is that what you do with God—ignore him?"

Trudeau rolled his head to fix his eyes on Matt. "No. I don't ignore God. I just don't think about things I can't see, touch or hear."

"Doesn't make Him go away, my friend." Matt let his words linger before he said, "Something to think about."

Chapter 6

"Is Duck here?" Matt strained to find a face on the woman behind the old screen door. Darkness in the enclosed porch and the hall behind her concealed her features.

"That's his nickname. My father's Cedrick Howell. How can I help you?"

"I'm a private investigator. I'm trying to track down some information he may have from his job with the park at Silver Creek Falls." Matt placed his identification against the screen.

"Volunteer—he volunteered." She unlatched the hook and eased the door open. "I'm Helen, his daughter. Don't know how much he'll remember."

Matt followed her down the unlit hall. Thick, maroon colored carpet silenced his footsteps into the living room. The television screen in the corner provided the primary source of light. Afternoon sunlight filtered in around the drawn shades. Dark wood paneling on the walls displayed framed photographs with a nautical theme and certificates Matt couldn't read.

Helen placed a hand on Duck's shoulder to distract him from the Lucille Ball rerun. "Dad, Mr. Kinler would like to talk about when you volunteered up at the park." She punched the remote to pause the program.

Matt shook the elderly man's hand and moved around a coffee table to settle on the end of an overstuffed couch.

From across the coffee table, Duck fingered his dark glasses. "Excuse these glasses and the dark room. I had cataract surgery this morning."

"I'm sorry to bother you, but this is important."

"No bother."

"I'll keep this short." Matt leaned forward with his elbows on his knees. "Do you remember a little Vietnamese woman who may have met you at the park?"

"I think … ah … was her daughter the one killed up there?"

"Yes. Do you remember taking her down along the south boundary to the site where her daughter died?"

"Uh huh." He rubbed his chin. "Just off Lookout Mountain Road—on the Shellburg Falls' side."

"You did better than I thought you would, Dad," Helen said.

"Hard to forget something like a murder." Duck crossed his arms on his chest. "I used to hike the trails a lot."

"Dad spent his life at sea." Helen pointed to the framed certificates and photos of ships mounted on the wall. "He said he volunteered so he could walk on dry land. If a job required anyone to walk a trail, he'd do it."

Duck flashed an amused glance at Matt. "One of the perks."

"How'd you learn where the daughter had been killed?"

"A lot of cops going by that day. I got curious so I hiked down the lane. Talked to the deputy who kept people out of their way."

"A lot of people go by?" Matt asked.

"Wouldn't say a lot, but hikers, mountain bikers, and horseback riders go through there now and then."

"Did you tell the mother you saw another man hanging around the spot where her daughter was killed?"

"Hmm … no, I told her a man had hung around, but I didn't see him—someone else told me."

"Remember who?"

"I think one of the mountain bikers from Shellburg. Don't remember his name." Duck shook his head as he studied his hands.

"Dad told me about this." Helen placed a hand on Duck's shoulder. "He'd bumped into one of those bikers at the trail junction near where the body had been found."

"Yeah." Duck said. "Don't remember much, but he had just chased a guy off who had acted weird around where the body had been found."

"Did you ever report that to the Sheriff's Office?"

"No. I think I told the biker he should call—said he would."

"When did this happen?"

Duck shook his head. "Not sure."

"You quit two years ago, Dad. How much before that?" Helen asked.

"Wish I had my journals. I'm sure I wrote that down."

"He kept a record of everything in pocket journals," Helen said. "But we've misplaced his collection."

"A habit from my merchant marine days," Duck said.

"Any idea how I can find this biker?"

"Dad told me there's a mountain bike club in Salem that maintains the bike trails at Shellburg," Helen said. "Forestry's district office up there should have a contact number."

"I'll check." Matt placed a business card on the coffee table. "If you run across those journals, please give me a call."

Matt fought the noontime traffic as he searched for the bike shop. The lady who answered the phone at the Forestry office had the club's information handy when he called. Trudeau needed some good news. If he could dig up a name or description of the weird guy who hung around the murder site, Matt could give Trudeau another lead in the cold case.

The shop was operated out of an old, detached single-car garage at a residence north of city center. Matt parked his truck at the curb and paused on the sidewalk. His call had gone to voice mail. A breezeway ran between the small, white single-story house and the garage. Above the passage hung a hand-painted sign. Red letters on white read "Bike Shop."

Behind the garage, Matt found the proprietor up to his elbows in grease and oil. Mountain bikes and parts were stuffed or stacked in every corner of the garage.

"Vincent?" Matt waited on the concrete pad outside the garage. This had to be a first. He couldn't recall a garage with pull-up doors front and back. Cluttered garages, he'd seen.

"Yep. What's ya need?" The young man left the bike frame clamped on the work stand and faced Matt. He wiped his hands on soiled shorts.

"I'm told you're the one that keeps up the bike trails near Shellburg Falls."

"The club does." He grabbed an open bottle of water and drank.

"I'm working a homicide where a woman was killed up there about ten years ago."

"Before my time, but I think I remember Phil Hyatt talked about a murder up there. He's one of our past presidents, but not riding anymore. I don't remember anyone else who mentioned any killing."

"Is he still around?"

"Yep. He's a school teacher."

Matt left the bike shop and jumped in his truck. Before he entered traffic, he placed a call and left a message for Hyatt. He hated to wait, but without an address or the name of the school, he had no choice. Heavy traffic through the business district slowed his return to the hospital. Stuck at a light, he rolled his shoulders and relaxed the tight grip on the steering wheel. Buoyed with thoughts of the first good lead in years, his mind raced with the potential offered by the mysterious man spotted near the falls. He took a deep breath and exhaled as the light turned green.

In the hospital parking garage, he left the truck and headed to his friend's room. He covered his mouth as a yawn escaped. Maybe tonight he'd get to sleep in his own bed. He walked through the lobby and onto the escalator, but this time he rode—no two at a time.

When he entered Trudeau's room, he found the bed empty. On the white board, someone had printed a schedule. Imaging fifteen minutes ago and then off to speech therapy. Matt checked with the nurse at the desk. The doctor had not scheduled Trudeau for discharge. Drained from a lack of sleep, Matt called Anna and headed for home.

♦♦♦

The fragrance of baked bread greeted him before the dogs. Anna, hands in oven mitts, greeted him with a kiss.

"Bet you're exhausted." She released him and moved over to the oven.

"Close to it." He emptied his pockets on the kitchen counter beside the house phone.

"Go take a nap while I finish up in here. Tell me about your day, later."

Matt plopped in his recliner and fell asleep with two furry companions.

The sound of his cell phone woke him. He heard Anna's hushed voice. "Just a moment. I'll see if he's available."

Matt raised the back on his chair and rubbed his tired eyes.

"Honey. Phil Hyatt?" Her eyes questioned as she handed him the phone.

"Mr. Hyatt. Thanks for returning my call." He beckoned with his free hand for Anna to stay. Her breath tickled the back of his neck as she listened from behind. Matt explained to Hyatt why he had left a message.

"Then you do remember the guy?" Matt asked.

"Yeah. But—I may have seen him around before. This last time he acted real strange—weird."

"How's that?"

"I'd been running over our mountain bike course up there and decided to take a break. I headed up the trail toward Silver Falls Park. Near Lookout Mountain Road I heard someone wailing and moaning. There's this guy on his knees in the trail. He's bent over kind of rocking with his face on the ground."

"Did he hear you coming?"

"No. I startled him. I said, 'Mister, you okay?' He jumped up all scared like and ran up toward Silver Creek Falls."

"Anyone else around?"

"Don't think so. Late afternoon and there wasn't anyone else around."

"Where did he go? Do you know?"

"Ah—no. So weird, I didn't want to get too close, but I did follow him a little later."

"Can you describe him?"

"Not really. Been three—maybe five years. I haven't been up there much since I started teaching—don't have the time."

"Remember what he wore?"

"He had a dirty hoody on over his head. I got a glimpse of his face. Remember a really bad complexion."

Matt waited.

"Some coming back to me. He's about average build, maybe hefty a little."

"White?"

"Yes."

"Can you think of anything unusual about the place where you found him?"

"Didn't until I ran into the old man who always walked the trails up in the park. I bumped into him after the guy left. When I told him, he asked me where the guy was carrying on. I showed him, and he said, 'That's where the woman was murdered.' I didn't know about any murder. Happened before I started riding up there."

"Did you call the Sheriff's Office?"

"Yes. I called and talked to someone. Never heard back, but I didn't expect a call."

"You think he'd been up there before?"

"You know, I thought ... maybe. Not sure, but he may have hung around the falls with a bike. I think the reason I remember is because he didn't look like a bike person."

"When he was groaning and moaning, what time of year was it?"

"Had to be summer—I think late summer."

The call over, Matt stared at the cell phone in his hand. Anna had moved over to the couch. "Not sure what to make of this," he said.

"Could've been the killer—you think?"

"Or a really close friend—or a crazy."

"Matt, that's creepy."

Chapter 7

"Rise and shine." Matt jostled her shoulder. "You said you didn't want to miss the sunrise."

Anna stirred and rubbed sleep from her eyes. "Over the summit?" She raised the seatback. "Oh, look at the rosy colors—oranges too. Matt, look." She tapped her side window. "The red's reflecting on that snowy peak. Jefferson, right?"

"No—that's Mt. Washington." He pointed at three distant peaks. "And the Sisters over there." Through the windshield, the red glow of the horizon flicked through the trees as he guided the van around the sweeping corners. "Red sky by morning."

"My van's no ship and you're no sailor." She placed her hand on his arm. "We'll hope for good weather."

Matt raised her hand to his lips. "How 'bout we stop for breakfast in Sisters?"

"Suttle Lake's glassy calm this morning." Anna gazed through the trees and down the mountainside.

"Welcome to the high desert plateau." Matt tapped the button to open his window a few inches and inhaled the rush of cool dry air. "Ahh."

"Wait'll we get to the air with juniper and sage. Hey, you didn't get much sleep. Want me to drive?"

"You can spell me after breakfast. I'll navigate."

"What's the name of this place?"

"Donnybrook. We go north from Madras then east."

"Never heard of it."

"Not much there. Might be a ghost town."

"Long way from where the murder happened in Harney County."

"She's staying on her brother's ranch."

"You think Trudeau's sorry he couldn't come?"

"Probably some." Matt enjoyed the giant ponderosa pine on each side of the highway. "He's realistic. Recovery takes time and he wants this investigation to move. His eyes sure lit up when I told him of my plan. Good for his mental health to have something to look forward to."

"Do you think he'll recover back to where he was?"

"I hope so … at least not lose too much ground. We'll need to keep him in our prayers."

After breakfast Anna walked the dogs while Matt trotted over to his favorite bakery to snag a couple of apple fritters for the road.

He studied the map while Anna drove toward Redmond. "I hope we can make this a day trip. I'm not sure what kind of time we'll make when we leave the main highway."

"Well, that's why we brought my van so the dogs could ride along, just in case."

"Yeah, but it's embarrassing to be driving through cowboy country in a chick van. My pickup would've been better. I just hope we don't run into anyone we know."

"Okay, Macho Man." Anna smiled and slapped his arm. "Maybe we should buy you a cowboy hat."

"That'd be worse—hood maybe."

"Poor baby. Get the thermos and pour some coffee to go with our fritters."

Matt tossed the map on the dash to free his hands. "In Redmond, we'll head north. Above Madras, we leave the highway on Pony Butte Road. I'll drive from there." He poured and placed the pastries on the center console.

"Does that road take us to the ranch?"

"Sorta. We'll go through Ashwood first, but the road's paved—if I understand the map."

It was late morning as Matt drove east into the rolling hills. In the rearview mirror, he caught glimpses of the snowcapped peaks in the Cascade mountain range. The road climbed over the hills and through dry, rocky upland. Juniper trees and sagebrush dotted the landscape. Bunch grass sprouted in scattered clumps to announce the arrival of spring.

"Pull over, Matt."

"What's wrong?"

"Nothing. Up ahead. I want to pick one of those little flowers. There."

He lowered the window and waited. The fragrance of sage and juniper filled the cab as cool dry air rushed in through his window and out her open door. Ahead, he spotted low lying white flowers scattered among the sage. "Watch out for rattlers," he yelled.

"They better watch out." She lifted the edge of her jacket to expose her holstered pistol and dipped down to step between two strands of barbed wire. Inside the fence, she knelt beside a cluster of vibrant, lavender flowers to shoot pictures with her phone and pick a specimen.

Anna smiled as she cleared the fence, picked her way through the sage and climbed into the van. A stem pinched between her fingers held a single blossom with elongated, lavender petals. "Here smell—faint, delicate."

"Nice, but my smeller doesn't work so well."

"Bitterroot, I think. I'll have to look this up when I get home. Might be a little early, but I don't know what else they could be."

The narrow-paved road led over hills and through canyons. They enjoyed spectacular vistas with plateaus, canyons, arroyos and distant mountains. When the road dropped into the draws, dry crumbled basalt and rock faces gave texture to the steep sides of their route. A stray cow, two deer and a jack rabbit provided the only signs of mammal life until they reached Ashwood. One woman in front of a house waved as they passed.

"Suppose we're the first people she's seen in a while?" Matt asked.

"No. Could be not many people come out here during the week."

"Haven't met any cars since we left the main highway."

By midday, he spotted the weathered wood sign on the shoulder of the dusty road. The name "Harkness" had been painted in black once upon a time. Matt flipped the turn signal out of habit.

A strip of sparse dry grass grew down the center of the crushed, red lava lane. The white single-story ranch house had a small front lawn bordered on three sides with a display of various types, sizes and shapes of rock.

"Someone must be a rock collector." Matt parked near the house beside two old pickups. "Told you we should've brought my truck."

"Oh, nobody will notice, Smarty."

A woman smiled and waved as she waited on the covered front porch. She wore a long sleeve shirt. The untucked tail hung out over her jeans. From the sides of the straw hat a string tie hung down with the ends joined under her chin.

"Sarah, I'm Matt, nice to meet in person—my wife, Anna."

"You've got an oasis here." Anna swept her hand out over the grass.

"Your brother the rock hound?" Matt asked.

"Ah, Dusty'd rather do that than ranch." Sarah moved aside and motioned to the door. "Come in. I just came down from the barn to fix lunch. My brother might join us in a bit."

Over the fireplace hung the head mount of a mule deer. Horseshoes and pictures of cowboys adorned the honey-colored knotty pine walls. The crepe soles on Sarah's chukka boots squeaked on the wood floor as she moved across the room to the easy chair. "Jasper. Move."

A well-fed golden cat, unimpressed by their arrival, uncurled, stretched and yawned before obeying.

"She's the oldest—so spoiled. Dusty names all of his cats after some type of rock. Have a seat. I'll bring you something to snack on while we talk."

Anna chose the end of the couch and Matt the easy chair. He rubbed the polished face of a cut thunderegg as he studied the lamp on the table between them. "Don't think I've seen a cowboy boot used like that before."

"Or a cowboy hat for a shade." Anna leaned to peek up at the bulb.

"No switch—how do they turn it on?" Matt twisted in his chair to examine the lamp.

"That's quite the conversation piece." Sarah scooted several cut and polished thundereggs to make room for her tray on the coffee table. "He's got a thunderegg claim. Got 'em coming out our ears." She waggled her finger at the lamp. "Just spin the rowel on the spur, Mr. Kinler."

"Never would've figured that." Matt smiled as he lit the lamp and settled back in the chair.

"One of Dusty's big finds—garage sale up in Antelope." She served ice tea. "Help yourselves while we talk. You'll recognize most of this, but that smoked sausage has elk meat. That's baloney, venison and pork, and that's beef jerky."

"You didn't need to go to all that trouble for us," Anna said.

"My pleasure. When I heard you were interested in the murder of that poor woman—it was an answer to prayer." Sarah sat on the couch beside Anna. Hands clasped in her lap, she paused and dabbed at her moist eyes with a tissue wadded in her hand. "Okay." She sniffed. "This I know. Timmy didn't kill her. I knew my son. He'd camp with us, but he wouldn't hunt—didn't like the killing." She wrung her hands. "Had the mind of a child."

Anna placed a hand on her arm.

"Did you live nearby? How'd he find the body?" Matt leaned forward to grab a piece of jerky.

"We used to camp down at Buck Springs a lot. Usually before hunting season and Dusty would scout for deer to plan where to hunt opening day. Timmy rode all over on his ATV. That's how he ran across the body. On that morning, I hadn't fixed breakfast by the time he roared back to camp, eyes big as saucers."

Matt grabbed his glass and gulped down some tea.

Sarah smiled. "I should've warned you— spicy, huh?"

He wiped his eyes with the napkin and nodded. "Good—just caught me off-guard." Matt returned his glass to the coffee table. "So you called the Sheriff?"

"Yes. Told them Baby's Grave. Timmy wanted to watch the officers so I let him go." She shook her head. "Big mistake."

"From what I read, the detective blamed your son because he stole a bracelet from the body," Matt said.

A distant stare into nothingness as she spoke. "My son's hobby. He collected those silicon bracelets. Didn't matter what cause. He always wore half a dozen on his wrists. He didn't understand crime scenes or evidence—just spotted a bracelet he didn't have yet.

"When a deputy asked him if he took anything or disturbed the body, I know exactly what happened. Timmy would've been embarrassed and would've said 'no'." She blotted her eyes with a tissue and blew her nose. "My son wasn't a good liar—never was. I'm sure the deputy pressed and Timmy pulled the bracelet out of his pocket."

"They took him to the station?"

She shook her head. "By the time Dusty and I left camp to find my son, they had him cuffed in the back of a car grilling him. He didn't understand what had happened."

"That's when they released him."

"Yes, but the detective never left us alone. He'd drop by and question Timmy, stop him in town—on the road. My son changed from one happy kid to a depressed and troubled child."

"Sarah," Anna asked, "where's Timmy's father?"

"My husband died several years before this all happened."

"Oh, I'm sorry." Anna patted her shoulder.

"Another sad chapter. My husband had lost all of his inheritance—everything but our ranch with his day trading. I told him to quit—he wouldn't listen." She leaned her head back against the cushion and stared at the ceiling. "Found him hanging in the barn—same as Timmy." She rocked forward with her hands over her face.

"How awful for you. You've had more than your share." Anna placed a hand on her back and eyed Matt with a slight shake of her head.

Sarah grabbed a napkin and wiped her face. "I apologize. I'll be okay. Gets hard sometimes. My brother took me in after I sold the ranch. Helped to get away from the memories." She wiped her nose. A slight smile formed on her sad face. "The old bachelor needed someone to boss him around."

"Mind if I go out and find him?" Matt asked. "I've got to meet the owner of this lamp before we leave."

"He'll be in the barn."

"I'll stay here and visit," Anna said.

◆◆◆

As he passed the van, the dogs grabbed Matt's attention with their complaints. He opened the back door and let them explore along the edge of the rock border of the yard. They strained on their leashes to try to mark each rock. Matt discouraged the irreverence with firm tugs. After a drink of bottled water, he secured Sam and Eddy in their kennels. He left the back of the van open to keep them from cooking.

The noonday sun warmed his uncovered head as he strode across the hard-packed dirt and gravel between the house and the barn. A breeze carried the subtle scents of the desert. Matt surveyed the scene as he approached the large building. The unfinished board and batten siding had turned gray with age. The gable roof peaked above the hayloft door. A lone Herford bull ate from a bale of alfalfa dumped on the ground in the corral beside the barn. Three cats lounged outside the double-door entrance. As Matt approached, the brown, black and gray creatures fled back inside through doors left ajar.

The long center aisle led to another set of open double doors at the back. A snowmobile and ATV had been parked along the left side among buckets and shelves filled with rocks. Bales of alfalfa had been stacked along the right side.

A cowboy and horse appeared as silhouettes against the afternoon sunlight in the rear entrance. From the back, the short skinny man's bow legs reminded Matt of a set of parentheses. "Dusty?"

"Yo." Dark eyes squinted as he studied Matt. Years on the open range had etched wrinkles on the rancher's suntanned face.

"Your sister said I'd find you here." Matt admired the contrast between the golden tan coat and the black mane and tail on the muscled Buckskin behind Dusty. "Beautiful," Matt said.

"Thanks—name's Yoda." A toothy grin sprouted under a scraggly, unruly gray mustache.

"Yoda? Like in *Star Wars*?"

His expression turned somber. "Timmy named him—big *Star Wars* fan."

"Been a while, but I'm sorry for your loss."

The curled brim of the cowboy hat concealed Dusty's face as he nodded.

"Talked to Sarah about Timmy. Thought I'd ask what you remember."

"Uh huh. I got nothing." Dusty led the horse outside the entrance, unclipped the lead from the halter and slapped Yoda's rump. The Buckskin's hooves beat a rhythm as he trotted into the fenced pasture. "Don't need to stir up her hopes. Let things be."

"Hopes?"

"Timmy's been branded a killer." Dusty coiled the lead and hung the loops on a nail near the door. "Ain't nothing gonna change."

"They're wrong."

"Yep. But the Sheriff ain't gonna do nothing."

"You talk to him?"

"Yep. Came to Timmy's funeral. 'Sorry'—he said." Dusty fished a bar of dark brown tobacco from his shirt pocket and bit off a chunk.

"The Sheriff?"

"Yep. Guilty 'cause of the way his detective did us. 'Didn't know'—he says. He fired the guy."

"But he won't reopen the case?"

"Nope. 'Nothing to go on'—he says." Dusty worked the chew and spat on the barn's dirt floor. "Ha—a bunch of you know what. I told him 'bout the woman at Lonerock."

"What woman?"

"Oh—let me think." Dusty scratched over his ear and dislodged his hat. "Maybe year after Timmy found the woman at Baby's Grave another one turns up in Lonerock." He straightened his hat.

"Tell the Sheriff?"

"Detective. He didn't care. 'Case closed'—he says." Dusty scuffed dirt with the toe of his boot and covered the dark spots of spittle. "They can all rot."

"Dusty, where's Lonerock?"

"North of here, Gillam County."

"What can you tell me?"

"Not much. Ain't nobody going to do nothing anyway."

Chapter 8

"We may have thunder and lightning before we get home." Matt let the van coast over the crest of the hill to enjoy the panorama of Oregon's central plateau. On the western edge, huge, puffy, cumulus clouds hung along the distant peaks of the Cascade Mountain Range.

"Those biggest thunderheads are closer to Mt. Hood," he said.

"Phooey. If there's any lightning, we'll be too far south to see," Anna said.

"We've got several hours before we reach the mountains. You may get your wish." He tapped the brake at the bottom of the grade.

"I'll keep my fingers crossed." She sorted through the maps in her side door pocket and picked out the one she wanted. "Did you find Lonerock?"

"I think I left the map open to the area."

"Condon. You said southeast? Here." She tapped the map. "So we've got a third victim. Does that mean we have a serial killer, now?"

"Hard to say. We'll need more information." He pressed the gas as the grade pitched up another hill. "Maybe when we get to the highway you can drive. If I can get on the Internet, I'll search for a murder at Lonerock."

"So, Dusty didn't know too much." She returned the map to the pocket.

"No, and what little he had could be wrong."

Anna needed two hands to lift the thunderegg from the center console. "Heavy."

"And that's just half." Matt glanced over at the polished face of the stone. "She called it a thunderegg agate?"

"Yes. But I had the impression folks have a lot of different names for them." She traced her finger tip over the pattern. "Like a ragged outline of a star—five points."

"Pretty the way the different shades of brown blend."

"Another of God's creations to enjoy." She returned the rock to the console.

"Just gave it to you?"

"Sarah said they have so many they're running out of places to store them. Dusty has a private claim and adds to his collection every time he digs."

"Wonder how far he has to go."

"She said, 'His big secret's up high in the Ochoco Mountains,' but I didn't quiz her."

"Probably guards the location like some gold claim."

"Tell me again what he said about Lonerock?" she asked.

"Wasn't sure of the date, but a woman was found dead near the cemetery—naked."

"The town didn't look big on the map."

"He said there're a few people around, but it's listed as a ghost town. If we had more information, we could head up there, but we'd be flying blind."

"I'd rather sleep in our own bed tonight."

"Me too. Have you heard any more from Beth on where they are?"

Anna grabbed her phone.

"If I had concrete information on a murder up there, I'd ask Allen to drop by Lonerock on their way back from Idaho. Do a little legwork."

"I sent her a text."

"Said you had a good talk with Sarah."

"We did. She's a believer." Anna shook the thermos stowed near her feet. "Out of coffee. Better refill when we stop for dinner. You'll need to stay awake for the drive home."

"Let's stop in Redmond."

"Don't hit that jackrabbit."

"I see him." Matt veered to the center. "Wonder if he's the same one we saw coming in? Just dawned on me. We haven't met one car since we left the highway."

"I'd get lonely out here. Sarah says she doesn't mind." Anna lowered the window to allow a gush of dry desert air. "Um. This, I could get used to. Oh—cooled down." She closed the window. "Sarah told me how her life hit bottom when her husband took his life. Nothing left but the land and buildings on the ranch. No time to grieve with all the bill collectors hounding her."

"Can you imagine? That'd be tough."

"While she and Timmy sorted what to keep and what to toss into their moving sale, Timmy found a Bible in the glovebox of his dad's truck. 'Shocked' was the word she used to describe her reaction. Her husband hated to talk religion—no interest in God. Stuck between the pages she found two handmade bookmarks with 'John 3:16' printed on them."

"Did she think her husband had been reading?"

Anna shook her head. "Someone had stuck a bookmark in Psalm 53 and used a yellow highlighter to shade a verse about a fool says there is no God. Matthew 19 had the other bookmark. The highlighted verse there was the one about how it's easier for a camel to go through the eye of a needle than for a rich man to enter the Kingdom of Heaven."

"Must've been someone he'd met."

"She remembered, a week or so before his death, her husband complained about some guy who worked on the truck. That mechanic told her husband he was a Christian. Her husband said he told the man he didn't believe in any God. She thinks the man stuffed the Bible in the glovebox."

"Her husband never found it?"

"Apparently not, but she started reading. Took some time, but she gave her heart to God—Timmy too."

"Just when you think God's going to fire a fastball he slips in a knuckleball. I'm always amazed at how He works." Matt raised his hand. "The mechanic tried to reach her husband, but instead—God rescued her."

"She's in a good place—full of questions, but I'm not sure I answered some so well." Anna tugged at the seatbelt. "She's troubled about Timmy."

"Most mothers worry over their children, but they did go through some tough times," Matt said.

"She asked me if God would forgive Timmy for hanging himself. A friend told her no."

"Being a new believer, I understand why she'd be concerned," Matt said. "That view has been held in some circles for a long time."

"Yeah—I told her we believed the only sin God refuses to forgive would be when a person rejects God—and refuses to believe."

"A lot of ways to say that, but you captured the main point."

"She also wondered if someone like Timmy had the ability to believe," Anna said. "You know—could he understand the depth of his sin, repentance, Christ's death and resurrection, everything?"

"I'm not so sure people like us understand all that well," Matt said.

"Yeah." She smiled. "I reminded her of Jesus scolding the disciples for blocking children from Him. 'The kingdom of God belongs to such as these,' He said."

"We Christians are a funny lot. Busy ourselves judging whether a person is saved by observing how the person acts, talks and so on. God sees through all the baloney. He knows if a person's heart is broken and repentant or filled with evil and rebellion. We can't."

"Guess Timmy and Sarah are no different," she said. "We'll all stand before God one day while Christ pleads our case. I hope and pray God will be merciful and grant us life everlasting."

"He'll do what He said He'll do," Matt said. "That's what Abraham believed."

The sun had dropped behind the thunderclouds by the time they reached the highway. Matt remained behind the wheel and drove into Redmond. "How about here?" He signaled for the entrance to a family restaurant.

"Fine, but park near that row of bushes. I'll need to walk the boys before we hit the road again."

He chose a space between two knobby-tired pickups. "If you walk the dogs, I'll check for messages before we go inside."

Anna left the back door up while she exercised the boys.

He finished scrolling though the day's incoming and waited at the back of the van for his wife.

A man and a pre-teen boy exited the restaurant and headed across the parking lot toward Matt. Both wore jeans, big buckles, cowboy hats and boots. The man's long sleeve shirt had snaps instead of buttons and the boy had a tan tee shirt with the picture of a black bucking bronco.

Matt centered himself on the back of the van as the tall and short cowboys approached the truck on the driver's side of the van. Sam and Eddy towed Anna to the open door and leaped into the back. Matt kenneled the dogs and closed the door.

Anna sidled closer. "That truck's backing up. Let's wait."

"Good idea. Rides so high they may not see us."

The engine throbbed and the radio's western music spilled from the boy's open window.

"Okay, Dad. You're clear of that sissy van," the boy shouted over the sound of the music.

"I told you," Matt whispered in her ear.

Anna wrapped her arm around his waist and propelled him toward the entrance. "C'mon, cowboy."

Seated in a window booth, Matt worked with his phone. "Got a message from Duck's daughter. You know—the park volunteer."

Anna ordered their coffee and sent the thermos with the waitress. "What's she say?"

"Found his journal. The incident with the guy blubbering in the trail happened on August 27, but she's not sure of the year. The cover's missing and that's where her dad always wrote the year."

"Can she make an educated guess?"

"Three to four years ago. She's going to inventory his journals and see which year's missing."

"So—Mari Johnson gets killed ten years ago and now we find more murders that happened six or seven years after Mari's," Anna said. "Strange."

Matt ordered the special, Cowboy Burger and fries, and Anna a Cobb salad. Both turned to their Smartphones as they waited.

"Beth answered," Anna said. "They'll spend the night in Pendleton tomorrow. She has to be back in her shop Friday. She had scheduled some clients to get their hair done."

"Don't want to miss those, I know." A slight smile showed as he raised his eyes from the screen.

"Oh, stop it. Make me sound like some ogre." Her effort to pout vanished in an amused expression.

"You're fun to tease." He reached across the table to clasp her hand. "Gives me such joy."

"All right, you two." The waitress placed their meals and condiments on the table. An ample build, she wore a western shirt tucked at the waist of her tight jeans. "Sorry to break in on the moment."

"Oh, there'll be more." Matt shook the folds from his napkin.

"How long you been together?" The waitress refilled their coffee cups.

"Over forty years." Matt raised his eyebrows as he peered over his glasses at Anna.

"Three," Anna said with a chuckle. "Forty-three."

"You don't act like you've been together that long." The waitress scooted the condiments closer. "I ah, I mean you act like you still enjoy being together. Don't always see that."

"Thank you," Anna said.

She smiled as she tucked the tray under her arm. "We just celebrated our twenty-fifth. We still have fun together."

"So happy for you," Anna said. "What's your husband do?"

"He's worked for the irrigation district since high school."

"Water must be like gold around here," Matt said.

"Is to the ranchers. My husband has lots of stories." She snagged the coffee pot and left.

"Had a message from the FBI profiler." Matt worked to corral the hamburger piled high on his plate.

"You may have to take that apart to get your mouth around it." She waved her fork at his dilemma.

"Think you're right." Matt wiped his hands on a napkin and armed himself with the knife and fork. "She's not really a profiler. She studies the behavioral side of murders. Crime scene—victim's lifestyle—stuff like that, and offers guidance to the detectives."

"How can she help you guys?"

"She may've run into similar homicides or might have some ideas on what kind of person we should look for. Not sure."

"I'd guess with a cold case," she poked the fork into her salad, "you take any kind of help you can get."

From the disassembled mess, Matt enjoyed the barbeque sauce slathered on the fried egg, ground beef, bacon and cheese. He left the bun and roughage to resume his Internet search. The browser offered several dead ends before he found a headline, "Woman killed near Lonerock."

"Here it is. I'm going to send Allen the link—I'll copy you." He swiped and tapped on the screen.

"So Dusty was right."

"Could be. At least we better check it out." He displayed the article on his screen. "You can read later." He kept his voice down. "This happened about one year after Baby's Grave. The victim and a sister had been exploring ghost towns—got separated in Lonerock. They found her dead outside of town. Says the sister blamed herself for not insisting they stay together."

"Must be a story there." Anna laid her fork down, slid her plate to the side, and drank from her water glass.

His phone barked like a dog. He punched receive.

"Matt. Everyone is looking at us," Anna whispered as she held the glass near her cheek.

"Hold on," he placed his hand on the phone. "Sorry, honey. I forgot to turn off the ringer." He scooted on the bench. "I'll take this outside."

"Better," Anna said.

"Hey partner." Matt hurried through the waiting area and into the parking lot. "A lot's happened while you've been on vacation." He'd met Allen Mann, former professional wrestler, at a training conference for private investigators. Their friendship had grown into an informal business arrangement. Matt agreed to rent a desk in Allen's office and paid a portion of the operating expenses.

Matt briefed Allen on the murders and asked him to dig up the details on the Lonerock homicide in order to identify the similarities and differences in the crimes. Anna joined him in the lot. After he ended the call, he placed his arm around her waist. "Ready to go home with me?"

"If you promise not to make a spectacle of yourself."

"Cross my heart."

Chapter 9

"This can't be a queen. Look how close my feet are to the end of the mattress." With the pillow as a cushion, Allen used the headboard as a backrest. During his travels as a professional wrestler, motels seldom had beds to fit his six-foot five, heavyweight frame. At least, the motels he could afford.

"That's what the lady said when we registered." With her head propped on a pillow, Beth closed her eyes as she relaxed on her back beside her husband. "We could call the office."

"Nah. Let's make do. I'm too tired to go through the hassle."

"I need to get out of my travel clothes before I fall asleep." She sat up and scooted closer. "Did you find the online newspaper the lady at the desk told you about?"

"Yep. Matt's link gave me a start, but this *Times-Journal* has more. I'm in the archives." He positioned the laptop for her.

She studied the screen. "Uh huh. Does this mean an all-nighter?"

"I'll just check headlines from summer months, two and three years back. It's a weekly paper."

"Summer's when it happened?"

"Yep."

"Makes sense. You'd make a good detective." She curled her arm around his bicep and placed her head against his shoulder.

He savored the scent as her dark hair brushed his cheek. "I'd better be—been in the business a while."

"Right after you quit wrestling? Right?"

"Yeah. But while I built up time to qualify for a license, I took some college computer classes and snagged a job doing skip-trace work. Also installed security systems for a licensed P.I."

"What's skip-trace?"

"Finding people. Most of the work involved computer records available through the Internet."

"A whole different world than my hair salon business. It's fun to learn new things from you." She hugged his arm.

"I could say that about you."

"Oh yeah? What?" She released her hold and squirmed to study his eyes.

"Never bought a horse before." He stroked under her chin with his finger.

She grabbed his finger. "That tickles—you think Misty's okay?"

"Sure. They board horses all the time. Good reviews online."

"I miss her—can't wait to get her home."

"I'm glad they let us leave our trailer there. It'd be awkward doing my investigation with a truck and horse trailer."

She snuggled against his side. "I'm so glad you talked me into this. I always wanted a horse. When my husband drowned … my life stopped. You've given me a new start." They kissed.

"Didn't help when your daughter ran away," he said.

"No." She swiped at her moist eyes. "Then you and Matt rescued her."

He cleared the laptop from his legs to embrace her. "And you took your life off hold for me."

"I did." Her voice muffled against his chest. "And now I have a new husband and my very own Appaloosa."

"Yeah, but which one will sleep in the barn?"

She giggled as her fingers dug for a ticklish spot in his ribs.

"Stop. I give."

"I thank God you came along when you did. I love you." They kissed. "I'm going to brush my teeth and get some sleep. Please don't stay up too late." She rummaged in her zippered canvas bag and disappeared behind the bathroom door.

Allen resumed his search through the archived weekly editions. The headline "Murder in Lonerock" popped on his screen. Published over two years ago, the initial story and the weekly updates filled the small-town paper. He made notes as he read. With the murder unsolved, there'd be no access to the Sheriff's file. He'd need to find witnesses or sources to paint his own picture of the murder.

Beth slipped under the covers and scooted against him. "Find your story?"

"I did." He patted her blanket-covered hip. "Long day tomorrow—think I'll join you." He closed the laptop and sat on the edge of the bed.

"What all do you have to do?"

"I'll want to visit the crime scene in Lonerock." He unbuttoned his shirt. "There's a ranch hand who was the last to see her alive. Maybe look

him up." Allen placed the computer on the desk.
"We'll need to find Ruth Titus, the victim's sister."
He turned out the lamp and headed for the bathroom.

"Is she in Condon?" Beth asked.

"Not sure—doubt it."

Before sunrise the next morning, Allen slipped
into his clothes and tiptoed out of the room barefoot,
shoes in one hand and the laptop under his arm. He
climbed into the cab of their pickup and started the
engine. With shoes tied, he waited for the computer to
wake up. Although he didn't use social media for
himself, he did find the medium useful when he
needed information on others.

Allen rubbed a hand over the day-old growth
on his chin as he waited for the Facebook page to
load. Beth hadn't stirred when he'd prepared to leave
the room. He hoped to have their day planned by the
time she awoke. When he searched the victim's name,
references and links to Char Titus jumped into view.
He sorted through the list and found a link to the
Facebook page for Ruth Titus, who had posted a
biographical sketch of her sister. She also identified
her hometown where she cared for her mother, who
waited for a kidney transplant.

Ruth didn't reveal as much as many in today's
world. Allen always puzzled over why so many
people tossed privacy concerns aside and posted
personal details of their lives for billions of people to
find. He'd never expose himself in that way. Allen
had dealt with too many people who'd use personal
details for an evil purpose.

Beth teased him for being cynical and
distrustful of others. He couldn't deny the truth, but
his work required him to approach everyone with a
measure of skepticism.

A visit to the murder scene and a trip to find Ruth would require another night in Condon. Allen closed his laptop and headed for the motel office.

He squinted at the bright morning sun atop the eastern mountain peaks. The lady behind the counter sported a baseball cap over gray hair she'd tied in a ponytail.

"We're going to need to stay another night, if we can." He fished the room key from his pocket and displayed the fob with their room number.

"This time of year should be no problem." She used her smile wrinkles. "I'm just filling in this morning, but I'll mark you down."

"Who are the Knights?"

"The high school mascot." She touched the bill of her cap. "My grandson's the quarterback."

"What year?"

"Senior. He'd like to go to Oregon State next year."

"I hope he can." Allen stuck the room key back in his pocket. "You been in Condon long?"

"Yep. I grew up here." She studied him.

"Do you remember a murder in Lonerock—couple years back?"

"Sure do. Talk of the town, that was." She waved a hand toward the guest rooms. "Those ladies stayed here."

"The one that was killed?"

"Yes—her sister too." She placed her hands on the desk and leaned forward. "Sad day. Those kinds of things are not supposed to happen around here."

"Too bad they happen anywhere. The sister's not from around here?"

She shook her head. "John Day. Why'd you ask?"

Allen grabbed his wallet and slid out a business card. "I'm a private investigator. I'm looking into the murder."

"Somebody should." She fingered the card. "Mr. Mann, you should talk to Roscoe."

"Could he help me?"

"He retired from the Sheriff's Office, but he was there."

"I'd love for you to give him my name."

"Sure, but he went to The Dalles yesterday—no idea when he'll be back."

"I'll be going to Lonerock this morning. I can check back here when I return."

After breakfast, Beth had called the boarding stable to check on Misty and told the rancher they'd been delayed.

"She's better off there than penned up in a trailer with us." He flipped the visor down. "Sun's right in my eyes. Warm too." Allen lowered the window as he drove along the narrow, paved road. The rush of fresh air cooled his neck and face.

"I'm anxious to get Misty home." Beth touched his arm. "Allen, honey, too much breeze for me."

"Sorry." He raised the window to leave a slight gap at the top. "The sun's got a bead on me right now."

"That's just right." She brushed the back of her fingers on the side of his face. "I love the scent of sage in the air—the blue sky." Beth studied the sky through the windshield and side windows. "Not one cloud."

"No rain today—maybe no thunderstorms."

"Will we have time to find the sister today too?"

"Doubt it, but we may not find anyone to talk to in Lonerock."

"You sure you can find where she was killed?"

"The cemetery—can't be many of those."

"You think this is the right road?"

"Yeah. But I checked the odometer when we left. If we don't get there in twenty-five miles, then we'll worry."

"Don't get us lost up in these mountains." Beth studied the mountain range ahead.

"Foothills. The lady said we'd wind around along the base of the mountains—couple thousand in elevation."

"Rocky and barren—everything's gray and brown out here."

"There's some green fields." Allen motioned toward a distant ranch below them.

"Yeah." She grabbed their thermos. "Guess I'm glum because I miss all the green we have at home. Want some?"

"Sure. I could use a little coffee right now."

"Wild flowers! Up there—your side." She pointed with the thermos.

"Not all drab out here." The pavement ended and the gravel surface crunched under the tires. Rocks pinged and clattered on the underside of the truck. Allen glanced at the dust raised in the rearview mirror.

Twenty minutes later the road led down into the valley where the small settlement had been established over one hundred years ago. He slowed as they entered the town. "They got a paved street."

"They do." Beth studied the buildings and dwellings as they passed. "Wonder what people do here."

"No business district. The lady at the motel said about twenty people live out here."

"Post office." Beth snickered as she read the hand-painted sign.

Allen stopped beside the row of weathered metal mailboxes perched side by side on a wooden rail. "Somebody's got a sense of humor."

"There's the rock," Beth said.

He pulled over to the side of the road and parked in front of the small white church built against a huge rock. "Kinda like a giant just plopped a big chunk of rock down in the middle of this valley." Allen craned his neck and scanned the hills on each side of the valley. "Don't think it'd roll down here."

"It sure dwarfs the church."

"I'd guess a hundred feet high—almost that wide too."

"There's a woman over there," Beth whispered.

A full-bodied woman had appeared from behind the church and worked with a rake along the front of the building. "Let's go talk to her," Allen said.

As they approached, the woman, dressed in jeans, tan chamois shirt and raggedy sneakers, faced them with the tool's handle held as a staff. "Howdy folks." A smile graced her tanned elderly face.

"You the pastor?" Allen asked.

"Haw." She rolled her eyes. "Far from it." She stuck a thumb toward the side of the church. "I tend our gift shop back there. Town don't use the church much anymore."

"The sign says it's over a hundred years old."

"Yep. The rock and church are part of our history. A few of us sell our art work and crafts from the shop."

"Are you open?" Beth asked.

"Not 'til this afternoon."

Allen cleared his throat. "Ma'am. I'm a private detective. I've been asked to look into a murder up here … happened a couple years back. Do you remember a murder?"

"Yep. The only one to remember around here." She nodded toward the church entrance. "Sister waited on the porch over there until dark. Finally, she asked old man Hodges for a ride up to the cemetery to find her sister." Her eyes focused on a distant hill. "Found her all right."

"Mr. Hodges still live in town?"

"Nope. Died."

"Anybody still around who may have seen the victim up at the cemetery?"

"Maybe Luis Ruiz. He worked on a ranch near the cemetery. The deputy, who patrolled up here, told everyone Luis had been in jail for rape."

"Luis still work out there?"

"Not sure." She knit her brow in thought. "Can't remember last time I seen him."

"How do we find the cemetery?"

"Haw. Not much up there." She poked the rake's handle at a distant hill. "I'll sketch you a map so's you don't get yourself lost."

"Could you include the ranch where Luis worked too?" Allen asked.

Chapter 10

"This should be it." Allen passed the handmade map to Beth as he used his free hand to steer through the ungated entrance.

"I'm not sure I want to be around this guy, Allen."

"You'll be okay." He patted her on the leg. "But, if you'd rather stay in the truck, I understand. This won't take long."

"Just don't leave me where you can't see me."

Allen parked at the edge of a small manicured lawn. A sidewalk led across the yard to a single-story house. The dark green dwelling with white trim and its grounds stood in a stark contrast to the dry, arid surroundings. "Somebody does a lot of work to keep that up."

"Lots of water too," Beth said.

"I'll check if anyone's home." Allen eased out onto the graveled ground.

"Don't forget to keep an eye on me."

On the sidewalk, Allen paused as the throaty sound of a motorized vehicle echoed over the packed ground between the house and a large barn. He shaded his eyes to watch for the noisy machine. From behind the house, a ranch hand on an ATV roared into view headed for the barn. Rocks and dust shot out behind as the driver braked and churned into a turn to greet the visitors.

Allen leaned against the truck beside his open driver's side window. The old rangy man cut the engine and coasted close to Allen before he clamped the brake.

"Howdy, folks." The wide brim on the sweat-stained hat hid his eyes. He tipped his head back. "You lost? Don't get many visitors out here." He slipped out of his quilted nylon jacket and draped it over the handlebars.

"I'm looking for a guy named Luis Ruiz," Allen said.

The lanky man cocked an eye at Allen as he stroked the stubble on his chin. "Used to work for me. Why?"

"Understand he had some information about an old murder up by the cemetery." Allen pulled a business card from his wallet. "I'm a private eye. A friend asked me to look into the killing."

The rancher fished a pair of reading glasses from the pocket of his red wool shirt. "Reckon he did, Mr. Mann, but he's dead." Glasses stuffed back in his pocket with the card, he said, "Died in a traffic accident out on ninety-seven. Good worker."

"Did he say anything to you about the murder?"

"Yep." He raised a leg to sit side-saddle and faced Allen. "Luis talked to a stranger who'd camped up there before they found the woman." He waved a hand toward a hilltop behind him. "Guy had the hood up on his old truck. Luis thought he needed help. Didn't."

"Hmm. Did he ever describe the guy?" Allen reached inside for a notepad above the truck's visor.

"Reckon so—if I remember." The rancher studied the ground as he ran a hand over his forehead.

"Medium height, I think—a heavy guy. Wore a hooded sweatshirt all the time, but Luis said the guy had bad skin on his face, like from acne—ruddy skin."

"Did the guy say why he camped up there?"

"Yep." The man chuckled. "Geocaching. We'd never heard of such a thing. Guess the woman had been doing the same thing."

"Did the detectives ever find this guy?"

"Don't think so. He was nowhere around when they found the body. Had one of them little foreign pickups. Old, red four-by-four with a black canopy. Nissan, maybe."

"Guess the detectives talked to Luis," Allen said.

"Yep. They hauled him in and accused him of being the killer."

"Did he say why?"

"Yep. Luis had a criminal record. He'd told them he rode by the cemetery on this." The man patted the ATV. "He'd gone again in the late afternoon and spotted the woman alone inside the fence. She'd had her head down reading the tombstones. That's what most folks do up there."

"Do you think Luis did it?"

"Nah." The rancher shook his head. "He weren't no rapist—or killer. Did wrong and paid his time."

"What'd he do?"

"He grew up down in Madras. Had a girlfriend in high school—daughter of a bigshot rancher down there. She come up pregnant. When she told daddy they wanted to get married, daddy had a fit. Luis got charged with statutory rape and they put him in jail."

"He have other trouble with the law?" Allen asked.

"Nah. I hired him after he got out of jail. Hardly ever left here. The girlfriend's family wouldn't talk to him. He never learned what happened to her or their child. He'd go down there to visit his parents once in a while. Whole thing broke his spirit. Felt so ashamed, he didn't go anywhere."

"You're not too far from the cemetery. Did you or Luis ever see the stranger in the red truck up there before or after?"

"Nah."

"Been any other murders around here?"

"Nothing like what happened up there." He waved his hand toward the cemetery. "Friend of mine south of here—Donnybrook, said a relative of his got tangled up in some murder of a woman down near Burns. He thought the same killer was involved, but I guess the law didn't think so."

"Did you go up and check out the crime scene?"

"Nah. Later, after the body and all had been picked up, Luis and I went up. Nothing left."

"I think we'll go up and look around." Allen shook the rancher's hand and climbed in behind the wheel.

Within minutes, Allen accelerated up the gravel road to the cemetery. "No Luis, but we learned something."

"The land is so barren and lonely up here," Beth said.

"Yeah. This is the kind of place you don't visit unless you have a good reason."

"You mean it's dangerous?"

"No. I mean a man in a red truck wouldn't be camped up here unless he had a purpose to be here."

"Do you think he's the killer?"

"He'd be my first suspect." Allen parked near the entrance to the fenced graveyard.

Beth pointed. "There, Allen. That's the tombstone where they found the body. What'd the lady at the motel call it—the cherub statue."

"Must be—only one like it." Allen opened the door. "Let's take a walk."

"Not much here." Beth waved her hand over the dry dirt surface with scattered clumps of low dry grass and weeds.

"Don't need to mow the grounds," Allen said. "Nothing much grows." He ushered her inside the woven wire fence and they approached the raised marker topped with the standing figure of an angelic child.

"This gives me the willies, Allen. They found her body right here."

"I know." He wrapped his arm around her waist. "Yes, right there at the foot of the marker."

"I'll never understand how someone can be so cold and heartless." She leaned closer.

"We've encountered the evil that men do to others, you and I."

She smiled as she rubbed the back of her head. "I guess we have."

"I thank God for sparing you." They embraced.

"Like you said, made us realize how short our time on earth might be. We've been blessed."

Allen kissed her forehead and relaxed his hold. "The thing that puzzles me is how anyone could sneak up on another person up here." He scanned in all directions. "So open, hard to believe the woman could've been surprised. Wonder if she knew the killer."

Sounds of a revved engine and tires on the gravel road broke the solemn moment. An old Ford Bronco approached and parked beside their truck. The pear-shaped driver closed the door and ambled toward them. He wore cowboy boots and hat with jeans and long-sleeved shirt.

"Ha, hoped I'd catch you up here." The man extended his beefy hand, "Mr. Mann. I'm Deputy Roscoe, retired."

"Oh, the lady at the motel told me about you," Allen said.

Roscoe tipped his hat. "Ma'am. Since you'd asked about the murder, thought it'd be good to catch you up here."

"Glad you came."

"See you found the spot." Roscoe glanced at the grave monument.

"Yeah. My partner asked me to gather a little information about this homicide. He's trying to see if it might be connected with another one he's working."

"What's the private eye connection?"

"There's a retired detective in the valley who is a good friend of my partner. The detective's had a stroke. So we're doing the legwork for him."

Roscoe scraped his toe in the dirt. "What's this detective's name?"

"Trudeau—Pasqual Trudeau."

Roscoe peered out from under the curled brim on his hat. "Trudeau ... with the Sheriff's Office— near Salem?"

"The same."

"Uh huh. Think he and I took some homicide training together, long time ago." He hooked his thumbs on his back pockets. "He doing okay?"

"Last I heard he's recovering—going to have a game leg."

"Okay." He drew a deep breath and exhaled. "Trudeau, huh?" A studied glance from under the brim of his hat. "Okay. The victim's sister found her SUV up here." Roscoe jabbed his thumb back at the entrance. "You tell Trudeau when we got here, the victim's SUV had two flat tires on the driver's side. Right about where your truck's parked. Someone had let the air out. Found blood on the ground near the rear tire. Tests confirmed blood came from the victim."

"Allen. I don't want to hear all these details." Beth frowned. "I'll wait in the truck."

"I apologize, Ma'am." He tipped his hat.

"None needed, deputy. I'm just not a hardnosed investigator like my husband." Beth walked away.

"Hope I didn't upset her," Roscoe whispered.

"Not at all. What else can you tell me?"

"Found Char Titus flat on her back in front of this monument. Thirty-three years of age, white, single. No clothes, legs and arms out at forty-five degrees."

"How was she killed?"

"Asphyxiation by strangulation. Doc says the guy must've used a fine wired garrote. The front of her throat had a deep cut like a sharp knife, but the injuries indicated more than a knife wound."

"He kill her here or out by the SUV?" Allen nodded toward the parking lot.

"We think he killed her out there and packed her in here for the pose. Don't know if it is important, but he had her head pointed to the north. Wouldn't have noticed but the body wasn't aligned with the grave where he had her spread out."

"Did he leave any of her possessions?"

"From what I remember, he left the stuff she had in her SUV, but kept her clothes and purse … GPS too."

"Ever identify any suspects?"

"We learned a stranger had been up here before the homicide. White male, thirties, heavyset, bad complexion and drove an old red Nissan with a black canopy over the bed. Only person who saw this guy was Luis Ruiz—registered sex offender. He worked nearby."

"Did you eliminate Ruiz?"

"To my satisfaction, we did. He passed a polygraph, didn't find his DNA or fingerprints matching any we found in our crime scene. Only found partial palm prints. We did locate remnants of an old campfire where Luis said this stranger had camped."

"Never identified the stranger?"

"Nope." Roscoe crossed his arms above his ample girth and cocked his head. "You say Trudeau thinks he has a similar homicide?"

"He's not sure, but wants to explore the possibility. His murder happened ten years back. Then he learned of one south of here that might be connected. So he's broadened his search." Allen avoided disclosing too many details because he didn't want to taint information Roscoe might reveal.

"Well that's interesting. Maybe a year or so before our homicide, there'd been one down in Harney County. I thought they'd be related but the detective down there said no. He'd identified his killer, but the guy committed suicide."

"What made you think the two were related?"

"The similar MO and the business card we found placed on the ground between our victim's feet. The card came from a real estate agency in Bend. Had several realtors' names listed, but one was Judith Rhime. She was the Harney County victim."

"So, the detective in Harney dismissed the card found here?"

"He said we couldn't prove the card came from his victim. Says it could have been dropped by anyone."

"I'd think that'd be enough to take a second look," Allen said.

"Yep. What I thought." Roscoe cleared his throat. "Walk over to my rig. I got something you can take to Trudeau."

Allen followed the retired deputy to the back of the Bronco. Roscoe opened the rear hatch.

"I want you to take that apple box with you," Roscoe said.

"What's in it?"

"A copy of everything from my personal case file on this homicide."

"Very generous of you."

"Not really. I've got no help and nowhere to go with this. Trudeau, I trust. Let him run with this. If nothing pans out, just mail this stuff back to me."

Chapter 11

"Refill?" The waitress dangled the glass pot over the table.

"Sure." Allen smiled as he leaned back to avoid a repeat of her last splatter. "Think I've changed my mind." He pointed at the short-order cook behind the order window. "The smell of his bacon makes me hungry."

She swiped a rag over the coffee she'd sloshed on the table. "I'll bring you a menu."

He leaned forward to grip the warm cup between his hands. A gray-haired couple left the restaurant and passed his window to reach their truck. A bachelor for many years, Allen had jumped at the chance to marry Beth. Not until Matt and Anna, did he have an opportunity to observe the benefits of a lifelong companion. He admired his friends' relationship and hoped to model his marriage after theirs.

Thoughts of his wife caused him to glance at his watch. She'd be up by now. Befriended by the grandmother in the motel office, Beth managed to wheedle a ride to Maupin to spend the day with Misty. Allen had encouraged her after he realized how uncomfortable she had become when he discussed the distasteful things of murder with others.

With an early start, he arrived in John Day as the sun peeked above the horizon. Plenty of time to kill because Ruth Titus told him she'd be tied up with her morning chores until eight-thirty. He'd need to hustle after his visit. Beth had appointments scheduled in her shop tomorrow. After he picked her up in Maupin, they planned to drive straight home.

The breakfast special arrived. He picked a piece of crisp bacon from the plate. A smile formed as he reflected on how complicated his life had become. As a single adult, he always did what he wanted and when he wanted. Now he had to work around the needs and desires of another. The thought sent a warm ripple across his shoulders.

◆◆◆

Allen glanced at his scribbled directions. While the Facebook post said John Day, she actually lived nearby in Canyon City. After the short drive, he spotted the post office, which meant he had a right turn ahead. Several blocks later, he parked on the street in front of the old ranch style home. Allen checked the time before he stepped out and shut the door.

Through the picture window he spotted a listless woman in a recliner. Focused on a flat-screen television, she gave him no notice. Allen pressed the doorbell.

Her dull brown hair tied back with an elastic band, Ruth Titus answered the door. In her forties, she wore a dark blue blouse with a white apron tied at the waist of her denim pants. "Perfect time. I've taken care of mother for now." She made a passing introduction to Mrs. Titus as she ushered Allen through the living room to a table in the kitchen. Mother didn't stir.

"Do you have help with your mom?" Allen settled in the chair offered.

"Yes. The clinic sends a driver to pick her up for dialysis three times a week. While she's gone, I have three to four hours to do what I want. Coffee?"

"Sure. Thanks." He positioned an empty cup. "Glad you get a little relief."

"We're on the wait list for a kidney." She poured. "That'd be nice … if it happens."

"How long you been waiting?"

"Almost three years. Around the time of Missy's murder."

"That what you called her?"

"Only at home—she hated it." Ruth sat across from him. "She and mom didn't get along … why she left."

"Did she live around here?"

"Oh. No." A slight smile formed as she shook her head. "Char headed for the big city. Couldn't stand cowboy hicks—that's what she called 'em."

"Big city?"

"Portland. My sister, the rebel." A wistful expression formed as she gazed out the window behind him. "Turned her back on us—her faith—everything Mom and Dad stood for."

"How'd you two end up in Lonerock together?"

"Long story. Mom was getting worse. I had myself tested and rounded up everyone I could. None of us qualified as donors." She shrugged. "I called Missy—had to."

"How'd that go?"

"Ha." She leaned back. "Said no, at first. But we talked. After a couple of months, she had a test." She drank from her coffee. "They found Hepatitis B. Disqualified her, but we stayed in touch. We'd met in

Condon to spend time together. The first time since she had left home."

"So, you were just sightseeing?"

"No. Geocaching. Char taught wilderness leadership courses at a college. Things like whitewater rafting, mountain climbing, survival skills—all things outdoors. The geocache thing was a hobby of hers."

"That's how you wound up in Lonerock?"

She plucked a tissue from a box and dabbed at her moist eyes. "Our last day in Condon. We were going to see Mom the next day. I didn't want to go. We'd been tramping around for a week, but Char had to go—'FTF,' she said."

"FTF?"

"First-to-find. I guess that's a big deal—was to her. She'd found the new location listed on a website for geocachers. Had to be the first one there, she said."

"How'd you get separated?"

"Stupid. We found the cache not too far from that big rock behind the old church. You know it?"

"Yep. Been there."

"Well, Char opened the plastic bucket and found an envelope inside with directions on how to find another cache. I guess they piggyback sites like that. Anyway, she had to be FTF.

"On the way back to our car, I rolled my ankle on a rock. I couldn't walk. Char helped me hobble over to the porch on the old church. A lady in the gift shop gave us some ice for my sprain.

"With the sun about to set, my sister wanted to go make her find. My ankle hurt so bad I got mad at her. I said, 'You go. Come back and pick me up.' Last time I saw her alive." She grabbed another tissue.

"Did you know where she was headed?"

"The note had the latitude and longitude, and some silly poem. She used a map to figure the cache to be near the cemetery. That's all she told me."

"Was there anyone else around?"

"Just the lady in the gift shop."

"Understand you're the one who found her."

"Actually, Hodge found her … nice old man. Char didn't come and didn't come. As it got darker, the lady in the gift shop pitied me and called Hodge. He came by and drove me up the hill to find my sister." She paused to blot her eyes.

"I'm sorry to bring up painful memories. But with your help we might figure out who did this terrible thing."

"No, no I want to help. When we reached the cemetery my sister's SUV had a couple of flat tires, the driver's door was open, and she was gone. Hodge got out and looked around. My ankle hurt so bad I waited in his truck.

Inside the graveyard, he stooped over near an angel tombstone and the worried look on his face told me something was wrong. He hurried out and said, 'Ma'am she's gone.' I didn't want to believe him and tried to get out, but he insisted that I should stay in the truck while he called the Sheriff.

"Took quite a while for the deputies to arrive. Hodge finally helped me hobble into the cemetery close enough to see for myself." She dabbed her eyes and blew her nose. "Awful. Most painful thing I've ever experienced."

"How'd your mom take the news?"

"Hard. She didn't need more bad news piled on top of her kidney problems." She sighed. "We're a sad lot, Mr. Mann. Only family left are Mom and me.

Dad died in a logging accident when I was young and my husband lost his life in a hunting accident."

"You've certainly had your share of tough times."

"Hasn't been easy, but we've got a lot of support from our church."

"Good." Allen propped a hand against his jaw. "Did the detectives recover any of your sister's personal belongings?"

"I don't think so, but they've kept everything. I have a list of what they found at the scene." She tapped her temple. "This reminds me of something. I'm not sure, but Char usually wore one of those fitness type watches. Kept track of how far she went, how fast—things like that, but I didn't pay a lot of attention. The sheriff's inventory didn't list a watch like that, as far as I can remember."

"You think the killer may have taken the watch?"

"That's what I think."

"You said Char found a note in the cache near the church. Did she keep the note and envelope?"

"Yeah. But I don't think the detectives found it."

"Hmm. Let me ask you. Did Char ever look for property to buy down in the Bend area?"

"Not that she ever told me. I'd doubt it."

◆◆◆

Hours later, Allen rejoined Beth in Maupin. They loaded Misty into their trailer and headed south on Highway 97 for Redmond. He had resigned himself to a long night on the road.

"I'm eager to get Misty settled at our place," Beth said. "We had a good day together."

Allen reached across the console for her hand. "Everything happened so fast I wasn't sure things would work out for you."

"Me too." Beth clasped his hand. "But, it did. If not, I would've been happy to wait at the motel."

"My visit with Ruth wouldn't have been as tough as Roscoe's."

"I'd still be uncomfortable. Sorry I'm such a wimp, Honey. When we went through the right-to-work ordeal and I got shot, I realized how gruesome stuff sticks in my mind. I can't set it aside."

He raised her hand to his lips. "Not a wimp. I love your innocence. Makes you kind and caring. I'll try not to bring my work home with me."

"Well, it's not like you planned this detour."

Allen smiled. "No, but by morning we'll be back on schedule."

"I'll be able to keep my appointments and then get time with Misty."

"And I'll deliver Roscoe's case file to Matt."

"I'd like to pick up a snack in Redmond or Sisters before we head over the Santiam Pass."

"Sounds good to me."

"Do you think the Lonerock murder was done by the same guy?" she asked.

"Yep. We've also got the start of a description. Average height, on the heavy side, bad complexion, wears a hoody, and drives a small red pickup with a black canopy."

"You've got a long way to go."

"We do, but there may be more in Roscoe's box. By the way, did you check out the Facebook page Ruth made in memory of her sister?"

"I did. Touching. The timing of her sister's death makes the murder much more tragic. They had just started getting reacquainted after years apart. Hope her mother gets a new kidney in time."

"Are you still thinking about doing the test?" he asked.

"I am, but I'm not sure—big decision."

Chapter 12

Matt chambered a round, checked the safety, and holstered the gun on his waist. Anna had gone into the kitchen, while he prepared to go to the office. Through the open bedroom door, he heard her voice, punctuated with laughter. He loved her laugh—he loved her.

She'd either answered the phone or placed a call. The smell of burnt toast greeted him as he entered the living room. After he stoked and fed the fire in the fireplace, he joined her in the kitchen. "You're busy out here." He hugged her from behind and kissed her cheek.

"Didn't want to send you off hungry." In a robe and slippers, she scrambled eggs at the stove. "Just in time—if you'll set the table, I'll bring the rest."

"Sure." He opened a cupboard. "Heard you cackling on the phone out here."

"Ha. I don't cackle." She stuck out her tongue. "I did forget to keep an eye on the toast."

"Guess I used the term loosely." He carried plates and flatware out to the dining table.

"That was Beth. They got home late last night." Anna followed with a bowl of eggs and the plate of toast. "She called me from her shop."

"Bet she's tired." He pulled out her chair. "Allen sent me a text at three-thirty. He's going to be a little late."

"She slept while Allen drove. Oops—we'll need the blackberry jam before you sit down."

He returned from the kitchen and settled at the head of the table. "I'm eager to dig through the box he has."

"Kinda creepy to think we got a serial killer running around. Not supposed to happen in our Pacific Northwest."

"Remember Bundy. He rattled around the Seattle area for a while—then there's the Green River guy."

"Oh. Yeah. Now that you've reminded me. I push unpleasant things out of my mind."

"I suffer from selective memory on occasion."

"By the way," she said, "you never told me what you thought of the profiler."

"Oh. I learned right off—don't call her a profiler. She told me she worked with the FBI behavioral science unit, but refused to be labeled."

"Must mean something to her."

"Not sure what, but as long as she can help identify a killer I don't care what title she wants."

"What's her name?"

"Violet Pushkin."

"She related to the Russian poet?"

Matt laughed. "No. She bristled when I asked her that."

"She's a bit sensitive, don't you think?"

"Sensitive? No. Quirky? Maybe a little. She insisted on being called 'Vi'—not Violet."

"Did she retire out of the Portland office?"

"No. Some Midwest office—Chicago maybe."

"And she retires and moves out to Oregon. Didn't you say Cannon Beach?"

"Yep. She's as tall as me. Smart too, went to college on a volleyball scholarship. Majored in psychology and then got a law degree."

"Does she think you guys are dealing with a serial killer too?"

"Won't say yet. I walked her through both the murders, Shellburg Falls and Baby's Grave. I made copies of some of the stuff for her to study. Just those two are not enough to make a convincing case. Today, we'll go through this third murder when Allen gets in."

"Poor Trudeau, I'll bet he's sorry to be out of action."

"Told me he'd be in today, even if he has to crawl."

"Is he that bad?"

"Oh, no. Just his way to saying he's excited and ready to go. I think he's about back to where he was before this last episode. He doesn't need Linh Johnson anymore."

"He let her go?"

"Yep. But they're still pretty chummy. I think she visits him a lot."

"I'm glad he's not alone all the time." She placed her hand on his. "Matt, Mrs. Johnson has waited so long. You guys better not let her down."

"Hope not. We've turned a corner, I think." He glanced at their wall clock. "I gotta go."

An hour later, Matt smiled as he parked in his reserved space. Perhaps early arrival works better than the bright red paint. He unlocked the office and carried his bag and laptop inside. The copier to his right started to hum and whir after he pressed the switch. The two sets of crime scene photos on the back wall drew his attention as he arrived at his desk. So many tragedies, the victim's, the families and Timmy. How many more? Matt shook his head.

Matt positioned a second folding table on the end of the one stacked with the first two case files. One long work surface for them to spread the documents and compare the three homicides. He pulled a folding chair out of the back room. The coffee pot gurgled on the table at the end wall between the copy machine and the restroom entrance.

Through the front window, Matt watched Trudeau's old white pickup glide to a stop in Allen's reserved space. Amused, he moved to the front door to greet his friend.

With a bag hung from a shoulder strap, the retired detective wielded a cane in his right hand as he entered. "Thought I'd beat everybody here," Trudeau said.

"I got here early so I could have the coffee ready." Matt grabbed the back of his desk chair and rolled it to the work table. "Here. I'll get you a cup."

"I haven't had a chance … to use my door key yet. You guys are always here."

"Your time will come." Matt placed a cup of coffee on the table beside Trudeau. "Don't try to do too much today. You've been off for a while."

"I couldn't miss this. What's the profiler say?"

"Ah. Don't call her a profiler. Just Vi."

Trudeau raised his eyebrows. "We going to be able to … work with her? My agent buddy … gave a high recommendation."

"Oh, I think so—just don't use titles."

"Good enough." Trudeau drew a bundle of papers from his bag. "I've been through this stuff …

over and over. I hope … Allen's information meets my high expectations."

Matt noticed the change in Trudeau's delivery, not as quick or spontaneous, more deliberate. "You get my text? Allen's running late."

"No. I didn't check."

"No matter. Vi just pulled in. We'll get acquainted before the work starts."

"Good morning." Vi paused in the entrance. Tall and lanky, the broad-shouldered woman wore gray slacks and a dark blue blazer over a white blouse. "You must be Mr. Trudeau."

Trudeau had swiveled the chair to face her and waved his right hand. "Forgive me." He slapped his bum leg.

She hoisted her black fabric bag onto a bare spot on the table. "Where should I sit?"

"Right there beside Trudeau," Matt said. "I'll get Allen's desk chair for you."

"Over there?" She nodded toward Allen's empty chair. "I'll get it."

"Okay. I'll get your coffee," Matt said.

Vi visited with Trudeau while Matt pushed a straight back chair to the table across from them. The next hour passed as the threesome discussed the similarities and differences between the Shellburg and Baby's Grave homicides.

"So … you're not convinced the same guy did them," Trudeau said.

"Not what I said." Vi leaned back, removed the half-glasses and let them hang from a fine chain she wore around her neck. "The M.O. has enough similarities to suggest the same killer. The most compelling for me is the news clip and poem left in the cache where you found Mari—and the silicon bracelet found over the mountains."

"Yeah … I'm waiting to get the lab results on that," Trudeau said.

"After I talked with Sarah, I'm certain her son didn't kill the Rhime woman." Matt pushed away from the table. "I need a refill."

Vi finger-combed her graying, shoulder-length hair back to expose her ears. "I agree. Timmy's not a killer." She released her hair. "Something I've seen too many times over the years." She leaned forward to accept a refill. "There are occasions when homicide investigators target one suspect or one theory and overlook something obvious."

"Tunnel vision," Trudeau said.

"Not purposeful," she said. "They follow logical investigative steps, but focus on one line of inquiry and, if they're wrong, end up in what I call the cold case cul-de-sac."

"Have to back out … and start all over," Trudeau said.

Allen entered with a cardboard box in his arms. Across the side a colorful banner read "Yakima Apples."

"Hey, partner," Matt said. "You brought lunch?"

"You wish," Allen said. "Brought you more work." He placed the carton on the table near Vi.

Following introductions, Allen settled on the folding chair beside Matt and across from the others. He concluded a summary of what he learned in Lonerock. "Those are the highlights and Roscoe's box probably has the details. I haven't had a chance to go through his files."

Matt stood and worked the outer cover off the box to expose the contents. "Well organized, there's a crime scene section, photos, interviews, forensics—good."

Vi positioned her reading glasses on her nose. "I'd prefer to start with the crime scene description and photos, if I might."

Matt passed folders of documents and photos to her. "Here you go, if the labels are right."

"I'd like to read the autopsy," Trudeau said.

"Allen, interviews or forensics?"

"Let me go get lunch for everyone," Allen said. "I'll start when I get back."

"By the time you're back, I'll have the copies made," Matt said.

Time passed as the team read, ate, copied and organized the information on the third murder. To make space for his copies, Matt policed the wrappers and waste from the Italian sub sandwiches.

As Allen prepared to brew another pot of coffee, he sidled over and whispered to Matt, "We need to get some better chairs. That folding one is killing me."

"I agree." Matt kept his voice low. "Take the straight back. I'll be tied up with this copier longer than I thought."

"Gentleman." Vi removed her glasses. "The evidence from the two recent murders in Gilliam and Harney counties compels me to conclude the same man is responsible for both." She rolled the chair back and crossed her legs. "He probably has or will kill again."

"No disagreement, but you're certain the killer is male?" Allen asked.

"As certain as anyone can be in such cases. There's no clear evidence in either murder of an assault, but sexual overtones are evident. You're dealing with a male perp."

"What about my Shellburg murder?" Trudeau asked.

"Some factors in common." Vi ticked off the points on her fingertips. "Geocaching, female alone, strangulation and souvenirs, bracelet, watch and business card, but the card isn't as strong."

"The news clipping … convinces me the three are related," Trudeau said.

"That'd be the best premise as we proceed." She crossed her arms. "The seven-year period between your murder and the one at Baby's Grave interests me. The last two occurred nearly twelve months apart."

"Possible the killer ended up in prison somewhere after the first murder. Interrupted his string," Matt said.

"A logical possibility—happened in other cases," she said.

"If this guy's been arrested before, maybe his fingerprints or DNA have been put in national databases," Allen said.

"Possible," Trudeau said. "But so far, in all these cases, we've only got partial DNA from under Davies' fingernails and partial palm prints from the Lonerock woman's SUV. Partials don't work for database searches."

"Something about the two recent murders reminds me of a case study we did in my FBI days," Vi said. "A good number of years ago, there was a serial killer in Arizona. The press nicknamed him the 'Mineshaft Killer'. A reporter used the label as a title on a book he wrote on the guy's crimes. Billy Fergus chose to die in the gas chamber five to ten years back. The posing, the ritual-like nature—feels like Billy, that's how everyone referred to him. He used a piano wire garrote—one of his trademarks. The wounds on these most recent women are similar."

"Roscoe mentioned something interesting about the posing." Allen said. "He told me the body of Char Titus had been placed on the gravesite crooked. He couldn't figure why the guy would go to all the trouble of carrying her to the spot, spread her out a certain way, and not align the body with the grave. Left her body sorta crosswise. Puzzled him, so he checked and her head was pointed north. Didn't mean anything to him, just odd."

"Do you have the picture?" Vi asked. She studied the image.

"Wait a second." Matt jumped out of the folding chair and sorted through the Harney County case file. "Yeah, here's the sketch of the Rhime's crime scene. If they've got the north arrow right, her head's to the east." He passed the sketch to Vi.

"Didn't notice that," she said. "Hmm. Don't know what to make of it. Do you suppose there's a south and a west?"

"Not that we've discovered." Matt tapped the table in front of Trudeau. "I believe you guys circulated a flyer on your murder to all law enforcement agencies in the Northwest and asked for similar cases."

"Yes … when the first murder happened and I did it again before they retired me."

"How wide a net did you cast?" Matt asked.

"Not sure what the secretary did … usually the Northwest region."

"Would that include northern California?"

"Not always. Usually Oregon, Washington and Idaho."

Matt returned to the folding chair and leaned toward Allen. "We're not able to use the law enforcement systems, so maybe we should make some calls and do some Internet searches."

"While you guys work on that, I need to get home." Vi placed a hand on the copies Matt made for her. "I'll take these and send you a summary with my initial thoughts."

"When can we expect to hear back?" Trudeau asked.

"My, aren't we pushy?" She smiled and patted his shoulder. "You'll get my first take by email tomorrow, but it'll take a few days to do up a report.

Chapter 13

"Did Rhime's rig have flats?" Matt peered over his glasses at his partner. "Vi raises the question in this summary of hers. I don't remember if the crime scene report ever said." He dropped the analysis on the table and sorted through the stack of papers for the Baby's Grave murder.

"I've got the Lonerock crime scene report." Allen flipped through the report. "The victim's SUV had two flats—all it says. Doesn't say how they lost air."

"Here's the write up on finding Rhime's pickup." Matt paused to read. "Doesn't say anything about the tires."

"After what we've learned of the detective's work on that case, we can't assume anything about those tires," Allen said. "Oh—here, Roscoe wrote a note in the margin on this Lonerock report—there's no sign of puncture."

"Must've let air out through the valve stems. Think that'd take some time for two tires"

"Could be noisy—would depend how fast he let the air out."

Matt returned to Vi's analysis. "She says here, if the killer used flats, the purpose could be to distract and disarm the victims enough for them to accept assistance from a stranger."

"Makes sense."

"She talks about the news clip the guy left to tie the Davies' murder to Rhime's murder. Says it'd be a rare thing for a serial killer to do." Matt swiveled his chair to face his partner. "She believes this guy wants to brag—draw attention to himself."

"Arrogant slime ball."

"Yeah, she says the serial killer in Arizona liked to brag and taunt the police. Ended up being his undoing. The cops gleaned enough about him from his communiqués so that when one of his victims escaped they pounced."

"If our guy's a braggart—might help us." Allen tapped the tablet he'd placed off to his side. "We've got a general idea of what he looks like. I've listed this guy's features here."

"Vi suggests we work out a scheme so if he starts with the taunt, we can draw him out." Matt flipped a page on the analysis. "I've thought about this too. Here she's discussing how patient this guy must be as he waits at a remote cache site for an unaccompanied female."

"Makes you wonder how many times he's gone home empty handed," Allen said. "I'd guess geocaching is a group sport—not an activity you'd do solo."

"Maybe we could publicize the description we have to geocache groups. Somebody may have seen this guy hanging around."

"While you digest her thoughts, I'll check for homicides in northern California similar to ours." Allen rolled the chair over to his desk and woke his desktop computer.

"Here's something." Matt raised his voice. "She says most serial killers pick victims who share common characteristics or circumstances. Our guy picks female geocachers who are alone. But, out in the weeds—he can't be too picky."

"She wrote that?" Allen shot back over his shoulder.

"No. That's my unprofessional take."

"Where's the Lava Beds National Monument?" Allen asked.

"California. They've got Captain Jack's Stronghold—down near Tulelake." Matt rocked back in his chair. "Not far below the Oregon border."

"What I thought. Got it." Allen studied the screen.

"Why didn't I think of this?" Matt waved the summary. "She asked, did they ever find the cache in the cemetery? I don't think so."

"I don't remember Roscoe ever saying. They didn't find the cache listed online."

"We know the Titus ladies found it. This guy must erase his trail each time." Matt dropped his papers and went for a refill. "You got something?"

"Not sure yet." Allen worked the keyboard and flashed several browser screens before the printer jumped to life.

Matt stirred powdered creamer in his coffee, retrieved the print jobs, and carried them over to his partner. "Caught the headline on top, 'Keno woman missing.' Related to our case?"

"Not sure yet." Allen read the top story and handed the page to Matt before he continued with the others.

"The Banfield family reported their daughter missing when she didn't return from a hike." Matt scanned the article. "Hmm. No idea where she went. Dolly was forty-two."

"They found her." Allen passed the second page. "Dead in the lava beds—murder. Not sure, but the Feds may have this one."

Matt read while Allen tapped the keys and worked the mouse. "Okay. The National Park Service operates the monument," Matt said. "Their enforcement people could investigate or refer the case to the state or the FBI. They also may have an agreement with the nearest county sheriff. We'll have to check this out."

"Yeah," Allen said. "I wasn't sure. Let me pick up some numbers and we can make some calls."

"Find one for the reporter—maybe the Banfields in Keno too. I'll call those," Matt said.

"With no byline, you're stuck with the *Herald and News*. Here's the number." Allen passed him a slip. "I'll dig up what I can for the family."

Matt punched buttons as he listened to the options. "Good grief." He jabbed the zero. "Oh, hi. Could I speak with your editor—or whoever decides what stories to publish?"

"I'm sorry, sir. They're not available. May I take your name and number?"

"Ma'am, this is important. I'd be on your doorstep if I wasn't a couple hundred miles away. I must talk to someone about a murder story published around ten months back."

"I don't—please hold."

Matt cupped the receiver with his hand. "Got my foot in the door."

Allen remained focused on the monitor. "We'll see if they slam it in your face."

"Crime reporter. You have information on a murder?" the man asked.

"Oh, I'm calling about the Dolly Banfield murder."

"Hmm. I don't think that's been solved—do you have something on it?"

"I might—not sure. I'm a private investigator located in the Willamette Valley. We've got a murder up here that might be connected to Dolly's death."

"Have you talked to the sheriff down there?" the man asked.

"Not yet. I wasn't sure what agency had the investigation—being on federal land and all."

"Sheriff had the case. Do you have anything on the murders for our readers?"

"Only if I can be sure the two are connected. Do you know why Dolly went down to the lava beds?"

"As I recall, her mom said she'd just taken up geocaching."

"My victim geocached. Why don't we exchange numbers? After I talk with the sheriff, I may have a story for your readers."

"Was your homicide recent?"

"Ten years ago."

"Interesting—we talking some kind of serial killer?"

"Too soon to say." Matt exchanged phone numbers and finagled the name of the sheriff's detective assigned to Dolly's murder.

"Any progress?" Allen asked.

"She may've been geocaching." Matt told Allen what he'd learned and jotted the Banfields' number as Allen read from his screen. "Think I'll call the detective first." Matt rolled his chair from their work table to his desk and tapped the number on the desk phone. A clerk at the Siskiyou County Sheriff's

Office answered. Matt left a message for the detective assigned the Banfield murder.

"The line about a possible serial killer ought to get a quick response." Allen carried his cup across the room to the coffee pot.

"We'll find out." Matt drummed his fingertips on the notepad. "Hate to cold call the mother, but I sure need to talk to her."

"Probably be better in person. Only a five-hour drive," Allen said.

"My curiosity won't wait. Catch the detective's call for me?"

"After I use the facilities." Allen left his empty cup on the table and entered the restroom.

Matt dialed as Allen moved across the room behind him. He sighed as the message on the answering machine played. "Ms. Banfield, this is private detective Matt Kinler. Looking into a homicide similar to your daughter's. Please call—"

"Hello—hello, Mr. ah—investigator?" she asked.

"Matt," he said. "Are you Dolly's mom?"

"Yes … yes I am. Do you know who killed her?"

"No, Ma'am, I'm working on a homicide near Salem. The same guy in my case might've been involved in your daughter's death."

"Oh." The sound of her voice softened.

"Ms. Banfield, we'd like to catch this man— we need your help."

"I … I don't ... Dolly's gone. Can't bring her back."

"No. No, we can't. But we can stop this guy from killing more daughters."

"There were others?" she sniffled.

"We believe so. Maybe three others."

"I don't see how I could help." Faint sounds of her blowing her nose away from the phone.

"Could you tell me about your daughter?"

"Told the deputies everything ... just be repeating myself."

"But we haven't heard about Dolly. Did she live in K Falls?"

"She lived with me. Her father died in a mill accident many years ago. Just Dolly and me."

"What kind of work did she do?"

"Army. She never said much, but her job had to do with radios and computers—made sergeant." The mother paused. "She'd been to Iraq, Kuwait and, ah ... the last time in Afghanistan. That's where her convoy hit a bomb ..."

Matt waited for her to continue. A mother's pride had bolstered her voice. Grief punctuated her delivery.

"... never the same again. She healed up okay, but wrong in the head. Couldn't sleep—nightmares. One minute she'd be fine, next she'd freak out."

"Did she get help?"

"The VA ... but way too many pills for me. I got her started on a healthy diet and exercise and weaned her off the drugs."

"A good thing she had you."

"She'd bounced back. We'd planned her forty-second birthday ... excuse me."

"Sure. I'm thankful for your time and the opportunity to learn about your daughter." Matt recognized the classic symptoms of Dolly's PTSD, but her mother hadn't mentioned the disorder. No reason for him to bring up the topic. Allen answered the phone across the office.

"Mrs. Banfield, do you know why Dolly went down to the lava beds?" Matt asked.

She replied, "My daughter combined her hiking with a love for any new technology to keep track of her heartbeat, mileage, navigation—she'd started something called geocaching. I've never done it, but she became quite the fanatic. She liked being the first one to a new treasure. She checked a website and away she went. Last time I saw her alive..."

"I'm dreadfully sorry for your loss, Ms. Banfield. I can only imagine how much you miss her."

"I still talk to her every day ..." Her voice trailed off.

After Matt ended the call, he stared at his notes. No doubt—the man who murdered the others had also murdered Dolly, his fourth. He held steepled fingers under his chin. They had to get their hands on Dolly's file.

Allen's side of the telephone call from the sheriff's deputy didn't sound promising. Matt grabbed his cup and headed for a refill.

"Okay, thank you for your time." The phone clattered as Allen ended the call. "Wow—tight-lipped would be an understatement." He swiveled to face Matt.

"Anything worthwhile?" Matt stirred creamer as he returned to his chair.

"Helpful with all but the murder." Allen studied his notes. "The Sheriff's Office responded to help the park police with the initial crime scene. The park service had arranged for the county and state to have concurrent jurisdiction in the monument."

"Did the SO run down all of the initial leads on the homicide?"

"No. The case was referred to the California Bureau of Investigation. But if I read between the lines correctly, the deputies do catch leads, now and then."

"Did I hear you give out Trudeau's name with our local sheriff's address?"

"He hadn't seen the flyer on Trudeau's case. I'm going to fax the flyer and if he thinks the cases might be related he'll send information on their murder to Trudeau."

"Maybe we'll have Trudeau call him after you've sent the copy. Ask him to do a little schmoozing."

"He did let a few things slip." Allen located a note with his fingertip. "Her car had been disabled and they found her naked."

"Her mom told me she went geocaching and loved to be the first one to find a cache."

Allen dialed the number to send the facsimile.

"Trudeau had physical therapy today." Matt said. "I'll run by his house on my way home. If he talks to the Siskiyou detective, he might arrange for us to get the file.

Chapter 14

"Perfect." Sydney mouthed as he examined the two keys he held above the steering wheel. When he reported for work tonight, he'd return the master keys. He doubted his foreman would notice the dummy keys he'd substituted on the ring to conceal his plan to get copies. If the boss discovered his slight-of-hand with the keys, he'd be fired. A risk, but he didn't care. The copies in his hand would still work, until they changed locks.

He drove his old pickup from the hardware store into northeast Salem. A few days had passed since he'd checked for mail at the room he'd rented using the name Jose Garcia. His landlady rented out several rooms in her small house. But Sydney chose the converted single car garage to avoid roommates. The bare space had a side door, electricity and a concrete floor. Not much, but he thought of it as his post office box.

Rosa, the middle-aged Hispanic landlady, didn't speak much English, which was fine with him. He didn't need any lasting friendships or a lot of nosey questions. Once he received the credit card with his phony name at this new mailing address, he'd be ready. His damaged complexion often led strangers to assume him to be Hispanic. A mistake he had used to his advantage several times.

On the outskirts of the city, he left the road and drove down a dirt lane. As he passed the small kitchen window on the side of the house, he nodded to his landlady who waved from inside. Beyond the house, he parked in front of the roll-up door on the small detached garage. The structure with a moss-covered roof had no curb appeal, but the address and seclusion met his criteria.

Sydney dropped the tailgate on his red import and grimaced. The small electric heater had rolled forward. He ducked under the black canopy and strained to reach the appliance. The landlady's yappy little mutt bounced out of the house and danced near his legs. With Rosa on the back steps, he resisted the urge to punt the dog across the overgrown yard. He fished the garage key from his jacket, entered and locked the door behind him. Several pieces of mail had been left in the middle of the daybed. Junk except for the envelope addressed to Jose Garcia. He made a mental note, Rosa had a key.

He jumped in his truck and headed for the wireless store. After he activated the Garcia credit card, he'd buy a Smartphone, prepaid minutes and a wireless hookup for his laptop, all linked to Jose Garcia. Excitement coursed through his body. The false identity gave him a layer of protection from the cops and the new devices would make him mobile. More secrets to be kept from his mother.

Several hours later he returned home. Under a fruit tree, the neighbor leaned on a shovel and glared as he passed. Sydney ignored Mr. Barnes rather than give him an impulsive gesture.

In the house, Sydney rushed through the kitchen and headed down the stairs to his room. The audio from the television blared from the living room.

"Sydney, is that you?" Wanda yelled from the living room.

"Yeth, Mother." He shouted as he dropped the bag of purchases on the floor by the bottom step. If she spotted the wireless logo, there'd be no end to questions.

He climbed the stairs to speak with his mother, seated in front of her television. The elaborate recliner, with heat and a vibrator, relieved her pain and kept her stationary, a benefit to him.

"Why are you so late? That probation officer called again."

"I'll call."

"Mr. Barnes called. Someone tipped over his garbage can and broke the bags open in the street. I told him you wouldn't do that. You didn't, did you"

"Of course not, Mother."

"You must be tired after working all night. You're late getting home, what kept you."

"The foreman had me thtay to teach a thafety class for the other janitors."

"Oh, Sydney. You're doing so well. I'm proud of you."

"I try my best." He shuffled backward. "Mother, I'm going to get thome thleep."

She waved the television remote toward the stairs. "You go. I'll wake you to help with dinner."

In his basement hideaway, Sydney tore into the bag. He found the instructions and worked feverishly to get operational. Smartphone ready and synced with the laptop, he logged onto the Internet through his mother's wireless router. Since she relied on him to maintain her computer and router, he had usernames and passwords memorized. He toyed with using his neighbor's wireless router, but resisted the temptation. No need to risk Barnes discovering his vulnerability. Sydney had used him once and may need to again.

Keywords committed to memory, he searched for news stories on his handiwork. A slight smile formed. He liked the word "handiwork," one he'd borrowed from the book written about Billy's murders.

Not one story, not one mention, he growled, low and guttural. He wiped beads of sweat from his forehead. The stupid cops had his clue, but hadn't figured out the connection between his first and second murders. Seven years apart, different techniques—maybe he needed to give a different clue or use another approach. The intense desire for fame rivaled his urge to kill again. *Be patient, Sydney.* Billy told the author a lack of patience got him arrested.

Several souvenirs in his collection could grab the cop's attention. He hated to part with any of those. An anonymous letter or phone call might work, but those carried greater risk. Maybe he'd find an industrious reporter and dribble enough information for a story. Better yet, Jose Garcia could operate anonymously through an offshore proxy server. With an international IP address, he could fly under the cops' radar. Not forever, but long enough. Sydney sacrificed his sleep to spend several hours online.

"Yeth," he mouthed and rubbed his hands together in celebration. Worth every penny to have the ability to send email messages and remain anonymous behind a foreign server's address. Wanda would do the usual whine when he asked for a loan, but she'd relent and pull cash from her purse. The last time he drove her to the bank she came home with the usual five grand. The inheritance made her a millionaire, but, except for cash stuffed in her purse, their lifestyle remained the same. However, she did indulge in "necessities," the flat screen television, and the recliner, and the scooter.

Sydney turned his attention to the screen as he searched locations for his next cache. The last three had been dry runs because none of the geocachers met his criteria. This fifth kill had to be on the coast to complete his dream of a compass rose. He thought the nuance reflected his genius. When his "handiwork" became known, others would write of his brilliance as they had of Billy's.

"Port Orford, the most westerly point on America's west coast." He paused to read more. Information and images from several links and maps made his heart race. He sucked a deep breath before he resumed. The lighthouse at Cape Blanco captured his attention. Pictures and videos of the state park with camping, hiking and horse trails, trees and brush had Sydney wound tighter than an old clock's spring. He pushed up from the couch and paced the floor. Why had he missed this place? Ideal for his next kill. Each step he took had to be planned. He unbuttoned his shirt and fanned his bare chest. Powerful urges stirred as he imagined a pose at the foot of the lighthouse, urges hard to control. *Be patient.*

Day or night, his windowless sanctuary turned dark with a flick of the light switch. The stairway allowed filtered light from the main floor. In the darkest corner, he kept the precious nightlight, an obsession from his childhood. Fear of being alone in total darkness brought on panic attacks.

Sydney kicked off his shoes and curled under a blanket. His head swam in thoughts of the new opportunities he had created. The name Jose Garcia had become a person. He plotted how to use Jose's credit card, mailing address, wireless phone and offshore server to become famous. He drifted off to sleep.

◆◆◆

"Sydney." Wanda shouted down the stairwell.

He hated for her to wake him. Her whiney voice grated on his nerves and put him in a foul mood.

"Sydney. Answer me. Time to help with dinner."

"I'm up, Mother." He rubbed sleep from his eyes as he stumbled into the three-quarters bath. Before he headed for the coast, he'd send a message to the local newspaper. Had to have a hook to grab the editor's attention. The spam filter used by the newspaper's server may pose a problem. With an offshore origin, his email might get junked. He'd experiment tonight after he finished his work. Better to use the government's computer and server. One more layer of protection for him.

He trudged up the stairs and into the kitchen. Wanda waited at the table on her scooter. "What thould I fix, Mother?"

"We need to finish up the leftover lasagna. Maybe some salad."

Sydney removed a foil-covered dish and a plastic bag of pre-mixed salad greens from the refrigerator. "Mother, I need a loan." He moved to the counter below the microwave.

"Loan?" Wanda powered to the utensil drawer. "You borrow and borrow and never pay me back."

"I will, mother. Tho hard on probation to get a decent job." He set plates on the table.

"How much this time—a couple hundred dollars?"

"Oh, let me think." He slid the first serving in the microwave. "How about ten hundred?"

"A thousand?" Wanda raised her voice. "Why so much? Are you in trouble?"

"No, I told you I'd planned a trip to the coast. I'll have travel expenses and my truck needs some repairs before I leave." He placed the warmed lasagna in front of her with a bowl of salad centered on the table.

"How long will you be this time? I'd like some wine, Sydney."

"Better not—too close to your pain medicine, Mother."

"Just a little—I've had both before. Pain's bad today." She scrunched a frown.

"I'll be gone around a week. Hang around Astoria and then cross over into Washington—Long Beach, maybe further." He figured she wouldn't overdose on four ounces.

"Thank you, Sydney." She sipped from the glass. "You're a good son. I put my purse out by the recliner. There's cash in the wallet."

Dinner over, Wanda sequestered in her bedroom, Sydney gathered his laptop and new cellphone. Money in his pocket, he tingled with excitement as elements of his plan fell into place. During the short drive to check in with his foreman, he turned different messages and clues over in his mind. Had to be enough to catch the coppers' attention and force them to realize they faced a brilliant killer, one they'd never catch.

He picked up the office keys and left Ross by the company truck under the yellow arches. Music blared from an upstairs apartment near his office building. Sydney stuffed the cellphone in his pocket and carried the laptop under his arm. Near the back entrance, he fished the new duplicate keys from his pocket. A sly grin formed as the lock's bolt released to allow him entry.

Driven to finish early, Sydney pushed himself. Several times he had to stop to catch his breath. After two in the morning, he tested the second of his keys on the office where he did his mischief. In his haste to finish cleaning, he'd failed to try this key earlier. He used a USB cable to tether his laptop to the agency's desktop. As the units came to life, he jittered with excitement. The limp, sweaty coveralls hung heavy on his shoulders.

The keyboard clattered as he created an email address for the offshore server. The domain name after the "@" symbol might be enough to trigger a spam filter, but he figured "compassrose" as a user name wouldn't raise alarm.

The crime beat reporter plugged her email address at the end of her stories. Sydney selected her as his contact. In the subject box, he wrote, "Shellburg Murder-Unsolved?" The message read:

> *"One clue and they can't catch. Cops have met their match!*
> *To kill a work of art. Each better, each a part.*
> *Find me? A fool's errand.*
> *The All Points Killer"*

The first shot fired into cyberspace, Sydney worked the browser for more information on the south coast until his shift ended.

He found Ross in the driver's seat of the company van. The odor of fast food hit him as he spoke to his foreman through the open passenger-side window.

"Hey," Sydney said. A pile of food wrappers and paper cups covered the center console.

"Good. I can go home. You're the last one." Ross stuck his large hand out.

Sydney dropped the keys into the outstretched palm. "Something's come up." He tossed his coveralls through the side door. "I need a week off."

Ross frowned. "I can't—too short a notice."

"Man, I don't got a choice—family emergency—in Montana."

"If you go, I can't guarantee a job when you get back."

Amused, Sydney climbed in his truck and headed for home. Ross had tried the old "lose-the-job" threat, a threat lost on Sydney for he didn't care. Employment kept his probation officer happy and she pestered him less. He had to admit the janitor job had perks. There'd been no coworkers, no stupid boss over his shoulder, and he had the use of agency computers with access to the Internet. Although risky, he'd still have access to the offices with his pirated keys.

He'd arranged for his probation officer to come by tomorrow for a home visit. If his mother didn't mess things up with her mouth, his case officer would go away happy and lay off the frequent calls for a few months. For several years, other probation officers had followed the same pattern. He expected her to do the same. She didn't need to hear his vacation plans or of his possible loss of a job.

Chapter 15

"Must be important." Through the office window Matt watched Trudeau drive away. "A new development to discuss—all he said." He left the table to heat water in the microwave. "Nothing for us to do but wait." Matt tapped the timer buttons.

"We need a break—not new developments." Allen moved from the folding chair to his own desk chair.

"Hope they don't shut you guys down." Vi reached for the cup of hot water offered by Matt. "Quite a collection of egos circle around a hot case," she said. "Some may not want to share the spotlight."

"Trudeau doesn't need to be sidelined right now—might destroy him." Matt dropped a teabag packet on the table. "Just plain—okay?"

"Perfect," she said. "You guys have stirred things up. Maybe they've got some new lead—a suspect even."

"I recognized the name of the guy who called. He's the detective who manages the cold cases," Matt said.

"Let's go through the new information he left," Allen said.

"Yes. I want to get back home tonight." Vi sipped from her tea. "Since I arrived late, tell me again the origin of this information. It's on this other murder in northern California, right?"

"Yeah," Matt said. "Trudeau called down there and talked with the Siskiyou detective. The detective wouldn't send the stuff direct to Trudeau, but agreed to fax these reports to Trudeau's detective friend at the Sheriff's Office—marked for Trudeau's attention."

"Not a lot of pages." Vi fingered the edge of the short stack of reports. "Is this all they did on the murder?"

"The Sheriff's Office responded to the first call on the murder. They did the initial crime scene work. Then the state investigators took over. The deputy Trudeau talked to wrote these reports and that's all he had," Matt said.

"Which state agency has the case?" Vi asked.

"California Bureau of Investigation," Matt said.

"Ah," Vi said. "If he's still there, I may have a contact."

"You've worked with them?" Allen asked.

"No. I met this guy at a homicide conference. When I get home, I'll check my collection of business cards." She picked out a report and pushed the others toward Matt. "Without objection, I'll read the report with the crime scene walk through."

"Not from me." Matt offered two reports to Allen. "You choose. We'll trade off."

Vi flipped through the stapled pages. "No photos—just a schematic with rough measurements."

"The car wasn't parked too far from the trail to a cave." Allen spoke as he read. "Unlocked—two flats. First time I called, he said they found the car disabled—didn't say how."

"Punctured?" Matt asked.

"Don't know yet."

Vi held the report open in her hand and leaned back. "This has to be the same guy." She peered over her glasses at the other three crime scene photos arranged on the back wall. "Naked ... posed the same way." She carried the report to the back wall. "The same fine cut to the neck. The autopsy would have a better description of the wound."

"Maybe we can get our hands on that someday—and the photos. I'll bet they didn't find defensive wounds either," Matt said.

"Nothing in the car—no clothing," Allen said.

"This report mentions the body had been moved," Matt said.

Vi faced the work table. "Yes. This report comments on the sparse amount of blood under the laceration on her neck." Vi offered her report to Matt. "Trade?"

"With what we know of the others, it'd be hard to say this isn't the same guy," Matt said.

"One sick puppy. Do they ever just quit?" Allen asked.

"Usually not," Vi said. "They might have a break in their cycle of murders. Maybe get thrown in prison, or have health issues, or get injured— eventually die."

"That'd end it," Allen said.

"Hey." Matt spread the report on the table and positioned the crime scene schematic. He stuck a finger on the sketch. "Here. Whoever drew this showed the direction north. I realize this may not be exact, but the way he sketched the body—her head's to the south."

"I don't recall ever studying a serial killer where the compass orientation had been a trademark," Vi said.

"Is that what we have here?" Allen asked.

"Appears to be a distinct possibility," Vi said.

"If we discount Davies, we have one to the east, and one to the north, and this one to the south," Matt said.

"The first one, Davies—it appears the killer had been interrupted," Vi said.

"So, we may have a west somewhere?" Allen asked.

"Could be." Matt grabbed his empty cup and went over to the coffee pot.

"Maybe that's what they called Trudeau about," Allen said.

"We'll know in a minute." Matt pointed toward the front window where, outside, Trudeau climbed out of his truck.

The disabled detective, with shoulder bag and cane, shuffled into the office. "They heard ... from our killer." He eased into the office chair Allen had left for him.

"A call or what?" Matt asked.

"A reporter with our local paper ... got an email. The editor showed the message ... to the DA. They called me in to tell the DA ... what we have."

"Is the editor going to run a story?" Vi asked.

"No ... not yet. They'll hold off ... as long as they get an exclusive."

"Hmm. That might be a problem," Matt said. "Remember, I talked to the reporter in K. Falls. What if he runs with a story down there?"

"Oh—that's in the Saturday text you sent, right? Trudeau asked. "Forgot. Tell me again what you told him."

"Not a lot of detail, but enough for him to know there are other murders." Matt shook his head.

"I kick myself now. Felt I needed to give him incentive to help me."

"Give me the contact … I'll tell the prosecutor assigned to work the case."

"What'd the killer say?" Vi asked.

Trudeau fished a single piece of paper from his bag. "This is a copy."

"Let me make copies." Matt returned from the machine with copies of the email for everyone.

"Using a proxy server—in Canada," Allen said. "It'll take some effort to find him. Our country's laws don't touch those operations."

"I've heard of proxy servers. How exactly does that work?" Matt asked.

"Easy to set up," Allen said. "Google off-shore servers, select one, sign up, and pay a fee. That gets you a link to a proxy computer server with an International IP address. Here's what happens. You have your computer here in Oregon with an Internet connection. Then with your link to the proxy server, you send a message to a newspaper in Oregon. The newspaper only sees the server's domain name in Canada, or some other country, and has no idea who sent the message or that it came from you in Oregon."

"With a setup like this, a guy could do some real mischief."

"Yeah." Trudeau tapped his copy. "The editor told us that is why the newspaper's spam filter had blocked this message. He has the tech people check the spam bin … for anything interesting."

"That'd explain the date," Vi said. "At first, I thought they might've sat on it for a few days."

"Look at his username, 'compassrose.' Seems to fit with the different directions he's posed the bodies," Matt said.

"What caught the editor's eye … 'Shellburg Murder' in the subject box. He remembered the stories they ran," Trudeau said.

"He's taunting, again," Vi said. "He wants the world to know he's smarter than the cops."

"Gives you the creeps to learn this guy thinks murder is art," Allen said.

"Not just that—he relishes what he's doing. Proud, boasting he has killed more than once," Vi said.

"What do you think of the 'All Points Killer' sign off?" Matt asked.

Vi placed her copy on the table. "The 'all points' part echoes the meaning in his choice of a username." She removed her glasses and let them hang from the tether. "But, I think it's more than a reference to how he locates his victims. He wants control. He's assigning himself a nickname," she mimicked quote signs, "not leaving that to the newspaper or cops."

"What you're saying is, he's put a lot of thought into this." Allen waved his copy.

"Most of these guys do. Sometimes the plotting and planning give them more stimulation and satisfaction than the crime itself. Then, there are the times they can relive an event." She picked up the paper and studied the message. "These guys are hard to catch because they plan, but have no obvious connection to their victims—the random nature. But, if they get thwarted, rattled or frustrated in their efforts, they make mistakes."

"How do we get under this guy's skin—get in his head?" Trudeau asked.

"We'd have to give some thought to that," she said. "First, he wants publicity—notoriety—acclaim."

"So, we don't give him any?" Matt asked.

"Yes and no," she said. "We delay any news release until the publicity works in our favor. We also cast him in a bad light, never positives as to his being smart, clever and so on."

"Then we shouldn't use his 'All Points Killer' title?" Allen asked.

"Right. We need to assign him a nickname that'd drive him nuts," she said.

"How about calling him a 'wanna be'?" Allen asked.

"Something like that has good potential," she said.

"Maybe call him 'The Wanna Be Killer'," Matt said.

"Killer might elevate him. Make it just 'The Wanna Be'," she said.

"Let's not get carried away. We got a problem," Trudeau said. "The DA and the Sheriff's Office … they're going to form a task force on this case."

"So we're out?" Matt asked.

"Not what I'm saying. Wait until they decide." Trudeau swiveled in the chair and spoke to Vi. "I've asked them to let me be a consultant on their task force. If you're interested, I'll ask them to include you. They'd pay expenses and a small stipend."

"Yes," Vi said. "I'm not well known out west. I'd be able to add an official task force to my credits."

"Hey, you can use volunteer work with our agency in your resume," Matt said.

"We're not well known out west either," Allen said.

"Yeah, there is that," Matt said. "Plus, we need to decide on a name for our business." He toyed with his empty coffee cup. "Guess that'd leave me and Allen out in the cold. A bummer, huh partner?"

Allen shrugged. "Yep. But I'd understand."

"I plan to continue my work here." Trudeau slapped a hand on the table. "You guys will be here and I want you involved. Let's wait until the DA decides on my role—and Vi's."

"How soon will he make a decision?" Matt asked.

"I'm supposed to meet with the Deputy DA and the detectives later. Might get word then."

♦♦♦

Matt glanced at the sunset in his rearview mirror as he headed for home. The disappointment he'd felt when Trudeau delivered the news had lost the sting. Anna would be disappointed too, especially after their visit with Sarah and Dusty. But she'd probably take the news better than he did.

Darkness settled in their private stand of trees well before sunset. Matt parked at the bottom of the front stairs. The canine greeters met him as his feet touched the ground. "Hey guys." Matt ruffled the furry heads before he grabbed his bags and climbed up to the porch. The front door stood open. The smell of baked goods made him hungry. He inhaled the fragrance.

"Sure good to be home." He spotted his wife at the kitchen sink.

"Busy day?" With a towel in her hands, she met him at the dining table and they kissed.

"Interesting day. We got more on the lava beds' murder." He wiped a fingertip across a smudge on her forehead and touched his tongue. "Hmm. Chocolate."

"Guess I missed some." She wiped the spot with the towel. "Is it gone?"

"But not forgotten. When do I get more?"

"You don't. I made cupcakes for Beth. She's invited several of us for a ladies' night. You boys will be on your own tonight. I've got to get ready." She headed for the bedroom and back over her shoulder said, "You'll have to tell me about your day when I get home."

He moved into the kitchen and emptied his pockets on the counter beside the phone. The message light flashed. He discovered fresh coffee in the carafe.

With a full mug, he settled in the recliner with their dogs and selected his favorite source for news.

Anna, dressed in a white blouse and dark skirt, hurried from the bedroom. "There're leftovers from last night in the fridge. I shouldn't be too late."

"You take such good care of me." Matt smiled.

She leaned down for a kiss then grabbed her black wool jacket and purse.

"I forgot to check—the messages," Matt said. "Saw the light. Do you know who called?"

Anna stopped at the door. "Trudeau. Wants you to call. I had icing up to my elbows and didn't answer."

Trudeau had good news. Matt and Allen could assist Trudeau and Vi, whom the DA had selected as consultants for the task force. One condition troubled Matt. The DA wanted the regular sworn detectives to do all active investigation. Matt and Allen could identify leads, but the actual coverage had to be done by the Sheriff's detectives.

He mulled his status from the comfort of his recliner. Trudeau said his most persuasive pitch had been the rapport Matt and Allen had established with the victims' families. Fair enough, but restrictions on his role as an investigator didn't set well, never had. He'd find a way to make this work.

Chapter 16

"Theee'th here." Sydney, behind his mother's chair, used the sheer curtains bunched to the side of the picture window for concealment. The white sedan parked on the street screamed government vehicle. He caught a glimpse of the sidearm before she slipped into a red blazer. Trim and fit, she strode toward the driveway.

"Should I get out of my recliner?" Wanda asked.

"No, Mother." He hoped to limit any contact his mother had with the visitor.

"What ith he doing?" He'd pressed his face into the curtain to gain a view of his neighbor, who had hailed the probation officer. Mr. Barnes and the officer moved out of sight as they talked.

"Who are you talking about?" Wanda paused her movie.

"Our neighbor. Here theee cometh." Sydney moved to the front door.

All business, she studied him eye to eye. "Do you have a table where we could talk? I have some papers to fill out."

He led her into the kitchen and pulled out a chair.

"Do you need me?" His mother raised her voice.

"No, Mother."

The interview followed the pattern of others he'd endured. The officer delved into his computer use. "Do you own or have access to computers?"

"No, he doesn't." Wanda arrived on her power scooter.

He resented how she always stuck her nose in his business.

"Do you?" The officer eyed him.

"No."

"He's got a friend who would love to play computer games with him."

"Have you been playing, Sydney?"

"No—how could I?"

"Don't you have a computer, Ms. Smythe—an Internet connection?" The officer studied Wanda.

"Yes, but I keep my laptop and router hookup in the bedroom. Sometimes I use them at night. Sydney never does."

"My I inspect your browser history?"

"Well … I guess so." Wanda fidgeted on her perch. "Sydney, would you get my laptop from the nightstand—please."

"Thure, Mother." Sydney made a quick trip into the bedroom and placed the computer on the table.

The officer worked the keys.

"I wish you'd let my son go geocaching," Wanda said.

"Why can't he?"

"His last officer said he couldn't use any computer things—Smartphone or any GPS device."

The visitor paused. "Smartphone's off limits, but if the GPS device is just a receiver—no other functions—I might give permission. Do you have one to show me?"

"No," he said. And she'd never find it.

"What'd you do with it?" Wanda asked.

"Thold it, Mother." He grew uneasy with his mother's participation. She often said the wrong thing at the wrong time.

The probation officer closed the laptop. "Before I finish up, I'd like to inspect your room and truck. That's the one in the driveway?"

"No problem." Sydney said. He had nothing to fear. He'd hidden the damning possessions in his storage unit across town.

"I got a good report back from your employer. Always makes my job easier when you're working."

"He's such a good worker," Wanda said. "He's getting a vacation."

The officer raised her eyebrows. "Really. You just started."

"Only a few personal—"

Wanda interrupted. "He's going up the coast—loves the coast."

"No—not now," Sydney said. "I've talked about a trip. Can't afford one."

"But—"

"Mother, pleath."

"You'd be permitted a trip to the coast. No out-of-state travel without permission."

"North—Cannon Beach would be the only place I'd go." He didn't want her to think of him being on the south coast.

After the probation officer left, Sydney drove across town. The officer hadn't shown a high degree of alarm over his vacation days or travel within the state. Those issues wouldn't have come up if his mother had stayed in her recliner. She thought she was being helpful, but he didn't want her help. He had secrets and her meddling might expose them. He hoped his PO wouldn't call Ross to ask about any vacation.

◆◆◆

Rosa waved from inside the kitchen as he passed. Sydney entered his garage apartment. The landlady had left a stack of mail for Jose Garcia on the table. He leafed through the junk mail.

After a stop at the storage locker to retrieve his prohibited devices, he planned to drop by his favorite hotspot and browse for news and messages. There'd been nothing in his mother's newspaper or on television about an old murder investigation.

Sydney chose a back corner in the coffee shop, a small regular coffee the price of admission. Not a drink he relished, but he fit in with the other geeks. Linked to his off-shore server, he found no reply from the reporter. The spam filter must have blocked his message. Maybe the reporter had to research the Shellberg murder. After all, ten years had passed. He decided not to send another email yet.

Home in his basement room, Sydney relived the past with his picture files. Invigorated, he packed for his trip. He'd drop by his storage locker tomorrow. Because his mother had been a persistent snoop, the unit became the best place to hide the clothing and souvenirs. The secrecy and security of the locker convinced him to keep it longer than he'd planned. When he picked up his kit in the morning, he'd also find the dog tags from his last kill. Those had to be the clue to leave with his next flower. They'd be much more obvious than his previous clues, but he needed to draw attention to his handiwork. Early in the morning, he'd head out of town.

◆◆◆

"Mom?" Winter Vanderscoot called as she stood at the kitchen counter. No response meant her mother hadn't come out of the bedroom. She touched the slices of sourdough bread to her nose, enjoyed the scent, and loaded the toaster.

"Did you call me?" Dressed in waitress garb, Eva Vanderscoot entered from the living room.

"I'm fixing a late breakfast and wondered if you wanted anything." Winter placed a box of dry cereal on the table.

"Nah, I'll get something at work. Might have some tea with you."

The toast popped up while she served their tea. Winter grabbed the toast and sat across from Eva. "Wish you didn't have to work, Mom."

"Don't know how else to pay bills." Eva bobbed the tea bag on a string. "Since your father died, I've had to supplement what we get from the state and Feds."

"I thought after Dad was killed you got enough to buy this place."

"I did. Really lucky to find this two-bedroom bungalow—only a mile inland. I wanted to raise you here, on the south coast." Eva smiled over the cup cradled in her hands. "So young, you don't remember—do you?"

Winter shook her head as she dug a gob of raspberry jam from the jar. "I wouldn't have much memory of Dad if we didn't have your pictures and stories."

"You weren't quite two." She sipped from the tea. "We'd tried for years. Your father—so proud—busted his buttons."

"The Chief and the other old timers talk about him around the department. Call him a hero." Winter held a spoon in one hand and her long blonde hair in the other to keep the tips out of the bowl of cereal.

"They'd remember because he'd been stationed here in Bandon." Eva gazed out the kitchen window. "He was a hero, Winter. Rescued a young mother and her baby. They'd been kidnapped by an escapee—a killer."

"Long time since I read the news story, Mom. Just doing their job. He and his partner check a suspicious car and get shot. Dad died."

"They'd killed the bad guy," Eva said. "When help arrived, they found the mother tied, gagged, blindfolded, and stuffed down in the back seat with her baby."

"I remember Dad's partner said they didn't have a description of the escapee's car and had no idea he'd kidnapped anyone—there'd been no reports."

"Yes. They spotted a suspicious car in a turnout, driver's door open and no driver. Your dad approached from behind on the passenger side and his partner on the driver's side. The killer jumped out of the bushes—ambushed 'em." Eva's eyes turned distant for a moment before she continued.

"Your father went down first, but when the killer fired over the car at his partner, your dad, from the ground, emptied his gun in the guy. The Superintendent, the one with your dad in his graduation picture—" She nodded toward the living room. "—said all six kill-shots came from your dad's gun."

"The Chief told me they still talk about Trooper Vanderscoot in the State's training." Winter gathered her dishes. "Didn't get to know my dad, but the stories and respect others have for him make me proud—I feel a connection."

Eva reached across the table to clasp Winter's hands. "You're his flesh and blood, Winter. His pride and joy."

Her moist eyes met her mother's. She nodded, withdrew her hands, and carried the dishes to the sink. "Everyone called him 'Scoot.' They call me that sometimes."

"I understand your interest in police work, Winter, but I do wish you'd find something less dangerous to do with your life." Eva met her at the sink and they embraced.

Winter, a head taller at five-ten, held onto her mother. "I really haven't decided yet, Mom."

"You've said that, but all of your classes at the community college point that way. Almost every day I hear you say how much you enjoy the volunteer work with police support services."

"Oh, I know, Mom." She released her hold. "It's just—everyone we've hung around with have been law enforcement."

Eva plucked a tissue from the table and dabbed at her eyes. "I don't know how we could've made it without our friends in blue. Couldn't find a better support group."

"When I stop to think about what I'm interested in—law enforcement trumps everything else. Must've got a gene from Dad, if there is such a gene."

"You may have." Eva smiled before she blew her nose.

"The Chief thinks I should apply to be one of his reserve officers after I finish my classes." Winter returned to her chair. "He says I was meant to be a cop. Said I have the right instincts—a nose for the work—called me a huntress."

"What's he mean? Was he teasing you?"

"I'm not sure. I don't see it."

"You've always excelled in sports. Maybe you should be a coach—you're good with kids."

"I've thought about that. I really like camping and hiking. Wonder what kind of jobs I could get with the Forest Service."

"Go online."

"Rex has me excited over this geocaching thing."

"Heard you talking to him. I don't get the point, but you've always enjoyed games—competition."

"We're going caching together on his next days off."

"When's that?"

"He's on the road three more days, then three off. I think he told me he's the only trooper on the south coast highway tonight—for a few hours at least."

"Big responsibility for one trooper."

"Maybe he meant just part of the highway. I'm going to call him from the police department later. If he has the time, we're going to meet for dinner in Port Orford."

"I'll be at work. You be careful, Winter."

"Oh, I always am, Mom. I can take care of myself—got my phone, mace and gun."

"Just don't make risky decisions. Whenever I hear of bad things happening, it is usually because the victim decided to go somewhere or do something they shouldn't. Believe me, I've heard too many sad tales from customers."

"I promise, Mom."

"Listen, take my SUV. I'll use your little beater tonight. I heard on the news they expect fog to move inland sometime this afternoon."

"Oh. You don't have to do that."

"I know, but the SUV has better lights. I want you to come home safe."

Chapter 17

"Okay, Mr. Garcia. Here's the key and your receipt for one night." The hefty lady jabbed her fat finger on the motel diagram. "Here's your room. No need to check out, just leave the key in the room when you leave."

Sydney grabbed the key and slip of paper as he left the office. On the way to his room, he stopped to pull the laptop out of his truck. Secure in the room, he hooked up the computer and waited. When the password request popped on the screen, he entered the one listed on his room receipt. With access to the Internet, he checked a few sites and then linked to his off-shore server.

His plan didn't include a night's stay, but this room provided him a place to lay low if things didn't go as planned. Sydney gathered his gear and headed for the truck.

Earlier, when he left in the middle of the night, Wanda hadn't stirred. He'd left her a note. The trip south on the freeway took him past Cottage Grove, then west to Reedsport and south on the coast highway. His travel time to Bandon had been close to his estimate.

After this short jaunt, he'd be able to find a place to hide his cache near the lighthouse at Cape Blanco.

A fog bank had hung out over the ocean when he reached the coast and remained offshore all the way to the motel. Now, in the parking lot, he felt the damp chill from the silent invasion of fog. He tugged the hoody tighter at the neck to ward off the cold. Not a coastal dweller, the sudden change in weather surprised him. As the fog moved inland and thickened, sunlight gave way to a dusky daylight. He inhaled the strong smell of the salt air. Second-thoughts on this operation crept into his mind.

He hoped the conditions didn't worsen as he drove south. The density of the fog varied as he traveled. In places, visibility shrank to a few car lengths and in some stretches, grew to a comfortable distance. Sydney switched the defroster on high and double-checked the headlight switch. Settled behind a long-haul truck, he relaxed his death grip on the steering wheel. The lights and his assumption that the driver had experienced these conditions before gave him a measure of confidence.

When the truck slowed on long climbs, Sydney remained behind. During one slow, steep stretch he caught sight of a sign with the mileage to Cape Blanco. A quick calculation approximated what the odometer should read as he reached his destination.

The fog thickened as he left the highway and headed west toward the lighthouse. Sydney crept along the unfamiliar road. No other traffic, the ribbon of pavement led through a thick gray cloud.

The end of the road surprised him. He stomped the brakes. Through the windshield, he studied the lighthouse wrapped in fog. A trail led uphill to the tall, white column. With each rotation, the beacon at the top swept a bright beam out into the dark cloud.

Sydney spotted a small, white, single-story structure with a red gable roof at the base of the column. He wondered if anyone lived there. Didn't remember any mention of a caretaker in his research.

He scanned the surrounding area, unsure because of the fog, but there wasn't much vegetation other than a few windswept bushes scattered in the coastal grass. The barren land, with little cover, reminded him of Lonerock, but much damper. He decided to backtrack and find a place with more brush and trees.

Downhill from the lighthouse, he found a narrow road to the right. Sydney parked on the shoulder and studied a copy of the brochure and map he'd found on a website. Off the main road, ahead he'd find the campground.

Thick brush marked each shoulder of the road. Shrouds of fog churned and curled in the headlights. Sydney toured the campsites along the narrow lane and spotted several that were occupied, but he may have missed others in the fog.

On the other end of the campground, the host's RV sat along the lane leading to an exit. Sydney eased past the last campsite and paused at the intersection. A quick check of his map showed the beach to his right and a horse camp to his left. He headed for the camp.

After a short distance, he slowed for a ninety-degree left turn and stopped in the middle of the narrow road. He ran his fingertip over the map. Fog obscured the long straight stretch of road ahead and the riding trail off to the side. Sydney unbuckled the seatbelt and strained to catch sight of the trail through the passenger side window.

He tossed the map on the seat and eased forward to find the horse camp entrance on his left.

Inside, he circled past the corrals and campsites along a paved lane. A plan formed in his mind as he found the camp empty. Cut off from the main campground by trees, brush and fog, he searched for a place to hide his cache. Sydney needed the victim to park and leave her vehicle for the time and distance required for him to deflate the tires without notice.

Dissatisfied with the choices, he pondered his options at the camp entrance. He headed back the way he'd come and parked on the shoulder close to the sharp turn. The map showed the horse trail across the road from him. He traced the line where the trail branched away from the road at the corner and continued straight through brush and trees to beach access in the distance.

Sydney threaded the sheath with the commando knife on his belt, donned a pair of gloves, and grabbed the dark green ammo can before he left the truck. From the corner in the road, he hurried onto the horse trail and headed toward the beach. The thick moist air dampened any sound. After seventy-five measured strides, he paused to listen. The eerie fog veil blocked the road from his view.

Off the trail at the base of a small tree, he placed the ammo can on the ground and drew the knife. With the tool and gloved hands, he scraped and dug a hole for the cache. He'd loaded the can with treasures to make the ruse believable for hunters of no interest to him. One last check, he positioned the harmonica, a small plastic firetruck, the Barbie doll, and a fabric artificial rose. With the logbook on top, he closed the lid. He tucked moss and duff around the cache and placed some dry branches on top to make the find more difficult.

The conditions made this spot ideal. After he recorded the GPS location on his handheld device, he made one last visual check of the spot. He welled with excitement as he strode back to his truck.

He checked the map before he headed for the highway. The fog could work to his advantage or be a curse. While he'd be concealed, so would those who might be a threat to him.

Sydney drove south and stopped for gas in Port Orford. As highway traffic appeared out of the fog and then disappeared, he realized he'd grown comfortable with the low visibility.

A sudden chill shot down his spine at the sight of a northbound state police cruiser. He checked the rearview mirror as the car's taillights disappeared in the fog. Why the reaction of alarm? The cop couldn't read his mind. As a precaution, he'd need to remember to drive through the campground to check for danger signs before he staked out his cache.

The station attendant had given him directions to a restaurant where he could find a Wi-Fi hotspot. Sydney carried his bag to an empty table and positioned the chair to prevent snoopy eyes from peeking at his work. He ordered from the menu board, opened his laptop and waited.

His meal cooled on the table as he tapped the keyboard. Thrilled with his connection, he worked through his off-shore server. He'd used a different geocache website for each operation. With a new account created, he logged in with "Msmuffet" as his username and a favorite password. He then entered his cache site's description and location, and a challenge to be the first to find it.

Sydney logged off and stashed his computer in the bag beside his chair. During his meal, he ticked off the steps he'd follow when he shut down this coastal venture. He'd delete his account on the geocache website and drop the email he'd created for this cache. After he retrieved the ammo can, he'd head for home. Sydney drew a deep breath as memories of past trips to the coast flashed in his mind. Maybe this wouldn't be another failure.

The sound of a siren riveted his attention. He rocked forward to catch a glimpse of flashing lights as a state police car sped by in the fog. Headed south, Sydney wondered if this was the trooper he'd seen earlier, headed north.

A Cape Blanco, Sydney finished a last tour of the campgrounds. He'd checked for police cars around the historic buildings and the lighthouse. Fog continued to blanket the campground. The number of occupied sites appeared to be the same as last time. In the exit, he waited at the stop sign for two older pedestrians who had been out for a hike. The woman carried a piece of driftwood. With knit hats pulled snug over their ears and collars up, the couple kept their eyes to the ground as they trudged past and toward the campsites. Sydney drove left toward the horse camp. He paused in the ninety-degree turn to the left and eyed the horse trail where his next victim would travel in search of his cache.

From the corner, he traveled straight for a few hundred feet and pulled over onto the left shoulder to park against traffic. In the passenger side mirror, he had a view of the area where any treasure hunters would enter the trail. Sydney jerked on the hood release and went outside to prop the hood up. He'd learned a stranger with a disabled truck caused less alarm. Bent over his engine, he'd be able to peek and follow the activities around him.

Sydney opened his door, grabbed his kit under the driver's seat, and unzipped the black canvas bag. He dug the coiled wire **garrote out and returned the commando knife. The dog tags had become wedged into one corner. He fished the tags and chain out from under his gear and studied them for a moment. The garrote he'd need first, the tags later. He tucked the tags in a back pocket and stored the coiled wire with the wooden handles** in the front pouch of his hoody. He patted the front pocket on his pants to feel for the valve stem tool. As a precaution, he placed the black bag on the floor near the door. He hoped the knife or mace wouldn't be necessary, but he wanted them handy.

As he leaned on the front fender, Sydney ran the next kill through his mind. Once she parked near the trail, he'd wait until she left the vehicle to find the cache. He'd creep along the shoulder behind his truck. The brush and fog would conceal his advance. After she left the road and entered the horse trail, Sydney would hurry to her vehicle, loosen two valve stem cores, and move back into the brush and wait. They'd always squat down to inspect the flat tires. He smiled at the memory of those moments of ambush.

A child's excited voice shot out of the fog from near the sharp turn. Sydney moved to get a view of the road behind his truck. A man, with slow, deliberate strides, appeared to be focused on an object in his hands. The talkative child skipped and danced about the man's legs as they advanced.

Sydney spit a silent curse and struck the fender with the heel of his balled fist. Geocachers in the campground with an Internet connection had not been factored into his scheme. He clenched his teeth as he fought to control his anger, his rage. Everything he'd planned ruined by an old man and a yappy kid.

"Cool, Grandpa," the kid shouted.

Fog and distance muffled Grandpa's reply.

On the edge of the road, the man held the GPS device chest high and shuffled his feet until he faced down the trail toward Sydney's cache.

"Are we there yet?" The kid hopped up and down.

Grandpa left the road and led the child onto the trail.

The kid trotted behind. "Transformer—like before?"

Propped with his arms on the fender, Sydney hung his head. Ruined, everything ruined by an old man and a snot-nosed kid. He checked the time. Not as late as he thought. Patience came hard to him. He hated to scuttle his plan too soon.

Noise from a harmonica announced the return of the geocachers. Sydney eyed them as they followed the road back to the campground. The dissonant sound faded. He shivered as he grabbed a jacket from inside the truck. The fog had thickened. Quiet had returned to his kill zone.

Chapter 18

"There's an accident with injuries north of Gold Beach." Winter read from her phone before she settled in the chair beside her friend's desk. "Got a text from Rex, he might be late."

"Honey, if you plan to spend your life with anyone in law enforcement, get used to your plans being changed," Sal said.

"You sound like my mom." Winter liked Sal, sassy, assertive and a heart of gold.

"Sister, maybe."

"No." Winter chuckled. "I didn't mean old like my mom—smart like her."

"Ah—thanks, but I'd say experienced."

"When we trained as volunteers, you said you'd worked for other departments. I never asked where."

"Too many—followed husbands. Seaside, Brookings, Toledo, but I'm not married now." Sal flaunted her bare ring finger.

"Are you waiting for a job here?"

Sal scrunched her face. "Not sure what—may try something else this time. Do what your mom's doing."

"That's all I can remember her doing." Winter shrugged. "The Chief wants me to apply for the next reserve officer opening. Mom's not wild about me and police work."

"Look, Winter. You choose what appeals to you. If police work's in your blood, go for it."

The desk phone buzzed and Sal answered. She listened and said, "Sure." With a hand over the mouthpiece, she whispered to Winter. "A call only a volunteer can handle."

"Hattie, this is Sal. Haven't heard from you lately." Sal toyed with the curly phone cord as she listened.

"How long has she been gone?" Sal winked at Winter.

"Two weeks? Why didn't you call earlier?" Sal tapped an index finger on her temple.

"Oh, you just learned of her disappearance. What was she wearing?"

"Feathers? What color?" Again, she winked at Winter. "Red, brown and black?"

"Does she have a name? 'Hen'—just 'Hen'. Okay, I'll get this out to patrol."

Amused, Winter listened as Sal talked her way out of the call.

Sal hung up. "Lonely lady. I think she calls in just to talk to someone. Harmless." She leaned back in the chair. "I remember when she called to report a dead body. Our officer arrived and found she had been watching a true crime show and called in what she'd seen on television."

"A lot of people wouldn't be so patient—nice of you. While we're out maybe we can watch for her chicken." Winter snickered with her friend.

By early afternoon, Winter had finished her volunteer duties and waited for Sal, who had asked for a ride home. Seated at a desk, she woke the idle computer to kill time on the Internet. She viewed the news, coastal weather and traffic, and then she checked her favorite geocache sites.

"I'm ready," Sal said.

"Just a minute." Winter scratched a quick note from information displayed on the screen.

"What's so important?" Sal asked.

"I told you about my new hobby. Here's a new cache at Cape Blanco. Maybe I could be the first to find it. I've never done that."

"What do you win?"

"Nothing. I can brag." Winter pushed away from the desk. "This'll be cool." She brushed her long hair back behind her shoulders. "I'll stop at Blanco, find the site, and meet Rex on his dinner break. He'll be jealous." The thought brought a smile.

"You're not going alone?"

"It'll be light out."

"But the fog makes it pretty dark. Don't do anything foolish. You told me those hunts take you off the beaten path."

"I'll be careful. Besides, I always carry protection."

Winter dropped Sal off, checked with her mom and sent a text to her trooper friend. She suggested their favorite eatery in Port Orford.

Eva told her of a stout storm with wind and rain headed for the south coast. With Cape Blanco nearly the farthest point west on the Oregon coast, she didn't want to be tramping around in a big blow. The fog had thickened. She checked for the headlight icon and punched the accelerator.

Three-fifty showed on the dash clock as she signaled for the lighthouse exit. Winter drove a short distance before she found a spot to pull over. With the engine running, she checked messages on her phone.

Rex had cleared the accident and planned to meet her in ninety minutes. She didn't tell him of the "FTF" cache. She wanted a surprise. Winter scrolled and tapped the GPS application and waited until she could enter the latitude and longitude for the cache.

She eased out onto the road with the phone on the console where she had a view of the screen. Fog deepened the late afternoon darkness and made visibility worse, minute by minute. She'd better hurry or scratch her plans. The sun above the fog would set around seven-thirty, but it'd be dark much sooner.

Winter drove with one eye on the road while she tracked her advance on the small screen. The little map showed a left turn to her destination. She'd been to the lighthouse before, but never ventured down this road. The sign indicated a horse camp ahead. Her graphic on the phone showed the main campground farther to her right on the other side of the equestrian complex.

She passed the entrance to the horse camp. Her route on the screen showed the destination ahead and near a sharp right turn.

Startled, she made a quick swerve to avoid an old disabled truck parked on the right shoulder, headed the wrong direction. Seemed an odd place to park with no lights and the hood propped up. She didn't notice a driver. Must have gone for help.

Winter viewed the display as she eased around the sharp turn to confirm where she believed the cache to be hidden. When she reached the back entrance to the main campground, she reversed course and returned to pause in the ninety-degree turn. She studied the surroundings and decided to complete the turn. Parked on the narrow right shoulder, she jabbed the emergency flashers. She wouldn't be long.

The flashers reflected off the fog and blurred the view of the road and images ahead. The lights would warn other drivers to steer clear of her mom's SUV. She strained to study the faint outline of the truck parked on the left shoulder. Still no sign of the driver. The thick fog and darkness made her re-think the risk. After a glance at the screen and a mental calculation, she had less than one hundred meters to go. If she planned to be a cop, this was no time to conjure up danger without good reason.

Winter adjusted the holstered pistol inside her waist band. From her gear bag, she stuffed a small can of mace in the left jacket pocket and grabbed her small flashlight to carry in the other.

Beside the SUV, again she eyed the old truck before she focused on the phone's screen. She moved to the back of the SUV and followed the route onto the horse trail. With each step, the trees overhead and dense foliage choked out more and more available light. She paused on the trail to pull out the flashlight. The beam didn't make much difference—weak batteries.

She spun and crouched to identify the source of a noise—one slight sound. Nothing, she transferred the flashlight to her left hand, Winter fingered the butt of her pistol with her right. The sound had been faint. Could've been her imagination.

As she played the dim beam of light on the trail, she remembered her mother's flashlight. A cop friend had given Eva one of those large metal LED models. She recalled her mom saying she kept the light in her SUV. To be safe, she decided to go back and get the brighter light.

◆◆◆

Twenty minutes earlier, Sydney had shivered in the cab of his truck. This operation had been a waste of time. On the cusp of darkness, he had a decision to make. Go back to his room in Bandon, return early tomorrow and stake out this cache again—or pull the ammo can, erase his electronic trail and try a different place on another day. He hated no-show trips, but like Billy told the reporter, "Sweet success rewards patience."

He'd wait until four-thirty to decide. The cool, damp air chilled him to the bone. To avoid drawing attention to himself, he'd kept the engine off. Whatever happened, he'd soon be able to have heat.

Beyond the horse camp entrance, headlights approached from the main road. Dimmed by fog, the lights moved closer. Sydney yanked on the door handle, rolled out onto the ground and pressed himself against the side of the truck. With the interior light disabled, his exit would go unnoticed. The sounds of tires on the damp pavement passed. He remained frozen in place.

As the sounds faded, he eased forward to catch a glimpse of the vehicle. He recognized the shape as a SUV. The brake lights lit for a moment before the SUV rounded the sharp turn. His hand brushed the kit bag as he twisted to push off the ground. A silent curse, as he grabbed the bag, jerked open the door, and placed the kit back on the floor. When he'd jumped out of the truck he didn't notice the bag fall. He wanted the knife easy to reach. Next time he'd be more careful with his feet. Sydney moved to the front of the truck and closed the hood. Time to pull the cache and wait for another day.

With the hoody drooped to eye-level, hands in the front pouch, he felt the wood handles on the coiled garrote. He thought of what could've been as he left the truck behind and headed for his cache.

Wait. Dead still, alert, Sydney listened. Sounds of a vehicle followed the flash of lights on the bushes and trees at the sharp turn. He dove for cover off the road.

The SUV reappeared. His heart raced as he waited. Could this be the one? Sydney eased through the bushes as he worked closer to the corner. He wasn't sure if the driver met his criteria or of the driver's intentions, but he'd be ready. The SUV stopped on the shoulder near the turn. The hazard lights flashed. Concealed across the road, he had an angled view of the front of the vehicle. He studied the driver through the windshield to identify the gender.

He gasped at the sight of her. The interior light shone on her long blonde hair. Outside, she bunched her hair to hang down her back and donned a dark baseball cap with bold white letters on the front, but he couldn't make them out. The door locks sounded. She glanced at his truck, held a device chest high and headed for the trail behind the SUV.

She's a tall one. He drew a deep breath to calm his nerves. Along the shoulder of the road, he used the SUV as cover. Positioned directly across from her vehicle, Sydney waited to ensure he could work unnoticed. Just a few moments, all he needed.

Sydney held his small tool as he slinked to the left rear wheel. A few twists on the core and the whoosh of air sounded. A quick peek at the trail to make sure she hadn't returned. He took a knee at the left front wheel to work with the stem at the bottom. The tool and stem cap tumbled from his gloved hand. Cursing silently, he jerked his glove off and ran his hand over the pavement under the SUV to find his tool. Disgusted with himself for the waste of precious time, he felt the small wrench. Feverishly, Sydney worked on the valve stem core. The air whooshed.

◆◆◆

Moments earlier, Winter had heard noises out on the road near her mom's rig. A quick side-step off the trail, she paused in the brush to assess the situation. A flash of movement near the back, left side. *Too soon for Rex*. She drew her gun from the holster. The first sound had been a rush of air. She heard something drag or scrape on the pavement and then a spurt of pressurized air. *Someone's messing with my mom's tires*.

She sprang for the trail, sprinted for the SUV and jumped into a combat stance in the road. "Freeze, Mister. Don't move." The man, his back to her, knelt beside the front wheel.

He spun on his knees and froze. "Pleath, don't thoot." The hoody on his head didn't conceal the spark of fear in eyes locked on her gun.

"What did you do? My tires are flat?"

"No—No, not me." Head shaking, his arms shot above his head as he rose.

"Nobody else here. You did this."

"Are you police?" He eyed her cap as he shuffled backward.

"Yeah, Bandon PD. I ought to arrest you." She didn't have handcuffs, zip-ties or any way to restrain the man.

"Pleath. I didn't do thith." He shuffled farther away.

"Freeze. Right where you are." She used her command voice. With the gun leveled on the man, she slid the phone from her pocket and punched the quick call for Rex.

"Pleath. I'll get help for you." He inched away.

"Mister, Stop. On your knees." The call went to voicemail. "I need you. Cape Blanco horse camp. Now."

The man continued to shuffle away, dropped his hands and sprinted for the old truck.

Winter cut her pursuit short.

The man jumped in the old truck and sped away.

She unlocked the SUV and climbed inside. If she'd subdued him, she would've had no way to restrain him. And he had an ugly and dangerous look to him. She'd wait for help. In the glove box, she found the number for her mom's roadside assistance.

Winter told the company to meet her in the main campground. She needed to find a more public place to wait. After a text to Rex, she headed toward the horse camp entrance.

On the side of the road, she caught sight of a dark object. She unzipped the black bag and spotted a commando knife, mace and other items. A glance back at the SUV confirmed the old truck had been parked at this location. She zipped the bag and tucked it under her arm.

Chapter 19

Sydney barreled north through the fog. Distance, he needed distance from failure, from a woman who might recognize him, report him. A near head-on collision as he passed a second pokey driver in the fog got his attention. He released his white-knuckled grip on the steering wheel. Flow with the traffic, don't attract attention, but he had to get off the coast.

His truck—she'd probably remember type and color. The shirt and hoody stuck to his back. Beads of sweat ran into his eyes. The maps hadn't shown a clear route inland until he reached Bandon. Locals might have a route, but not Sydney. He cursed and hammered his palm on the steering wheel. Maybe he should lay low in his motel room. No, he had to get off the coast highway. He had to assume the description of his truck and his appearance had been sent to lawmen north and south.

An old, red Nissan pickup with black canopy would likely be on the lookout sheet of every cop on the coast. Not like he'd hurt her, but he couldn't afford to be caught and questioned. *Billy, what would you do?* Dump the canopy, change the profile of his truck. Sydney leaned over the wheel as he strained to find a side road in the foggy darkness.

Stuck behind a line of travelers, he scanned the right shoulder ahead. In the darkness, lights of a first responder flashed. Sydney tucked close to the motorhome in front of him to avoid notice by the southbound driver. A police car blew past.

Minutes later, Sydney spotted an intersection and made an abrupt right turn. The sign read One, Two, or Three-mile road, he couldn't remember. Didn't matter because he only wanted to drop the canopy. Under high-tension power lines, he parked on a dirt lane. With the aid of a flashlight, he used his tools to disconnect the canopy from the bed of his truck. He flipped the aluminum shell onto the ground and left it on the side of the lane. Maybe some farmer could find a use for the thing, if not, he doubted the cops could trace where he'd bought the cover. The truck and canopy predated his prison days.

Sydney jumped in the truck and headed back to the highway. Chilled by his sweaty clothes, he cranked up the temperature and fan speed. The truck, what about the truck? At the stop sign, he wondered if, being a cop, she'd picked up his license plate number. Then he remembered the motel in Bandon, they had the plate number. The truck had to be dumped.

What's the matter with me? He drew a deep breath. She caught him deflating her tires. Never laid a hand on her. Nothing. No one knew what he'd planned to do. Billy told the author what he did to avoid arrest, after his last victim escaped. He'd shaved his head and changed his style of clothing, but the cops had a car description. Caught him clean shaven, with his buzz cut, and new duds, but same old rig.

Northbound again, after he distanced himself from eminent danger he'd get rid of the truck. Yes. Maybe he'd push it into a ravine and report it stolen. Better yet, he'd torch it. Or he'd torch it and then dump it over a cliff. Sydney followed a semi into

Bandon and remained a safe distance through town. A road sign marked the turn-off for Coquille. He signaled as he checked the rearview mirror for any sign of danger. Headed inland, he relaxed with the hope he'd dodged a bullet.

Off the coast, the weather changed. A stout wind cleared the fog and raised havoc with the trees and foliage along the edge of the narrow highway. Rain pelted the windshield. Sydney welcomed the darkness and miserable conditions. Free from prying eyes, he drew comfort as the mileage rolled up on the odometer.

She saw my face! He shuddered at the realization. She'd describe him and might recognize him in a line-up or in one of his old mug shots. The only good witnesses were dead ones. He couldn't remember if Billy said that or someone else. A Bandon cop she said—had "BPD" on her cap. No choice, she had to die. Maybe not the beautiful death he'd planned, but dead nonetheless.

Fingertips played over his scar-furrowed face. His mom had tried to get him to go to a plastic surgeon after his prison time. He hadn't cared. Years of ridicule and scorn-filled glances had taught him the folly of friends, companions or his mom's ultimate, marriage. He shook his head. What'd marriage do for her? Stuck with an ugly son, a dead husband and a lonely existence. Wealth, she did have money.

With a changed appearance and a new truck, he could avoid being recognized. What would he tell the probation officer? He'd think of something. Going back to his old job wouldn't be a good idea. He'd become Jose Garcia to everyone but his mother, the probation officer and old man Barnes. He had to remember the pesky neighbor. Maybe when he talked to a surgeon, he'd ask for a Hispanic look. His landlady, Rosa, knows him as Garcia. He'd need to move to a different rental before the surgery.

◆◆◆

I should have plugged him. Winter returned to the kitchen table with her tea. She scrolled through her messages. Rex said they hadn't found the guy. Eva had left for home. She gazed out the window. Rain droplets and streaks on the glass refracted the light from the neighbor's outdoor motion lights. When the wind whipped his trees and shrubs, the whole neighborhood lit up. Her mom joked about having free security lights. Winter held the citrus-flavored tea near her chin to enjoy the fragrance before she sipped.

The grandfather in the campground had told her the disabled pickup had been parked near the horse camp when he and his grandson found the cache. So much for being first-to-find. The guy didn't bother them, but he sure tinkered with her SUV. The tow truck driver found the valve stem core removed from one tire and loosened in the other. Glad the creep didn't puncture the tires. Neither she nor her mom needed a major expense. Part-time work and school expenses didn't leave much for her to help with household expenses.

At first, she figured the guy planned to steal something or had vandalized the SUV. Nothing made sense, when she'd first spotted him. But after she found the bag with the zip-ties, tape, and knife, she realized he'd intended more than mischief. Winter'd had no time to dwell on the ordeal until now. After the stranger fled, she had to get her mom's SUV fixed, tell Rex what happened, and get home. Now, in the quiet, she realized the man intended to do her great harm. To steady her hands, she pressed hard on the table.

The flash from headlights outside alerted her to a car in the driveway. Her hand brushed the butt of the gun tucked inside her waistband. Her mom rushed past the picture window headed for the front porch. In the small living room, mother and daughter embraced. Neither spoke.

"Oh, Winter." Eva eased her hold. "You gave me quite a scare." She moved away to drop her purse beside a chair.

Winter swiped at her moist eyes. "I wasn't scared until now—first time I've had a chance to think about it." She plucked a tissue from the box on the end table.

"Sorry I wasn't here for you. I had to close up tonight, otherwise I would've been here. When you called …" She rushed again to embrace her daughter. "I can't lose you too. Not ever."

"You won't, Mom. I'm okay."

"I need some coffee." Eva headed for the kitchen. "Where's your boyfriend?"

"He and every cop on the coast are after the guy. When he's off-duty he'll come by." Winter returned to her chair at the table. Her tea had cooled.

Eva filled the tea kettle and lit the burner on the stove. "Tell me what happened." She sat across from her daughter.

As Winter finished, Eva doctored her second refill. "I'm glad you had your gun—and know how to use it." She moved the sugar to the center of the table.

"Me too. It's a good thing he didn't have the knife on him." Winter picked out another tea bag and grabbed the kettle from the stove.

"Could you've shot him?"

"If it came down to him or me—you bet." She returned the kettle.

"You sound like your father." Eva had a wistful smile.

"Mom, I could. I can't describe how I felt, but I had no doubts. Knew what I was doing the whole time."

"You've always been confident."

Winter held her hair as she bent over her tea to test the temperature with her tongue. "I didn't fall apart until I got home and everything hit me." She reached for her mother's hand.

Eva clasped her daughter's hand. "You okay now?"

"I'm fine now. Don't tell anybody, Mom— even Rex."

"I won't. There were times your Dad came home after a bad incident and he'd relive what happened—I could tell. That's the only time he'd show any fear."

"Post-traumatic reaction, a label my firearms instructor uses. Now I understand what he means."

"Does Rex think they have enough to find this creep?"

"If they don't find him tonight, probably not. I really didn't have much. Too dark for me to catch the license number. The only hard evidence I had was the bag he dropped on the ground. Probably fell out of the pickup—didn't have any weapon in his hand when I found him letting air out of your tires."

"Too bad he didn't leave his wallet too." Eva drank from her cup.

"One thing unusual. He spoke with a lisp— trouble with the 'S' sound."

"That'll be helpful when they catch up with him."

"Rex didn't find any identification in the bag. A GPS like geocachers use, the knife, zip ties, duct tape—that kind of stuff."

"That's an odd collection."

"Yeah. Rex said the detectives will check out the stuff in the bag. He told me to keep in mind the bag may not belong to the stranger."

"Maybe he'll know something by the time he gets here."

"I doubt it, Mom. He told me that vandalism complaints don't have a high priority. But, he's going to push as much as he can."

"Why wait for them? We got Google. Check for news stories about vandals going after vehicles." Eva jumped up and carried her coffee into the living room to their desktop.

Amused by her mother's initiative, Winter remained at the table with her tea. She wished she'd thought of doing her own investigation. Maybe a side effect from what she'd experienced. The only sound she heard were clicks from her mother's keyboard. Winter drank from the fragrant orange-flavored tea.

The printer clanked and whirred in the other room before Eva returned and slapped papers on the table. "Read these."

Winter drew the printed pages over near her cup. "Mom. These aren't anything like what happened to me. Spray painting, scratches, smashed windows— didn't happen to me."

"Well, I'll give these to Rex."

"He told me they'd send a notice to all the police departments around to check for incidents similar to mine." Winter cocked her head and studied her mother for a moment. "You surprise me, Mom. Thought you didn't want me in police work and here you are being the big detective."

Chapter 20

Matt clomped up the steps and paused on the porch with hands on his knees to catch his breath. Too long since his last run. The dogs boiled out of the house when he opened the door. No lights in the kitchen, Anna hadn't stirred from her night's rest. He eased the door shut, leaned on the porch rail, and monitored the border terriers down in the yard. The scent of the old evergreen forest tinged the cool spring air. Maybe he'd hire an expert to determine the age of his trees. Friends in the timber business had given age estimates of almost two hundred years.

He shed the outer layer of his running outfit and draped the light nylon jacket over the front handrail. As normal breathing returned, he resolved to get back to his regular schedule. He pressed a finger to his neck and checked his pulse. Sam and Eddy scrambled up the steps and jockeyed at the door to be first to enter.

Inside, Matt kicked off soiled running shoes. He removed his glasses, grabbed the towel from the coat rack beside the door, and dried his head as he went to the kitchen counter to check his cell phone. After too many nighttime interruptions, both he and Anna had decided to leave their phones in the kitchen at night.

He hadn't taken the time to check messages before he left on his run. A text had arrived after midnight. As he leaned on the counter, Matt read from the screen. Trudeau said the state lab found the material in Mari Davies' silicon band to be the same material as they found in the wrist band left with Judith Rhime's body. Aloud, he said. "Nothing I can do about it." He drew a deep breath and exhaled a sigh.

"Don't know why you're telling me." Matt talked to himself as he assembled the drip coffee pot and loaded the grounds. "You're on your own. I've been benched." He filled the tea kettle and lit the burner.

"Who's been benched?" Anna asked.

He whirled from the stove. "How long have you been there?"

"Not long. I heard you yakking out here as I came out of the bedroom." She entered the kitchen. They kissed. "Your shirt's sweaty. Better change or you'll catch a cold."

"I'm too mean to get sick." He smiled as he brushed a finger under her chin. "If you finish the coffee, I'll go shower."

"Deal. What had you so upset out here?"

"Oh, nothing. Just feeling sorry for myself. I've been cut out of the murder investigation—right when they catch a break."

"What kind of break?"

"The lab confirmed what we thought—the two wrist bands matched."

"Trudeau will be happy."

"Yep. He notified me with a text in the middle of the night."

"Don't take your demotion so personal." Anna placed a hand on his back. "You're not in law enforcement anymore—remember?" She searched for a dry spot on his shirt to wipe her hand.

"Gets me frustrated. Want to help but can't do much. Oh, well." Matt headed for the bathroom.

By the time he returned, Anna had breakfast on the table, sausage gravy and biscuits. He signaled thumbs up. "Yum. Thought that's what I'd smelled when I came out of the bedroom."

"We've been on the go so much lately, I thought a breakfast together would be nice."

"A good Saturday thing to do. Besides, I've got nothing on my schedule."

"I'll find something for you. I don't need you underfoot, moping around all day."

"Now, now, Honey." He ladled gravy over his biscuits. "You know how I need a little therapeutic whining now and then."

"Yes, I do." She poured refills of coffee from the carafe. "Just keep your therapy session short."

"Already over." He posed with a loaded fork near his mouth. "A cure for many ills." He swallowed and reached for her hand. "You keep life fun."

"Oh, you do your share." She released his hand and pushed away from the table. "Tell me about your demotion again while we clean up. I'm not sure I got all of the details when you called."

"Not many details," he said as he carried a stack of dishes into the kitchen. "The prosecutor doesn't want me or Allen doing any active investigation."

"What does that look like?"

"Right now, we've got a copy of most everything from the case files. Allen and I can work in the office with Trudeau and Vi until we're blue in the face. If we identify an interview to do or a document to get, we have to tell the sworn detectives and they'll do the work. We sit and wait."

"Not much satisfaction—I get that." She set the cookware beside the sink.

"We're not cut out completely. I told you about the newspaper getting an email from the killer."

"Yeah, he used 'compassrose' in his email address."

"The prosecutor let us stay while they discussed whether to respond. After Vi gave her opinion, they put together a reply."

"Do you know what they're going to say?"

"Not exactly, but Vi suggested they put the guy down, don't credit him with anything. She says he wants recognition so they must avoid any praise."

"Praise for murder?"

"Not murder, praise for being clever, smart—attributes like that." He loaded the dishwasher. "They're going to accuse him of being a phony, a fraud—a wanna be sitting in a basement in his pajamas making things up."

"Aren't they afraid he'll get mad and kill again?" she asked.

"Vi says, if we get him agitated, he might make a mistake and expose his identity when he tries to prove his role in the past murders. She also hopes to distract him so he'll delay more killing until we catch up with him." Matt poked the washer's start button.

"Big risk," he continued. "She believes he's methodical and has a timetable for his murders. Unless we knock him off stride, he'll keep to his schedule. Then, he may just do both at the same time, campaign for recognition and keep killing."

"That's so scary, Matt." She moved close for a hug. "Gives me the shivers. I hope Vi is right about the distracting."

"Me too, Honey." He kissed her forehead. "Me too."

"When will the editor run a story?"

"He'll wait for the prosecutor to give the green light. But only if he gets an exclusive."

After cleanup duties, Matt carried his laptop and phone into the living room. He tossed more wood on the fire and fanned the coals to life. The pitchy fir popped as orange and yellow flames danced behind the glass screen. The scent from the fire accompanied him to his recliner.

He adjusted the chair to the nap position and switched the television from his news channel to a baseball game.

By the time Matt awoke, the postgame show played on the screen and Anna had curled up on the couch with their terriers and a book.

"How long you been there?" he asked.

"Not long."

"Who won?"

"I don't know. I was reading and you had the sound muted."

He raised the chair back and tapped the mute button. "My fire's hungry again."

"I heard your phone. You didn't stir."

He worked his phone and read. "Hmm. Trudeau sent me two messages."

"Is he working at home or in your office today?"

"Doesn't say—he's got some new stuff. This first one's huge. The fitness wristwatch the killer took from the Lonerock victim ended up on the victim in the lava beds."

"Matt, I know you don't mean this, but when you detectives call the dead ladies 'victims,' I get those 'fingernails on a chalkboard' chills. They have names—Mari—Char—Judith—and this new one, Dolly. When you use detective talk you dehumanize the ladies—so impersonal."

"You're right. I don't use 'victim' to diminish them. Never thought too much about the label, but maybe I use 'victim' to avoid an emotional connection with the deceased. I've got to be dispassionate. I'd risk the loss of my objectivity if I developed a personal attachment."

"I understand—just, please use names at home." She rose from the couch, leaned down for a kiss and headed into the kitchen. "More coffee?"

He studied the second text message. The victim's car at the lava beds had two flat tires. The killer had loosened the valve cores.

Anna returned with his refill. "You didn't tell me the second message."

Matt slid the phone back on his side table. "Dolly's car had tires flattened the same way as the other ladies."

"Thank you, Matt." She scooted the dogs to reclaim her space. "I appreciate the use of her name."

"You're very welcome, Mrs. Kinler." His phone toned and he answered.

The reporter for the *Herald and News* identified himself and asked, "Mr. Kinler?"

"Yes. That's me."

"I wondered if there'd been any new developments."

"Not since we talked. We're still sorting through our information." Matt raised the chair back and leaned forward. His mind raced to find a way to deflect the reporter's questions. Matt couldn't afford to be the source of any story published in Klamath Falls.

"You said your murder might be related to ours down here—any progress yet?"

"Not to where we're confident enough to go public. By the way, while I have you—I talked with a prosecutor up here and he mentioned he may call you. Did he?"

"Hmm, no. What'd he want to talk to me for?"

Matt cleared his throat. "I—I'm not exactly sure." He dare not get on the prosecutor's turf.

"Got a name and number. I'll call. Remember, we got a deal. You scratch my back—I'll scratch yours. With an exclusive big crime story on a serial killer—I'd be a star around here."

"Wait a minute—I didn't say anything about any exclusive. I told you there may be a story of future interest to your readers—that's all. We just traded information and nothing else."

"You're a weasel—Kinler. You better not back out now. I'm tempted to go with what I have."

"Wait. I'd be glad to exchange information, but publicity at this time might ruin our chances to catch this guy up here. And I can't be a hundred percent sure your murderer is the same as ours." The one hundred percent standard kept his conscience clear.

"Look Kinler, I'm not going to be jerked around. You try and you'll be sorry."

"Calm down—I'll play straight—" The call ended before he finished.

Matt jumped to his feet and pulled the shirt away from his sweaty back. "I've got myself in a pickle now."

"I gathered your friendship may be on the rocks."

"Now there's an understatement." Matt explained the background of the conversation. "I can't prove my side, but I'm sure I didn't promise him an exclusive. I only told him there may be a future story." He paced between his chair and the fireplace. "The DA will never have anything to do with me, if this doesn't go well. The prosecutor promised the Salem paper an exclusive, if they'd help trap the killer. Now I have this reporter saying I promised him an exclusive."

"Pickle works," she said.

"Oh. Wow, Honey." He wiped his hands back over his head. "If that paper down there runs a story now, they might blow everything up."

"Why would that be?"

"Because this killer wants—publicity— notoriety—fame, as he sees it. That's the only incentive for him to communicate. If he does, maybe we can frustrate him into doing something stupid. But if the paper down south publishes a story, he'd probably stop talking to anyone. No longer need to."

"There's not much you can do—is there?"

"No." He returned to his recliner and grabbed the cell phone. "I'll send Trudeau a text. Lay out what's going on in Klamath Falls."

Chapter 21

Sydney gasped for air as he pumped the pedals. Lights of the distant city reflected off the high cloud ceiling. He stopped to catch his breath. From the edge of the rural road, he glanced back over his shoulder. The flames from his burning truck cast an orange glow above the orchard and backlit the column of dark smoke.

In the distance, a siren wailed and lights flashed to signal the approach of a first responder. He hauled the bicycle down across the ditch and into the brush. Crouched out of sight, he'd hoped to be farther away, but unfamiliar roads, darkness, and his poor physical condition made the ride harder than expected.

After the firetruck passed, he scrambled back onto the road, adjusted his backpack and resumed the ride to town. He planned to ditch the stolen bike and catch a taxi once he reached the residential streets of Salem.

Another rest on the side of the road to catch his breath and stop the pounding in his chest. Behind him, the glow of the fire had faded. Exertion to achieve fitness had never appealed to him. But tonight, because of the Cape Blanco disaster, Sydney had no choice. Memory of that cannon she waved in his face flashed to mind. She could've killed him. Although a knife wasn't his weapon of choice, if he'd had his, the outcome might've been different. But, she escaped.

Sydney remembered how Billy said the one that got away had been his downfall. There'd be no downfall this time.

The truck fire and his cover story addressed the immediate concerns, but what about his kit? He growled through clenched teeth as he mounted the bike. Anger simmered as he pictured how he'd placed the bag on the floor of his truck. He'd already knocked the kit out of the truck once before—a big mistake.

He cranked the pedals as he tried to recall what the kit bag contained. The knife, the GPS, light line, tape—a chill rushed down his spine as he tried to think how any of those items might be linked to him. Gloves had always been a precaution, but there may've been something he forgot. Never had he targeted a woman, but this time he'd need to find that Bandon tramp, a matter of self-preservation.

The taxi driver left him on the sidewalk one block off Center Street. In the dark on the tree-lined street, Sydney slung the backpack over one shoulder and checked the time. Even if his replacement worked slow, the office building should be empty by four o'clock. What he had to do wouldn't take long. He strode at an easy pace as he headed for his previous job site. A slow approach allowed him to study the windows for telltale movement or lights.

Sydney waited in the shadows and surveilled the two floors of the building. Convinced the janitor had finished for the night, he moved into the alley and fished a set of keys from his pocket. Inside, he pulled a pair of coveralls from his pack to disguise himself. He couldn't believe his good fortune when he'd found these coveralls in the thrift store. Baggy fit, but similar to the ones handed out by his previous employer.

Eyes and ears keen for signs of danger, he crept up the stairs to the second floor and the office with his favorite workstation. As he waited for the computer to boot up, he recalled how furious he'd been the first time he'd read the editor's response. But Sydney had tamped down his anger, and now he'd reply.

Linked through the state's system to his off-shore server, he typed an email. He seethed as he tapped out his message. The editor called him a fraud, a phony. He'd show them, but he'd be careful. They're baiting him, but he'd not fall for their tricks. The edits and revisions purged his initial venom. Done, he read one more time.

> *"The cops don't get it and now you.*
> *Ignorant too?*
> *Death cuts a fine line.*
> *Truth lies from north to south, east to west.*
> *One artist, one trail, one masterpiece.*
> *The All Points Killer"*

He added a postscript before he hit send. *"If you don't recognize my work, there may be other editors who do."*

Sydney cleared his digital trail, locked up the office and snuck down the stairs. Once in the alley, he made sure he had no witnesses before he called 9-1-1 to report his stolen truck. The operator told him to wait for an officer to arrive.

The first light of dawn greeted him as he moved from behind the building. He set the backpack on the sidewalk and waited.

The officer took his report in a straightforward manner, as if she'd received vehicle theft reports several times each shift. He explained how he'd parked to go inside and clean the building. When he came out, he'd found that someone stole his truck. He assured the officer the truck had been locked and showed his ignition key. She agreed that his truck may have been hotwired.

The officer obtained a description of the truck and took his insurance and contact information before she left. His claim of nearby employment had been risky. The janitor's outfit had helped, but the officer focused on the truck's description, his contact information and his insurance.

Buoyed by his clever brilliance, Sydney shed the coveralls, hoisted the backpack on a shoulder and cleared the neighborhood before he called a taxi.

His appetite to kill again had to wait until he'd repaired the damage from Blanco. The urge to stalk, to dominate, to overpower burbled deep within. Patience, Billy would say. He hoped he had the self-control. The Bandon cop had to be silenced.

The taxi driver left him at the foot of the driveway. In the front window, Wanda watched from her recliner with surprise written on her face. Good. He found his key and unlocked the front door.

"Hello, Mother." He shook off the straps and placed the pack near the stairs.

"What happened to your truck?" she asked.

"Thumbody thtole it."

"What—that old wreck?"

"Yeth, Mother. While I cleaned the office building." He had to reinforce what he'd told her when he left last night. "I filed a police report."

"We'll need a copy for an insurance claim. Won't be worth much."

"The officer said we could get one downtown."

"Before you go to bed," Wanda raised her cup, "get me a refill, please."

Sydney took the cup into the kitchen. A plan formed as he poured the coffee. She had resumed her morning program by the time he returned. "Mother, I'll need a new truck. How much could I borrow?"

She muted the sound but continued to watch. "If you find a used one in good condition, we'll talk price."

"After I get some sleep." He snagged the backpack on his way downstairs.

Sydney hooked up to the Internet. Several used pickups met his criteria; midsized, four to five years old, four-wheel drive, and a canopy over the bed. An extended cab would be nice. Price didn't matter to him, only to his mother. He'd borrow her car and check out the trucks after more urgent matters.

Sydney dove into the research on how to change his appearance. He checked websites for plastic surgeons who advertised facial reconstruction and liposuction and explored hair plugs. The possibilities grew with each site he visited.

Surgeons in California and Mexico captured his attention. He liked the idea of going out of state to have his surgery. There he could heal and return to Oregon without bruises or discoloration. Food and lodging expenses would jack up the cost, but Wanda had the money. His only challenge—sell her on the idea. The prices listed in Mexico would appeal to her, but he'd never been south of the border. He dialed his friend.

"Hey, Angel."

"What's up, Dude? I don't hear from you much."

"Thorry, I'm not good at keeping in touch. I hoped you could help me."

"Sure, if I can."

"I'm trying to find a plastic thurgeon in Mexico. On the Internet, I found a few in Mazatlán. Didn't you thay you grew up there?"

"I grew up inland—Rosario. We've got lots of family down there. No surgeons."

Sydney explained his plan to drive south of the border to have surgery and stay until he recovered.

"Pick me up on your way down and I'll be your guide. I've been out on the Maz beaches a lot. We'd have a good time, Dude."

Not what he had in mind. Too much time together meant Angel might ask questions that Sydney didn't want to answer. He'd read the rules and requirements for driving his personal vehicle into Mexico. Angel might be handy, but his gamer buddy didn't need to know his business.

"I'll think it over. I'm just planning. If you hear of a good thurgeon down there, let me know."

"I'll make a few calls."

As he hung up, another problem occurred to him—out of state travel. His probation officer would need to approve. If he snuck off and the officer called, maybe Wanda could stall for time. But, she wouldn't be good at stalling. He logged onto his off-shore server. The editor hadn't given a response to his latest.

Midafternoon, Sydney trudged up the stairs to fix a snack. As he glanced in the living room, Wanda slept, her head drooped forward. The sound from her television followed him into the kitchen.

Sydney fried a couple of eggs, slathered toasted white bread with mayo and assembled a sandwich. He grabbed a sugared soda from the refrigerator as he moved to the kitchen table. The television went silent.

Wanda arrived and parked her power scooter across from him. "You'll ruin your dinner."

"Nah." He stuffed the last bite in his mouth.

"We'll plan to eat before you go to work."

He swallowed and gulped from the soda can. "Not working tonight."

"You've been off a lot lately. Aren't you afraid they'll fire you?"

"I don't care, Mother." He swiped a gob of mayo from his cheek and licked his finger. "I told them I had to get a new truck firth." She didn't need to know the truth.

"When are you going to find a new truck?"

"Right now. I'll need your car."

"Could you fix some tea for me before you leave?"

"Thure, Mother." He wiped a hand across his mouth and then on his pant leg.

"Maybe a couple of cookies too."

Sydney refilled the kettle and turned on the burner. "I met a girl, Mother."

"Oh—Sydney." Her face brightened. "I knew you'd meet someone nice—at work?"

He rummaged in the pantry for cookies. "Not at work." A package in hand, he placed them on the table. "I haven't really met her yet ... but I want to."

"That's a start, Son. Where?" She opened the package.

"When I drove out on the coath." He grabbed a box of tea bags, a cup and spoon for the table. From the kettle, he poured the steamy water.

"Such good news, Sydney. I'd like to meet her. Do you have a picture?"

"Not yet." *When I do, you won't see it.* Back in his chair, he said, "Mother, when I meet her I don't want to thcare her off." His fingertips played over the scarred cheeks. "You've talked about plastic thurgery. Could you afford to help me?"

Wanda, bobbing the tea bag, paused and studied her son. "You always got so mad before— what's changed? You sure?"

He shrugged. "When I thaw her … I decided I had to meet her." He tapped a cheek. "Don't want her to be afraid of me." *Actually, Mother I don't want her to recognize me until it won't matter.*

"Well, Sydney. I want the best for you. I'll get the name of a good Portland surgeon and make an appointment."

He shifted in the chair and crossed his arms on the table. "Mother, I'm hoping maybe I'd go to California or Mexico."

Her eyes widened. "My, you are full of surprises, Son."

"Mother, I don't want to be ugly anymore." *That'll get her.*

"Oh, Sydney." She reached across the table to touch his arm. "You're not. Let's see what we can work out."

"One problem, Mother."

She plucked a cookie from the package. "And what is that?"

"Probation officer. I don't know if I can travel out of the state."

"Hmm." She sipped from her tea. "How long does the surgery take?"

"Probably need three days altogether," he said.

"Maybe she doesn't need to know."

"Probably not for a few days, but I'd need another week or so to heal and let the cuts and bruises clear up."

"Couldn't you heal at home?"

"Ah, Mother. If I'm all cut up, I don't want people we know to theee me—like Barnes." He pointed toward the neighbor's property.

"It'd be hard to keep your absence a secret very long."

"Well, I don't hear from the probation officer very often. If you get a call, just take a message. Thtall her until I get home."

"I'm not comfortable with that, Son."

"Pleath, Mother." He feigned the sad puppy expression with his scarred face. "I don't ask for help very often."

"No." She stared into the dark tea. "No … you don't." She raised her moist eyes to study him for a moment. "Let me think about this."

"Thankth, Mother." He scooted the chair away from the table. "There are a couple of trucks I want to check out. When I come back, should I bring one of our favorite pizzath?"

"That'd be nice."

In the garage, the reluctant engine coughed to life after several tries. Wanda's old Impala didn't get much use. Low mileage, decent condition, he backed the maroon sedan out and onto the street. His neighbor glared over the large container placed at the curb for tomorrow's garbage pickup. Sydney punched the gas and sped past Barnes as the car belched a cloud of dark exhaust.

He smiled at the rearview mirror as his neighbor fanned both hands at the cloud of petroleum-rich emissions. First, he'd move out of Jose Garcia's place at Rosa's. Then he'd head across town where another landlord advertised a trailer for rent.

An hour later, Jose Garcia's scant belongings in the trunk, Sydney drove to a southside address. The neighborhood appeared to be more rural than a city suburb. A woven wire fence surrounded the overgrown, unkempt property. An elderly man in denim shirt and pants waited near the entrance to direct Sydney inside. He closed the gate.

Sydney parked beside a weathered thirty-foot travel trailer. A thick extension cord on the ground ran from the trailer to a small single-story house. Chalky white paint and a moss-covered roof adorned the dwelling.

"Are you Mithter Franklin?" Sydney met the man outside the car.

"Yep. Drop the Mister—just Franklin. You Garcia?"

"No—no, he's my brother. I'm Thydney. He wanted me to get a place for him to live."

"What's he got, a broken leg or something?"

"He's in California and moving up here."

"He got a job up here?"

"Janitor—that's what he doth."

The man opened the door for a tour inside the trailer. Bed, water, electricity and an address met Sydney's criteria. "I'll take it."

"For your brother?"

"Yeth, my brother."

"First and last month now—security deposit and I'll give you the key."

"For the gate too?"

"Nope. Don't lock the gate. Just keep it shut." Franklin tapped his fingers on a rental agreement he'd placed on the counter. "Got some ID?"

Sydney presented his driver's license.

"Smythe? What happened to Garcia?" The old man frowned as his eyes flitted between the license and Sydney.

"We're thtep-brothers—different fathers."

Franklin studied the license and Sydney. "Well … okay, let's have the green and I'll give you a receipt."

With the one-page rental agreement stuffed in his pocket, Sydney headed for home. He took a detour to arrange for Garcia's mail to be forwarded and another to pick up pizza.

He entered through the back door. "Thorry I'm late, Mother." She waited on her scooter at the table. He slid the warm pizza box in front of her.

"I heard you drive in—almost gave up."

When I'm gone she'll have nobody to listen to her whiney complaints. He slammed the drawers and cupboard doors as he gathered plates and utensils.

She flipped the lid up and out of the way as he set the table. "Did you find a new truck?"

"Nah—maybe tomorrow." He pulled the hoody off over his head and flung it toward the head of the stairs.

"The police called." She picked a wedge of pizza. "They found your truck all burned up in an orchard—over on the eastside."

"Umm," he nodded with his mouth full.

"You don't seem surprised."

He shrugged as he swallowed. "I'll get the report and thend a copy to our insurance."

Chapter 22

"Poor Trudeau—you guys just got here." Matt dropped the community stir stick and carried his refill to their work table. "You'd think they covered everything new when your task force met this morning."

Vi tapped a pen on the table beside her notes. "We discussed the Klamath newspaper and the new email our killer sent to the local editor here. Trudeau complains about being called in all the time—but I think he thrives on being bothered."

"He'd be disappointed if they didn't call." Matt settled in his chair across from her. "Being needed helps with his recovery."

"I'm sure he'll fill us in when he returns," Allen said. "Before the interruption, you said the prosecutor put the fire out down south."

"Yeah," Matt said. "I got a call from the reporter down there. Really ticked because his editor put a muzzle on him. I don't know how secure he is in his job, but he talked about going rogue."

"According to the prosecutor, strong-arm tactics weren't needed," Vi said. "After he explained that the detectives had a suspect and any publicity could jeopardize the case, the editor agreed to hold off."

"Any deal to give the paper an exclusive story?" Matt asked.

"That wasn't clear to me," she said. "I think the prosecutor offered to cut them in on all information specific to the murder in the lava beds."

Allen rocked back in his swivel chair. "Probably be a moot point when they go public with the Shellburg murder, Matt."

"True enough," Matt said. "Let's get to the reason we all came here."

"Okay, you've got your copy," Vi said. "Here's the interpretation the task force had. You can pitch your thoughts into the mix." Glasses perched on the bridge of her nose, she read from her notes. "The first two lines of this email contain his boilerplate condemnation of law enforcement, stupid, ignorant and so on. But he challenges the editor to get smart. Don't be like the cops. The third line gives him some bona fides, with the reference to the method of killing where he writes, 'Death cuts a fine line.' He's authenticating himself as the killer."

"Except for Mari Johnson," Matt said.

"True, but I think we agreed he'd been interrupted and didn't finish there," Vi said.

"Yeah. Other differences too, but that's the only logical explanation for now," Matt said.

"He adds more authentication in the fourth line with reference to the four points of the compass." She pressed a finger to her notes. "This fifth line is loaded. 'One artist, one trail, one masterpiece.' A stretch here," she removed the glasses. "But I think he hints of multiple murders tied together. I believe he's alluding to the clues he's left to link the killings."

"I'm certain, after the two messages," Allen said, "This guy's the killer or has direct knowledge. Find him, you'll have the sicko."

"Interesting when you read his first email and then this." Vi waved her notes. "He's obviously frustrated because he hasn't been proclaimed by law enforcement to be the murderer. Look at the P.S. where he threatens to go to other papers if this editor doesn't get it."

"This guy's a psycho," Matt said, "calling himself an 'artist' and his murders 'masterpieces'."

"He thinks he's brilliant—a genius who won't get caught," Vi said. "A trait shared by many in our prisons."

"Well, if he wants publicity, he'll get his wish, kind of," Matt said.

"Yeah, well when the DA faced the fact that we couldn't keep a lid on this..." She nodded at Matt. "...we discussed a possible role for you as a spokesman for Linh Johnson. Go that route to open the door for publicity while denying him the accolades he hungers for."

"I'm intrigued," Matt said.

"As I told the DA, something has to be done to anger him—frustrate him so he'll show himself or do something irrational. So far, he's been cunning, methodical and lucky. He never seems to repeat a location. The consensus among task force members puts his next attempt to kill on the west side of the state." She raked her hair back behind her ears with her thumbs and released with a toss of her head.

"I assume their guess is based on the locations and positions of the three bodies we've had in central Oregon," Allen said.

Vi nodded. "This guy will kill again and again, until he's stopped. After Shellburg, he's been lucky to avoid mistakes—came close at Lonerock."

"We've speculated about why he's made return trips to where Mari Davies was killed," Matt said. "If he's haunted by what he considers failure there, do you think he'll continue to visit again and again?"

"I believe he will, but the frequency is a big unknown," Vi said.

"The only visit we've heard about happened in late summer," Matt said. "But the news clipping about Baby's Grave showed up this last winter. No way we could mount a 24/7 surveillance campaign."

"How about we stake out the place with trail cams?" Allen asked.

"Hey. Good idea. I'd forgotten about those," Matt said.

"They've got a lot of technology in those things now. Digital, infrared, memory, and some have wireless features," Allen said.

"Check on what's available. Then we'll figure how to scrounge up the money." Matt spotted the familiar white truck outside the front window. "Trudeau's back."

Allen vacated his swivel chair. "He can sit here. I'll go to the other side."

The old detective, soft-sided briefcase slung on his shoulder, caned into the office and settled in the chair beside Vi. "We might've caught a break." He dug a folder from his case.

"Got my attention." Matt waited across the table.

"They've tried to track the killer through his emails. Our tech people say … the first message came from a state server ... they may be able to identify the office. Soon … they hope to pinpoint the actual computer."

"If I recall," Vi said, "the message came in during non-business hours."

"Middle of the night, I think," Allen said.

"Correct." Trudeau raised a copy from his folder. "The second email … more difficult for us because the guy used that off-shore server—in Canada. The IT people don't know if they can get around the server he's using. May take time."

"How long before they'll have a fix on the state computer?" Matt asked.

"Not sure—guess this guy used different workstations … or corrupted the digital trail. I didn't understand what—but they're confident."

"When they've got the computer, I hope it's time for a full-court press. If they need bodies to run down any leads, I'm ready," Matt said.

"Not you." Trudeau cleared his throat. "The prosecutor plans for you to help us go public … with the murders. He likes the idea of you as the spokesman for Linh Johnson."

"Did you talk with her?"

"Yep. I called her. But the prosecutor wants … to go over the release with both of you … before you get in front of the cameras. Linh's probably on her way there now."

Matt gathered his laptop and papers and headed out the door. On the way downtown, he called Anna.

"Don't hold dinner, Honey. I'm going to be late."

"What's going on? Can you tell me?"

"I'll need to tell you later. We're going public. Might want to record the news tonight."

"What channel?"

"All of them will carry this story."

♦♦♦

Hours later, Matt drove up to the house and parked near the bottom of the front stairs. He returned Anna's wave as she stood at the window to check on who had arrived. The lights accented the cedar interior behind her. The dogs scrambled down the steps to greet him. A touch, a tousle before they made the rounds. Matt waited for them to finish.

Inside, Anna had settled on the couch. "Didn't think I'd be this late," he said, bending to kiss her.

"You have dinner?" she asked.

"Picked up a burger." He emptied his pockets beside their house phone in the kitchen and left his bag on the floor in their home office.

"I recorded the news for you. Wasn't quite what I expected. I've got it paused on the screen for you."

"Yeah. All part of their game plan. The prosecutor wanted to try me as a spokesman for the Johnson family. Members of the task force had agreed with Vi. The killer wants to be authenticated— famous. In order to get tips from the public, they wanted to go public with the murders and at the same time downplay any task force or any claims by the killer. Hope I did okay."

"Oh, I think so. I just expected the Chief Detective or DA to stand at a podium and give some official pronouncement. Not you." She smiled.

"Can I borrow this?" He grabbed the remote and pointed at the picture. "I haven't seen myself yet."

"Okay, but where are you guys?" she asked.

"State Street, beside the courthouse." Matt moved beside their large flat screen. "See this big rhodie behind us? You remember those big rhododendrons."

"I do. Go ahead and play. Sorry, but I flubbed up all the introductions."

He tapped the play button and his image appeared on screen in midsentence. "…representing the family of Mari Davies, who was murdered over ten years ago near Shellburg Falls. Mari's mother is here today to ask for your help in finding the killer of her daughter.

"The Sheriff's Office has received messages from a demented person who claims responsibility for Mari's death—and the deaths of other women. Mari's family wants the public to know they don't believe these false claims and has appealed to law enforcement to ignore the lies of this wanna be killer."

On the screen, a close-up of Linh Johnson appeared as Matt spoke.

"Nearly ten years ago, Linh Johnson said goodbye to her daughter, an avid geocacher. Mari went by herself to be the first to find a new site. She never returned. Witnesses may have seen a man with a bad complexion wearing a hoody sweatshirt.

"Anyone with information on this murder is asked to call the Sheriff's tip-line number on the screen."

He switched back to Anna's live program.

"Matt, they had your name and number on the bottom of the screen."

"Yeah, I volunteered to let them use it. They want to sell the idea that this was a family effort—not law enforcement. They've hooked up a trap and trace in case the low-life calls to torment the family."

"You'll get a lot of nutty calls. What if the calls overload your phone?"

"Had a flood already. I silenced the ringer. They've fixed my voice mail to dump into a folder on the cloud so my phone won't burst. I've got access to sort through them."

"Linh looked uneasy beside Trudeau on the screen."

"She's a private person, but very determined to find who killed her daughter."

"She recruited a good ally in Trudeau."

He checked the time. "That story's been on twice, plus posted online. I'd like to screen the calls before I call it a day. Think I'll fix a cup of tea. How about you?"

"No. Too late for me."

Two cups of tea later, Matt rubbed his itchy eyes. The hands on the clock approached midnight. He yawned as he scanned his notes on the voice mail messages. "Nutty calls" Anna called them. A long shot, but he didn't mind. He'd struck out before.

Amused, he tapped the pad as he remembered the callers. One guy named Barnes reported a neighbor with a bad complexion who had killed his dog. Others offered little more than names of suspicious people.

As he moved his fingertip through the notes, he stopped on a call from a woman named Eva. A man in a hoody had let air out of the tires on her car when her daughter had parked near a campground. Eva said she'd found the story online and wasn't sure her information would help. He lit up his browser and queried the area code and number. No subscriber information popped up, but the area code and prefix appeared to be used on the coast around Bandon.

Before he headed for bed, he sent a text to Allen and asked him to get more information on Eva.

Chapter 23

"Owooo." Sydney bent over the sink and eased the toothbrush from his mouth. His hands gripped each side of the sink as he examined his heavily bandaged face in the mirror. Doubts spun in his mind—what had he done? Yesterday, the doctor told him the number of incisions, but he'd been too loopy to remember much after he awoke from the surgery.

No matter the outcome, nothing could be worse than before. He turned his head to view each side and used light touches around the incisions. The road trip, Angel, the border crossing, the last few days whirled in his mind. Woozy, he steadied himself. Maybe he'd remember better when he could quit the drugs. Odd to have surgery as the reason for his first visit to Mexico. Sydney had no time to tour before the operation. Maybe he'd check out the city and the western coastline while he healed.

The nurse told him the doctors usually released patients with similar operations on the third day. Angel had borrowed his new truck, but planned to be back in time for Sydney's discharge. Today, he wouldn't do well alone, tomorrow might be different. A painful rinse of his mouth and he returned to his bed. The new wrap and bandages the nurse applied to his midsection helped, but the effects of the liposuction hurt with each twist of his midsection.

While he preferred to travel alone, his friend had been handier than expected. Angel's cousin worked for a Mazatlán travel service catering to Canadian clients who came for facelifts and all forms of body enhancement. The cousin also reserved a luxury bed and breakfast suite on the waterfront for him to use while he recovered. Purified water, Wi-Fi, satellite television and an Internet connection—what more did he need? Wanda blanched when he'd handed her the quote, but she had agreed to his plan.

"Ah, Señor. The doctor cocked his head to view Sydney's face.

He winched at the doctor's light touches during the exam.

"Swelling going down. No infection. You have place to stay in Maz?"

"Yeth."

"I'll check in tomorrow. You're doing well." He ran gentle hands over Sydney's midsection. "Plan to check out by noon. You'll need to come back so I can check on your progress a few more times."

"How long will it take to heal?" Sydney asked.

"In a couple of weeks, most bruising and redness gone, Señor. You'll have look you wanted. No more red acne scars—cheeks tight and smooth, nose straightened, and we enhanced the cheekbones."

"Thank you, Doctor."

♦♦♦

Noon the next day, Sydney waited in the hospital lobby. He spotted his silver-gray pickup approach the entrance. Angel parked and hopped out. The used Toyota had low mileage, an extended cab, and looked nothing like his old red truck.

"Hey, Dude." Angel, plump and short, always had a smile on his large round face. Sydney remembered how surprised he'd been when he learned Angel had been convicted for embezzling. He didn't look like a swindler.

"Do you want to drive?" His friend offered the keys.

"No. You know the traffic lawth. I heard you don't want to get a ticket down here."

"Yeah. Nothing good happens with that." Angel withdrew the keys and headed for the truck.

"You know the way to my hotel?"

"Resort, Dude. You're in a beach resort. Cool."

Sydney recoiled from the pain as he tossed his bag into the small back seat. Slow and casy, he slid onto the front passenger seat. Scrunched down to hide his bandaged face from gawkers, he tried to memorize the route in case he had to drive himself. From what he'd seen of the city, a wide, divided thoroughfare followed the city's oceanfront.

South of city center, the sunlight glistened off the waters of the Pacific. The beach on his side alternated between stretches of sand and sections of rock. Angel slowed on the divided four-lane and moved to the inside lane while Sydney called out the numbers on the buildings along the inland side of the boulevard.

"There. The white thtucco," Sydney said.

"I'll do a U-ey up here." Angel pointed at the next intersection.

"Are they legal here?"

"Yeah, unless some fedérale don't like it." Angel checked ahead and behind. "We're all clear."

They parked at the curb near the white building. "My cousin said you don't need to fill out any paperwork. She handled everything. Just pick up the keys. I'll go with you because they might not speak English."

"You go. I'll wait in the truck. I've done too much moving around."

Angel trotted ahead on the sidewalk veered into the arched entrance to a courtyard on the right side of the building. Beyond the arched entry, two closed garage doors lined the front of the first floor of the three-story stucco building. Sydney leaned forward and craned his neck to view the terraced upper floors. He didn't remember which floor had been reserved for him. Each upper floor appeared to have a walled outdoor living area across the front.

From somewhere above, he heard the sounds of children at play and small dogs barking. Movement at the front wall of the third-floor terrace caught his eye. Young girl faces popped up and disappeared as the children screamed, yelled and giggled from inside the top-floor terrace. He leaned back as a sense of dread swept over him. The second floor, with yappy little dogs and noisy children above, didn't promise a restful stay. He exhaled a heavy sigh.

Out of three things he hated most, he had two right here, little dogs and children. Add someone stupid and he'd have a trifecta. A sharp whistle caught his attention. Angel with his big smile waved from behind the short privacy wall on the second-floor terrace. He acknowledged his friend.

Minutes passed before Angel reappeared, this time at the first garage door as he worked a key. He swung the door up and open. A secure place for his truck did little to lighten Sydney's disappointment over the third-floor neighbors. His friend jumped in behind the wheel, drove from the curb and wheeled into the small single-car garage.

"There you go. Get your stuff and I'll take you to your room."

"I'll grab what I need right away—get the rest later." Sydney eased his duffle from the back seat and met Angel at the tailgate. "Thome of the thingth I want are toward the front. Could you get them?"

Angel raised the back of the canopy and dropped the tailgate. "You'll have to point out which bags."

A commotion of children and dogs erupted beside the garage and spilled from the arched entry onto the sidewalk. Each of the two pre-teen girls had a hyper Chihuahua tugging on a leash. The girls followed their noisy pcts south and away from the resort. The dogs barked at everything, moving or not.

"Hope they're leaving," Sydney said.

"I don't think so, Amigo. From what I heard in the office, they'll be here a few weeks."

"I'll try to avoid them." From the back, Sydney selected the items for Angel to set on the tailgate. When they finished, Sydney had a bag hung on each shoulder and held a lighter one in his hand. The larger and heavier duffle held his laptop. His midsection only hurt if he made quick moves.

He waited for Angel to climb out from under the canopy and lock the truck. The girls and dogs sounded closer. From the corner of his eye he caught a glimpse. Long black hair, big brown eyes—they chattered and giggled. The yappers yapped.

Angel joined him as they moved out onto the sidewalk. His friend closed the door.

Sydney faced the girls.

Their eyes bugged out at the sight of the bandaged stranger. "Momia," one screeched as they spun away from Sydney.

Angel yelled something in Spanish.

The taller of the two tangled in her leash and fell to the sidewalk. She screamed in terror as she clutched her knee. Both Chihuahuas had worked themselves into a frenzy to defend their keepers. The shorter girl released her leash and jumped to aid her playmate.

Freed, the fierce defender churned toward Sydney. A sharp pain shot across his stomach as he swung the smaller bag to stop the attacker. He missed, lost his balance and tumbled to the concrete. He writhed from pain in his midsection as the little beast tore at his pant leg.

Sydney kicked at the rat dog. "Thtop. Thtop."

Angel grabbed and jerked on the leash to restrain the dog.

"Owoo. Ahh." Sydney tried to right himself. "I hope I didn't tear something." In slow motion, he got to his feet and growled. "I'm going to kill—" His eyes locked on one of the most beautiful creatures ever.

Daggers in her eyes, she spewed hatred in a Spanish tirade. Angel stepped between Sydney and the furious woman. Dumbstruck by her well-formed body and long dark hair, Sydney gaped. His stare added fuel to her fire.

Angel used rapid Spanish to quell the flame.

Sydney understood none of their words, but his friend prevailed.

The gorgeous woman consoled the girl with the wounded knee, and led the girls and yappy pets past Sydney. She opened the other garage door and disappeared inside.

Angel sidled close and whispered, "Let's get out of sight, Amigo." He collected two bags.

Sydney gritted his teeth at the spikes of pain as he grabbed his bags.

A shiny, black Mercedes sedan backed out of the garage onto the boulevard. The darkened windows blocked any view of the occupants.

"A beautiful woman," Sydney said.

Angel placed a hand on his shoulder. "Mi Amigo, forget you ever saw her. Don't let your eyes rest on her, don't speak to her, if you bump into her, go the other way."

"Whoa. You make her out to be a black widow—a she-devil."

"Worse. La Familia Michoacán."

"I thought this was Sinaloa Cartel territory."

"Yeah, but a lot of the smaller cartels have formed alliances. One word to her husband—he'd cut your heart out, Amigo."

"I'll keep clear of her. But that dog's history if he tries me again."

◆◆◆

Recovery had gone well. Sydney had shed most of the bandages and the pain had dissipated, but redness showed near the incisions on his face along with a few persistent bruises.

He lounged on his terrace to watch the sunset. Since Angel's warning, he stayed back under the upstairs overhang. Unnoticed, out of sight had been his motto. Angel had returned to his inland relatives after the first night so Sydney had used taxies to get to and from the doctor's office.

With Internet access, he used his off-shore server as if he'd never left Oregon. The sudden travel, surgery and recovery had disrupted his life and plans. Sydney brooded. There'd been no reply to his last email to the editor. With the confusion of recent days, he'd failed to check for news stories about his splendid murders. He'd renew his efforts soon. There had to be some way to gain notice. Perhaps he picked the wrong newspaper, a lazy editor. Maybe he'd follow up on his threat to find a different paper. Tantalize another editor with some teasers.

As the sun set on the horizon, he watched for the sun's last wink of the day.

Above, one of the little girls squealed. The dogs barked.

Cape Blanco and the long blonde hair of the one that got away surfaced in his memory. He grabbed his new hand mirror to admire what he had become. She'd never recognize him, until he spoke. For him to orchestrate headlines of her beautiful death with published stories on his brilliant work, would be such a rush.

He closed his eyes and savored the symmetry of it all.

Chapter 24

"Cougar?" Matt, at Allen's desk, tilted the screen for his partner. "I never thought about them being around."

"Yes." Allen leaned for a better view over Matt's shoulder. "The tail's sure long."

"If they're around Shellburg, they're probably up in my canyon. I never see any when I'm out running."

"You won't unless they want to be seen."

"Lots of deer—there's an elk."

"Thing takes good pictures, huh? Most at night—not the doe here."

"And hikers." Matt adjusted the screen for Allen. "How long will the batteries last?"

"Maybe three months, if we don't use the audio or video recording. Just still shots."

"And this one will transmit the pictures to your email?"

"That's how I'll set the thing up. But I have to get a signal booster. When I ran a test, nothing reached my inbox."

"Really cool. Should we get two of them?" Matt asked.

"Could, but I think this'll do what we need. I'll build a little box to mount the thing in."

"Weather hard on them?"

"Not supposed to be, but just in case."

"You can go set the thing up now if you want. I can work on these lists—tedious job," Matt said.

"Trudeau surprised me when he said they couldn't narrow the computer search down to at least a specific agency or office."

"Me too," Matt said, "all mumbo-jumbo. They only said the email came from a handful of offices—but these lists have a pot full of employees from those agencies." He lifted a stack of paper from the table.

"Vi helped weed out a lot of them when she said any serial killer will likely be a male," Allen said.

"Cuts well over half, but don't tell anyone we engaged in profiling."

"Mums the word." Allen cupped his mouth with a hand.

"Okay," Matt said. "They've run criminal history on all of the males. I want to verify they printed out the results of each query they made—we can't miss any." Matt rapped the side of the box on the table. "In here they've alphabetized all the arrest records found so far. We'll have to review these to pick out the guys who need a closer look."

"I'll take that box over to my desk," Allen said.

Hours later, Matt checked the time. He pushed the last stack of papers aside. "Done. All of the male employees on the agencies' lists have been run."

"I've been through all of these arrest records." Allen carried the box back to the table. "Not sure we've got any suspects in here. There's a half-dozen driving under the influence, a few marijuana possessions—several domestic violence."

"Trudeau said the detectives are chasing down the violence cases," Matt said.

"Then we're out of work."

"Not too satisfying—like eating left-overs." Matt reached for another bundle of papers. "Here are a bunch of sub-contractors who may have access to the buildings where these agencies rent space. You know—landlords, painters, carpenters, furnace guys—janitors."

"He wants us to go around and get a list of all of the workers who could get in the buildings—then what?" Allen asked.

"Give him the workers' names."

"This feels a lot like we're being used, Matt."

"Yep, but I tell myself this is for my friend. This case helps his rehab."

"Not too rewarding to do all the leg work, develop suspects and then stop so the detectives can have all the fun."

"When I told Anna that, she told me to stop whining."

"I know better than to argue with her."

Matt studied the screen on his laptop, "These buildings are near the State Capitol. Let's run over there instead of working the phones."

◆◆◆

After going from building to building, office to office, for several hours, Matt sat in his truck with Allen. He waited for his partner to complete a cell phone call.

"I gather they use the same sub-contractor for maintenance?" Matt asked.

"You got that right. Turns out to be a small circle of associates," Allen said.

"We've got names of all the employees now, except for the janitorial service. This Ross has custodians in each building on our list," Matt said.

"Since he works nights, he's probably home sleeping."

"Not today. I talked to his daughter on the phone. Mom hauled him off to ER and they slapped him into intensive care," Matt said.

"Anybody in the office, to help us?"

"Mom is the office. We'll talk with her," Matt said.

◆◆◆

State workers were headed home by the time they finished. Matt drove through rush hour traffic to their office. Allen unlocked the door and carried the lists of names over to his desk. Matt placed his bag on the long table beside the box of arrest records.

He fished his cell phone from a pocket and leaned back in his swivel chair. Anna answered as he crossed his ankles on the edge of the table.

"I'm running a little late tonight, Honey."

"Figured you were busy because I didn't hear from you. What's going on?" she asked.

"We've been foot soldiers for Trudeau."

"You don't sound happy. No progress?"

"Hard to say. We've tried to find the killer among the employees on those lists I told you about."

"Well, you must have the killer's name, unless the guy's a really good burglar."

"We'll keep digging. Allen and I are frustrated doing only the menial tasks."

"We've been all through that, Matt. You can always quit—not like you'd lose income."

"No matter. Hey, I'll be on my way in a few minutes. Let the traffic thin out before I head home. Allen sent our short list of janitors over to the task force. If the analyst kicks the results over to us, we might play with those before we close up."

"I'll start dinner," Anna said.

Matt dropped his feet to the floor, tossed the phone near his bag and glanced at Allen. "Any progress, partner?"

"The analyst sent the results of the criminal checks for the janitors. Not too many so she attached them to this email." Allen leaned close to his screen. "Not much here, but there's something goofy about a janitor named Smythe."

Matt moved behind Allen to study the screen. "Okay, scroll down ... No axe killer, just a computer hacker?"

"The analyst sent some old news stories. He'd hacked into NORAD and did hard time. He's been out several years—could still be on probation," Allen said.

"According to the cleaning company's record, he only worked about a week. Where before that?"

"Don't know," Allen said. "Here's the number for federal probation. If they supervise him, they'd know."

"But they may not tell." Matt reached for his desk phone and dialed. The receptionist wouldn't answer questions or confirm any information about Sydney Smythe. Matt left a message for the probation officer who handled Smythe to call Trudeau at the Sheriff's Office.

"Better give Trudeau a heads-up," Allen said.

"I think he's headed over here to pick up these names we gathered," Matt said. "By the way, when I told him about Eva, he laughed. Asked me if I knew how many reports the sheriff gets every week on vandals letting air out of tires."

"I'm inclined to agree," Allen said. "Haven't learned much from my queries. She's lived at the same address for about twenty years and has no record. Has a Winter living there—might be a daughter."

"I'm all in on this full-court press to track down the killer through these emails," Matt said. "But if Trudeau doesn't want to follow up with her, when things slow down I may give Eva a call."

◆◆◆

The next morning, Matt slid his plate to the side and opened the newspaper to the comic section. "After the recent run of stories on the Shellburg murder, the paper's tame today."

Across the table, Anna studied the grocery ads. "I don't mind happy news." She poured a refill from the carafe. "Anything else for breakfast?"

"No." He scooted his chair back and gathered his plate and utensils. "I better get ready to go." He leaned for a kiss before he headed for the kitchen. "Great coffee cake, thanks."

"Matt." She rose from her chair to face across the bar. "Beth called me yesterday. A client told her about some abortion doctor in Philadelphia convicted of murder. Troubles me, the awful things he did. Don't know why I hadn't heard."

"I shelter you," he smiled.

"Oh, stop it. You're always bringing your murder cases home."

"Guess I do. The name's Gosnell. He's doing life for several murders at his clinic."

"There's a book about what he did. Beth ordered a copy."

"Wow. That'll make for some heavy talk in the hair salon. Don't they just gossip and swap recipes?"

"Be serious, Matt. Nothing funny about the destruction of a precious, innocent life—a gift from God."

"No, there isn't," he said. "Far too many hold their power to end a life over the right to live."

"Yeah and they soothe their conscience by adjusting the moment life begins."

"Soothe all they want, God sets the moment and will have the final word."

"I heard you on the phone with Trudeau. What's going on?"

"The probation officer called him. The one I told you about last night. She invited him to send a detective with her on a surprise visit to that janitor's house. He said the detectives are shorthanded and asked if I wanted to go."

"You don't sound too excited. After being so blue over your demotion, I'd think you'd show a little enthusiasm."

Matt rinsed the dishes in the sink. "I'm in this to help my friend—nothing more than that. If this was a red-hot lead, they wouldn't send some washed up FBI agent."

"They'd have egg on their face if the janitor turns out to be the killer." Anna joined him at the dishwasher with her plate.

"Just a little yoke." Matt pecked her cheek.

"Very punny."

"From what I've learned, there's nothing to make me think this guy's a killer. A computer hacker who went to prison. One thing in his background makes me curious. Our killer has experience with servers and how to navigate over the Internet. Be interesting to size him up."

◆◆◆

Later that morning Matt arrived in Salem. The voice from the navigation app on his Smartphone directed him to the Smythe residence. He drove past the end of the driveway and parked at the curb behind a white four-door sedan. In the rearview mirror, he studied a young woman in conversation with an elderly gentleman. Short dark hair, she wore a navy blue blazer with dark slacks. She clutched a portfolio against her white blouse. Had to be her.

On the street, Matt moved to the back of his truck and waited. She glanced his way, ended her visit, and met him at the end of the driveway.

"Mr. Kinler, I'm Fran. I apologize for getting you out here. This may be a dry run." She released his hand.

"Call me Matt. What do you mean?"

She glanced toward the gentleman in the yard next door. "Mr. Barnes over there keeps an eye on Smythe for me. Hasn't seen him around for a week or so."

"That unusual?"

"Not to be gone, but the length of time is."

"Barnes … Barnes." He glanced at the neighbor. "A Barnes called our hot line after our press story. Talked about a neighbor with a bad complexion who killed his dog."

"I'd bet he's the caller." She nodded back toward Barnes. "Our boy has a bad complexion and I've heard the dog story before."

"Barnes doesn't know where Smythe went?"

"No, but we'll ask his mother—she's disabled. She'd told the neighbor that Sydney's hobby is photography. He goes on short trips to take pictures."

"Does your neighborhood spy know where Smythe goes to take pictures?"

"No. But, he better not go far. Can't leave the state without my permission."

"Does he have other restrictions?"

"Nothing unusual, except he can't have access to computers."

Matt followed Fran to the front door. On the porch, through the window he spotted an old black and white program playing on a large screen television.

"She may not hear the bell over the sound in there," Fran said.

Matt leaned toward the window. "I see her—moving slow."

Moments later, Wanda, aboard her power scooter, opened the door. "Oh." Her eyes widened on Fran. "You didn't call."

"No. I didn't. This is a surprise visit, Mrs. Smythe."

"Can you do that?"

"Yes, Ma'am."

"Well, Sydney's not home right now."

"When do you expect him?"

"I, ahh …" Wanda rubbed her swollen knuckles, her eyes flitted between Fran and Matt. "Don't know … he's on a trip."

"Where is he, Mrs. Smythe?" Fran asked.

Wanda held her misshapen fingers to her face and moaned. "I told him not to go … ohh."

"Where is he?"

She averted her eyes. "California."

"He should have called me first. I might've let him go."

Wanda plucked a tissue from the caddy fixed to the handlebars and dabbed her moist eyes. "You better come in." She powered back into the living room and invited them to sit.

"No, thank you. We'll stand," Fran said. "Could you turn down the sound, please?"

She grabbed the remote from the caddy. On the screen "Aunt Bee" went silent. "You're not going to arrest my Sydney, are you ... Miss?"

"No, but he may face a sanction. Why'd he leave the state?"

"You've seen the skin on his face—how he looks." Her sad-eyed expression focused on Fran. "Made him shy and embarrassed. For a long time, I'd begged him to get his skin treated. Finally, he agreed."

"What, like plastic surgery?" Matt asked.

"Yes." Wanda cocked her head to the side and studied Matt. "You look familiar. Have we met?"

"No, Ma'am." He handed her a business card.

"Maybe TV?" Wanda asked as she studied his card.

Fran interrupted. "How did he travel?"

"In his truck."

"The old red one?" Fran asked.

"No. New gray one. Someone stole his other truck—burned it."

"I'd like to check out his room, Mrs. Smythe."

"Can you do that?"

"Yes, Ma'am, I can."

"Okay. I don't want him to get in trouble. He's so talented—smart. As soon as he can use computers, I know he'll be able to get a good job." Wanda followed them to the top of the stairs. "Did you decide if he can use one of those GPS things, yet?" She raised her voice as they reached the basement.

"No, Ma'am, I haven't."

After the inspection, Matt followed Fran down the driveway. In the street, beside his truck she stopped to face him. "Strange, Matt. All the way outside, I'm thinking, where are all of his pictures? Most photographers I know have their photos plastered all over."

"Yeah. Not a big collection of books either," Matt said. "Most on computer technology and magazines for gamers. A couple books on geocaching. Does he do that?"

"Either did or wants to. He's asked permission to get one of those GPS devices. Until today, I'd planned to give him some slack. He could probably find one easy enough anyway—so common now."

"His face—what happened? Burns, cut up, what?"

"Really bad acne scars. Rough reddish complexion." She leafed through her folder. "One of the psych profiles suggests his extreme self-consciousness was worsened by the onset of acne and contributed to a more pronounced speech impediment."

"What kind of impediment?"

"Lisp. Has trouble with the 'S' sound."

"His new truck—all we have is silver-gray?"

"Yes, and his neighbor says it's a Toyota with an extended cab and canopy over the bed. Didn't get the plate number."

"Do you have the exact dates for his prison time?"

Fran flipped through pages in her file and slipped one out for Matt to read.

He thought aloud as he checked the dates. "Smythe entered prison after Mari Davies died and his release occurred months before the Judith Rhime's murder."

Matt glanced toward the house. Perched inside at the window, Wanda kept an eye on them. The worried expression on her face gave him pause. If she'd watched his appearance on television, wouldn't she be suspicious of her son?

Chapter 25

In the mirror Sydney traced faint lines left by the scalpel with his finger. Unnoticeable soon, the surgeon said of the trails he'd left behind. Bandages gone, no more visits to the doctor, he'd been cleared to travel. The decision to return to the states, his alone.

A mixture of anger, frustration and revenge soured in his gut. The stupid cops had no clue, the editor didn't catch on and now this jerk on the news. He hung his head as he placed his hands on the sink. How could they not connect the dots? Maybe they're toying with him. *A wanna be? I'll show 'em.*

Sydney squeezed the tube of ointment and applied the cream to cover reddened areas on his face. A smile formed as he considered how his mother might react. He paused to admire his new appearance before he left the bathroom. *The coppers won't recognize me.*

Today, Angel would return with his truck and they'd head for the border. Until now, bandages and surgical wounds had restricted his activity. But another reason to stay out of sight remained, the manic she-devil upstairs with the noisy dogs and children. Since she and her girls always had breakfast early, Sydney waited to catch the buffet at the last moment.

In the dining room, Sydney loaded a tray with his selections from the service line before he meandered around empty tables to his favorite back corner. The food had been good, but he'd never caught the names of the dishes when the server pitched them. He came to get his face fixed and had no interest in the language or customs of Mexico.

Most of his choices had been egg dishes, rice and tortillas because of his familiarity with them. This morning the server added some sauce with chunks of tomato and onion. He dipped the tines of his fork in the sauce to test the bite of the spice. The tip of his tongue recoiled at the hot flavor. He gulped from his water glass to douse the fire and quell the pain.

Outside the dining room entrance, sounds and commotion interrupted the quiet. His heart sank. The two girls from upstairs stormed into the room with two friends. The screams and squeals stopped when the taller girl spotted Sydney in the corner. She called a huddle, and as she spoke the girls shot glances at him.

The gorgeous woman arrived with a look-alike. Sydney shifted in the chair to avoid the hate-filled eyes. The spicy mess on his plate lost any appeal, but he didn't dare try to leave. No need to pass too close to the explosive woman. He picked at the rice on his plate and took an occasional drink from his mixed fruit juice. Compulsion to admire, to lust, to imagine, drove him to steal glances at the beautiful Latinas.

Across the room, an attendant slid two tables together for the new arrivals. After the entourage gathered around the joined tables, servers brought bowls and plates of food from the buffet line and placed them on the table family style.

Resentment welled at the scene of preferential treatment. He fought the magnetic attraction of his eyes. The she-devil caught him and glared daggers. She waved her fork as a pointer and raised her voice in a Spanish diatribe.

Beads of sweat formed on his forehead. The Spanish he didn't understand, but everyone in the room caught the meaning, as did he. Unnerved, he bladed his shoulders and moved his juice close to the edge of the table to drink without accidental eye contact.

"Amigo." Angel's arrival startled him.

"Oh." Sydney shifted to face his friend. "Didn't expect you tho thoon."

"Yeah." He pulled out a chair across from Sydney. "Dude—you haven't finished your breakfast."

"Not hungry." He offered his plate. "Hardly touched—want it? Too hot."

Angel's face brightened as he reached for the food.

Sydney scooted his chair so Angel blocked his view. "I need to kill time until the cartel woman leaves. Don't need any trouble."

"Si. Good thinking, Dude." Angel devoured the breakfast.

They waited until the women and children left the dining room. Sydney led Angel up the back stairs to his second-floor entrance. Angel connected the television and game console. Sydney finished packing.

Last night he'd viewed the recording of the outrageous statements by the guy who represented his first victim's family. Again, he couldn't believe the cops hadn't connected the murders. The idea they were playing with him recurred. Then they trot out some idiot who tries to make Sydney out to be some jerk, phony killer. *I'll show them brilliant. A legend—that's what I'll be.*

Sydney went out onto the terrace to wait for Angel. In a chaise lounge under the third-floor overhang, he gazed off into the distance. The blue, cloudless sky merged with the ocean on the horizon. The water danced in the noonday sun. But his mind didn't dwell on scenic beauty. The fouled effort at Blanco only whetted his appetite to kill again. Fine, she would've been his best yet. He closed his eyes to picture her.

Never had he stalked, he'd only set a trap and waited for his prey. In Billy's interview with the author, he spoke against the preselection or surveillance of victims. Such methods carried too much risk. A random kill lowered the odds of capture. All true, but Billy hadn't met Blanco.

Screams of young girls and voices of hysterical women spilled down from above and broke his train of thought. He rose and opened the sliding glass door to his unit. Angel dropped the controller as someone pounded on the door and shouted in Spanish.

Angel placed his foot in case he had to block the door before he opened. Sydney spotted a harried housekeeper, who waved her arms as she spoke in frantic spurts. Angel diffused the panic and locked the door before he returned.

He smiled. "The crazy woman upstairs lost one of the Chihuahuas. She accused us of stealing one named Hombre."

"That'th hith name, Hombre?" Sydney asked.

"Yep, I told her we don't like dogs."

"Got that right, 'thpecially the little biter"

"She said Hombre had run off before. They found him across the road, down on the beach."

"That explains what the maid wanted a couple days ago. Came to my door, but I didn't understand what she wanted. Good. Hope he gets run over."

The furor had died down by early afternoon. Before checkout, they planned to visit one of the north beaches. Sydney hadn't bared his slimmed body in public. Dressed in shorts, shirt and flip-flops, he headed for the door.

"You drive, Man." Sydney hung one strap of the day pack on his shoulder.

In the entrance, Angel said, "Wait, Dude. I got to go."

Sydney said, "Give me the truck keyth and your bag. I'll load up and wait in the garage. Don't forget to lock up."

On the front sidewalk, he unlocked the garage door as a car horn sounded in the distance. He caught a glimpse of a little dog on the sidewalk along the beach. Not a concern of his, maybe a city bus could finish the critter off. He raised the garage door, opened the lid on the canopy and lowered the tailgate.

As he transferred bags from the sidewalk into the truck, horns blared behind him, tires squeaked and skidded on the pavement. He glanced back over his shoulder. The little beast had targeted him and bore down with teeth bared. Sydney spun to launch himself onto the truck bed. The dog's teeth ripped at one of his ankles. He cursed, kicked at the dog, and leaped under the canopy. Below the tailgate the furious dog tore into the flip-flop Sydney left behind.

In a volcanic rage, Sydney leaped on the dog and clamped a hand behind its head to jerk his flip-flop from the jaws. Yelps and squeals erupted. He

spun to screen what he had to do from passersby.
With both hands, he silenced the dog. He didn't need
another scene with the she-devil. Drenched with
sweat, he panted as realization replaced his rage.
Gripped with fear of being discovered, his heart raced.

He plopped the limp body on the bed and
closed the tailgate. To conceal the remains, he
grabbed an empty white plastic bag.

"Dude!"

Sydney flinched. "Don't thcare me." He
locked the back lid on the canopy.

"Hey, Dude. What happened to you?" Angel
bent over to check the blood on Sydney's ankle. "You
kick something?"

"No. I tripped." He reached for his flip-flop on
the garage floor. "Gouged it."

"Hombre! Hombre!" The screams of the girls
carried over the traffic noise.

"Better get out of here." Sydney headed for the
passenger side.

Angel backed across the sidewalk and into the
street. Before the truck sped away, Sydney locked
eyes with the cartel woman, who stood on the
sidewalk, children beside her. Chills swept down his
back. He choked back a nauseous surge.

"What's wrong, Dude? You don't look good."
Angel wove through traffic as they headed for the
north shore beaches.

"Nothing. I'll be okay." He shifted in his seat
to check traffic behind them.

"Something's up, Dude. Better tell me." Angel
glanced at him.

"Really—no big deal." Sydney pointed ahead.
"Find a trash can—gotta drop thomething off."

Angel glanced at him, but didn't reply.

They traveled in silence for several long minutes before Angel pulled into a public parking lot and stopped near a trash can.

"Let me borrow the keyth to the back." Sydney took the key from the ignition with the keyring. "Wait here."

He moved to the back, grabbed the bag, and disposed of the evidence.

Angel accepted the keys and started the engine. "You killed their dog, Dude." He shook his head.

"I don't know what you're talking about, Man."

"Hey. I saw his little foot sticking out of the bag." Worry filled Angel's big round face.

"He attacked me."

"A little dog?" Angel covered his face with his hands.

"I just wanted it to be quiet—didn't mean to kill it."

"We're dead, Dude. La Familia—they'll catch us, cut off our heads and leave us in a ditch. Our families won't ever find us." He lowered his hands and stared up at the headliner.

"They don't know. They won't catch us."

"We gotta get out of town—now."

"Chill. I've got my computer and other stuff in the room. Can't leave without my gear." He couldn't tell his friend about the flower pictures.

"Okay, but we better hang out on the north end until midnight. Then we'll sneak back for your stuff."

◆◆◆

After midnight, traffic on the ocean front boulevard provided cover as they drove toward the bed and breakfast. Within blocks, Angel swung onto a side street to approach the back of the complex.

"We'll need to park a couple blocks away and go on foot," Sydney said. "They might be on the lookout for my truck." He pointed. "Here."

Angel parked at the curb.

"Only a block to the alley." Sydney fished his new commando knife from under the seat and tucked the sheathed weapon inside his waistband.

Together they moved along the dark street. No moonlight, but the ambient city light denied them total darkness. Sydney crouched before he sprinted across the street, which bordered the side of his resort, and ducked into the back alley. He motioned for Angel to follow.

Snug against the back of the building, he heard the sounds of cars as they passed out on the front boulevard. Dogs barked in distant neighborhoods.

"Follow me," Sydney whispered. "The cook might be in the kitchen. Be careful there."

They eased through the service entrance and hung close to the shadows as they worked their way to the back stairs and his second-floor entrance. Sydney froze at the sounds of a man who cleared his throat and spat. He squatted beside Angel and gestured his plan.

Angel remained as Sydney crept to the top of the front stairs. One step, a second step, he caught a glimpse of a man in the shadows near the arched front entrance. Backlit by the oceanfront lights, a stream of smoke shot out into the passageway. The smell of cigarette smoke drifted in the air.

Sydney retreated and made a noiseless entry into his room.

Chapter 26

The reflection of the border crossing shrank as he studied his side mirror. Sydney took a deep breath and exhaled relief. The weight of fear lifted the moment the guard waved them into the United States. The streets of Yuma bustled with activity. The cartels had tentacles into his country, but he'd baffled the cops and he'd avoid the drug lords too. Besides, how could anyone care about some little mutt dog?

"Hey. Pull over," Sydney said. "I can drive in my country."

"Si." Angel tapped the dash clock. "We'll be at my house 'bout dinner. Eat and play a few games. Want to?"

"No, Man. I gotta get home. My probation officer's probably freaked out by now."

"Think she's got a warrant?"

"Doubt it—told my mother theee wanted me to call. I'll wait 'til I get to Oregon."

♦♦♦

As he drove north through the San Joaquin Valley, Sydney flashed back to the strange press conference held by the family of his first kill. Any cop with smarts would've put two and two together by now. *Yet, this guy announced to the world that I'm a pretender. Trying to take credit for another killer's handiwork. Ha.* He clenched his jaw and beat the steering with the side of his fist. *They've got to be*

*toying with me. Trying to goad me into doing
something stupid. I won't play their game.*

Images of Blanco, her long blonde hair and
fine body, flooded his mind. Maybe a detour on his
way home. A different truck, new face, and slimmed
body, she'd never recognize him. He'd left his new kit
in the storage unit, but he had the knife he'd bought in
Mexico. The author wrote how Billy tried to avoid
any deviation from his well-drawn plans and methods.
Sydney's idol believed impulsive or spontaneous acts
carried the risk of disaster.

He'd followed his mentor's advice, but Billy
hadn't been at Cape Blanco. In the dark and fog, she'd
surprised him. The gun, the stance, he had no choice
but retreat. Seized by desire, he decided to detour
through Bandon. He might catch a glimpse of her in
broad daylight. A small town—if she's out on patrol,
he'd find an opportunity.

◆◆◆

The sun rose as Sydney arrived in Bandon's old
harbor parking lot. He found a spot to view the boats
tied in their slips. The boat launch ramp had the most
activity on this early weekday morning. Outside the
truck, he stretched the kinks out and inhaled the cool,
moist ocean air. He pulled a skull cap from his pocket.
Since the buzz-cut in Mexico, his bare head hadn't
been exposed to such cool temperatures. Seagulls
soared above on a stout breeze while others flocked
and complained on the docks and handrails.

Mid-afternoon, Sydney waited for the gas
station attendant to return with his change. He wrung
and squeezed the leather-wrapped steering wheel.
Stakeouts of the police department and repeated trips
through the business district had been fruitless—not
one sighting. Anticipation drained, he'd find an eatery

and head for Salem. Once he calmed the probation officer, he'd prepare for a serious return visit.

Sydney pulled into the parking lot behind a restaurant along the highway. Beside a large motorhome, he set the brake. The prison psychologist had asked him why he always chose to separate himself from others. He didn't think much about why. The way he'd always been. Hang in the background, don't draw attention.

With the truck locked, he rounded the front of the RV and headed for the side entrance. Inside, a few patrons occupied tables and booths. One section held a number of gray-haired couples.

A waitress waved and ushered him to the front dining area and a booth. He scooted to the window and glanced out at the front parking lot and highway.

It'd take time to grow accustomed to his new look. No one stared, no one noticed. She handed him a dinner menu. The back cover listed "Seniors' Twilight Specials."

"Would you like a moment to decide?" she asked.

He tapped the back of the menu. "Can I get the thteak thandwich thpecial?"

She covered her mouth and coughed to the side. "Yes, but we offer the same thing for people your age off the regular menu. Fifty-cents more, bigger steak." She nodded toward the gray-haired bunch and kept her voice low. "They come for the specials."

"I'll have the regular, pleeth."

A whole day lost for nothing. He poked his fries with the fork. Probably better this way, he might've been tempted to do something stupid. By the time he reached Salem, his mother would be in bed for the night. Maybe he'd use the trailer he rented for Jose Garcia and call his mother in the morning. There'd be several hours to decide while he drove. He shoved the plate away.

A familiar dark SUV parked in a diagonal space near the highway. Sydney stiffened and shifted for a clear view. He hadn't noticed before the driver had stopped with the back bumper to the restaurant. A woman rounded the side and stood near the left taillight of the SUV. He relaxed. Short graying hair, average height and weight, she wore a waitress uniform. The woman wasn't close to what he'd hoped.

He slapped a couple of twenties on the bill and grabbed his water glass. The waitress swung by and snatched his money. An Oregon State Trooper drove into the lot. Sydney shrank back as his eyes followed the patrol car. The angle of the car and the equipment on the dash blocked his view of the two officers in front.

The uniformed driver glanced at Sydney before he stopped at the back of the SUV. On the other side of the patrol car, an officer jumped out and appeared to hug the SUV driver. Sydney leaned over the table. Above and beyond the roof of the patrol car, he spotted braided blonde hair. Only the profile of her head showed while she spoke with the older woman. As he strained to see more, his elbow tipped the water glass. He jumped back and scooted away from the spill.

"Oh-oh." His waitress arrived and slapped a rag on the puddle. "Here's your change."

He leaned back. "Thorry." He accepted the cash.

"Okay—happens every day."

Sydney slid out of the booth as she mopped the spill. On his feet, he glanced out the window. She was gone and the waitress from the SUV walked toward the front entrance.

Disappointed, he headed for the side door. There'd be another day, another chance.

◆◆◆

"You better go pick up your daughter, Trudy." Eva stuffed her purse in a cabinet. "Show me where you are on your tables and I'll take over."

Trudy led her into the dining area. "All of my customers have their food, except the new arrivals at the front window. They're ready to order, I think."

"Got it—you go. I remember how much daycare costs."

"I'm glad to work with another single mother. You understand." Trudy patted Eva on the shoulder. "Saw Winter out there. Did she join the State Police?"

"No. She and her boyfriend went to some conference in Coos Bay today."

"You must be very proud of her." Trudy untied her apron. "Had to laugh." She nodded toward the booth with the recent arrivals. "A guy in that booth knocked his water over trying to watch you two out there."

"Had to be Winter, not me." Eva tied a bow and slid the apron to the front. "This guy from around here?"

"No—I've never seen him before. He sure talked funny."

"We get a lot of those, don't we? You go."

◆◆◆

Sydney slowed as he passed his neighbor's house. No lights meant he could avoid the nosey old man. Probably inevitable, but he wanted to keep Barnes in the dark about his new appearance as long as possible. That's if his mother hadn't blabbed. He sighed with a slight shake of his head.

One block beyond his house, he parked around the corner on a dark side street. With what happened in Mexico, he'd need to shed his truck. Wanda would whine, but he'd manage her.

He jogged past the garage light as the motion sensor lit up the driveway. In the darkness, he fished the key from his pocket, but no need. The backdoor had been left unlocked, as usual. Security had never been a big concern. Sydney crept up the steps, through the laundry room, and into the kitchen.

The bedroom light showed under the door. He rapped. "Mother?"

"Sydney? Oh—come in."

He stepped inside, as she muted the television.

She pushed herself up from the pillowed backrest. "Let me see you! Come here." She reached out to take his hands. "You're beautiful, Son. Smooth cheeks—no red scars. Look at you."

"Not beautiful, Mother."

"Oh, I'm so happy for you, Sydney. You'll find a wonderful girl now. I know it. You're so slim—what happened to your hair?"

"I decided to change everything—but the way I talk."

She sighed. "I wish we could fix that too."

"Mother, I can't thtay here—gotta hide."

"Why—what's wrong? The probation officer?"

"Not her. I'll call." He sat on the edge of the bed and played his worried best. "I had trouble with a Mexican cartel. They may thend a guy to find me."

"I've heard about them on the news. Better go to the police, Son. What'd you do?"

"No, Mother—too complicated. I'll lay low until there'th no more danger."

"Well, I don't know about these things." She leaned back on her stack of pillows.

"I'll need to get rid of my truck, Mother."

"What—you just got it." She raised up.

"I know—I know." He stood. "But the car dealer will honor the warranty and allow me to trade for another one. I'll tell him I got an oil leak."

"Do you?" She leaned back.

"I will."

"This is getting expensive, Sydney."

"A couple grand—not much."

"I'll help you—always have, but there has to be an end to this, Son."

"There will be, Mother. I need to grab some clotheth and get out of here."

"That reminds me." Wanda studied him. "I washed the clothes you had in the laundry room."

"You didn't have to do that."

"You were gone so long. I had to do some of my things. But, something fell out of your pocket in the dryer."

His throat tightened as he choked back fear. "What … Mother?" He searched his memory as sweat formed on his lip.

"Those things soldiers wear on a chain. Ah … necklace."

"Dog tagth?" Now he remembered. Cape Blanco had knocked him off stride.

"Yeah, the tags have a girl's name, 'Dolly.' Same as one of those women in the newspaper."

"What women?" Heat flushed from his neck to his new face, as Wanda queried him with her eyes.

"There've been stories about women murdered. I saved one of the papers for you—out on the kitchen table beside those dog tags. Oh—remember the private detective I told you about? His business cards out there too."

"Oh—ah, I didn't hear about any women murdered." He wiped sweat from under his nose and cleared his throat. "Yeah—I remember those tags. My boss sent me to clean rooms at the Veterans building one night. Found those outside on the sidewalk and put 'em in my pocket. Just forgot."

"I thought you'd like to read the story, since you found those. The one named Dolly was killed down near Klamath Falls. Do you think those tags belong to her?"

"Doubt it—long way from here." His mind raced. "I've never been down there, Mother."

"That's what I thought." She nestled into her pillows. "Quite a coincidence you finding a necklace with her name."

"Ah huh—ah. Maybe there's another woman with the thame name." His voice trailed off. He wanted those words back.

"Not likely, Son. You better tell the police what you found."

"Good idea. I'll read the thtory before I leave."

Downstairs, Sydney packed his clothes in a duffle bag. Big mistake to leave those dog tags where they could be found. She meant to spring the news on him—to test him. As far as she knew, he'd never been in Central Oregon—north or south. The stress left him limp. He slumped on the edge of the bed. She had her suspicions, but he'd work on her.

He carried the bag upstairs and slipped out the front door to avoid the motion light on the garage. No need for the neighbor to spy on his nocturnal travels.

Tonight, he'd be Jose Garcia and tomorrow get a different truck. During the quiet drive, the urge to kill raged in every fiber of his being. Maybe tonight a visit to Shellburg Falls would give him the release he needed—to relive the thrill. He changed course from the trailer and headed east into the foothills.

Chapter 27

Henry swayed in the driver's seat as his top heavy
mobile kitchen rocked over the curb. For years, he'd
planned to widen the driveway entrance, but there
never seemed to be enough money. He parked on the
worn grass beside his wife's SUV in the driveway.
Every day he and his business commuted to the vacant
lot he'd rented along the highway in Woodburn. Not
far, but he couldn't leave his food truck overnight.

Married with children, Henry Fuentes made a
good living with his truck. The rent he paid for his
favorite location had been negligible. Always frugal,
he kept his overhead low. His teenage children
worked for him, and he bargained for the ingredients
used in his popular tacos, burritos, and his very own
Mexican burger.

He set the brake, removed the keys, and
studied the text message. All afternoon he'd wrestled
with whether to call the number. At thirteen, Henry
had crossed into California. In Modesto, he took the
only job he could find, collecting money for drug
dealers.

With no place to live, no money for food,
what's a lonely thirteen-year-old supposed to do?
Cartels had operated in his homeland for as long as he
could remember. From the first day, Vaquero treated
him as a son and introduced him to the La Familia
way of life. Violence, drugs, death, and money

became commonplace. Being slight of build, Henry's mentor didn't send him on physical shakedowns. Rather, he trained Henry to deal with those whose violation of Vaquero's code required more than a broken and beaten body.

Vaquero gave him the nickname, el Término. A secret shared only by him and his mentor. Henry's build and unassuming manner helped him avoid notice or arrest as an accomplished killer for the cartel. Vaquero taught him the skills of stealth and how to plan each hit. Every assignment came with a silenced handgun and ammunition. Henry had never owned a gun.

Married at twenty, Vaquero approved Henry's move to Oregon. After ten kills, Vaquero, believed a shooter's luck might run out. Over the years, his old mentor had called upon him when the cartel had a special problem. With less influence in the Northwest, he understood La Familia had a smaller talent pool in his area.

Loyalty to Vaquero compelled him to make the call. Besides, the cartel never balked at his fee.

"Mi amigo," Henry said.

"El Término!" his old mentor said.

The conversation curt and detailed, Henry rewrote his scribbled notes. Before he folded the paper, he checked the information again. He ran a finger over the entries; gray Toyota, Oregon license plate number, and a description of his target. Two Salem addresses had been obtained by the Cartel. One from a plastic surgeon and the other from motor vehicle records by a cartel contact at the border. He called the number given to arrange for the gun.

◆◆◆

Later that night, el Término studied the houses on each side of the street as he walked around the corner. The targeted house had a light on in a front corner room. He paused under a tree near the curb. The light flickered behind the curtains. Years of practice had taught him to identify different lights he'd find in homes. Lights let him know if anyone was awake and where. Three o'clock in the morning also helped him evaluate the level of risk he'd face.

The black knit skull cap and leather athletic shoes matched his outfit. Cotton top and trousers ensured quiet entry and movement. One street light at a distant intersection and a neighbor's porch light didn't pose undue threat.

Up the driveway, he hung in the shadows. The red LED on the motion light flickered. He sprinted several quick strides and tucked in behind the garage. He paused for the light to time out. Darkness reigned behind the house.

El Término drew a knife and small flashlight from his custom-made tool belt. He crept to the backdoor to examine the door knob and lock. Standard. He tried the knob. Unlocked, a condition found more often than not. He eased inside. Up two steps and a moment to let his eyes adjust to the level of light.

Motionless, el Término waited to ensure he had the house to himself—except for the corner room. No sign of danger, he snuck through the kitchen, down the hall to the source of light he'd seen from outside. Left ajar, light escaped along the edge of the door. He peered through the gap. The woman slept with the sound on the television turned low. She'd parked a power scooter beside the bed.

He eased back into the kitchen to begin his search. The first floor covered, he headed down the stairs to check the basement. The space had been outfitted as a bedroom. He rummaged for any information on his target. The presence of few personal belongs told him his target must have moved out.

Back in the kitchen, he made a more thorough search. He opened a cupboard above the house phone. Stuffed between cups and glass tumblers, he found envelopes and papers. He gathered the collection and bundled them on the counter in his hands. The small flashlight clamped in his teeth, he thumbed through the bills and correspondence. Neither of the names his mentor gave him popped into view. Vaquero told him the name and address for Sydney Smythe had come from hospital records and Jose Garcia from a license plate record.

Nothing of interest, he corralled the unwieldy stack in his gloved hand. Above the phone, the bundle spilled from his grip, rattled the receiver, and scattered on the counter and floor. He stifled unspoken curses as he stooped to gather the old mail.

"Sydney?" A sleep-laden voice called from behind the bedroom door.

El Término rushed to finish.

"Sydney, answer me. Are you back—did you forget something?"

Out the backdoor, he waited in the shadows. If she investigated, he didn't want to trigger the motion light on the garage and telegraph his presence. The house remained dark, but he'd wait. Near the back corner of the garage, he spotted the outline of a pedestrian door. In the darkness, he found the knob and entered the unlocked door.

Pitch black in the windowless space, he shined the beam from his flashlight to survey the garage. Beside the door, he spotted labeled switches. He flipped the one marked for the outside motion light. The driver's side window on an old Impala had been left open. Close to the maroon car, he examined the interior with his beam. A crumpled paper had been stuffed above the visor. El Término removed the paper and read "Rental Agreement" at the top. Both names, a different address. He tucked the agreement in his pocket before he crept back outside. More research, more time would be needed.

No light or movement in the house, he moved toward the front of the garage to check for witnesses or the police. Clear, he crouched and slipped past the motion light. The switch had worked.

◆◆◆

After a night in the woods with his memories, Sydney drove to the dealership and slept until the business opened. When the salesman arrived, Sydney made his pitch. Except for the lisp, the man didn't recognize him.

The leak caused by the jimmied threads on the oil filter worked. By mid-morning, he drove off the lot with a red version of the same make and model truck as his gray trade-in. He headed for the trailer he'd rented for Jose Garcia. A few hours of sleep, then he'd visit his storage locker.

No sign of the landlord as he opened the gate. Good. He didn't have time to deal with introductions. Inside the trailer, Sydney dropped his bags on the floor. He wrinkled his nose at the stale air and opened a window over the bed. Fresh air washed over his face as he searched for the owner. No sign, he settled down for a long nap.

A short time later, the high-pitched whine of a small gas engine jolted him awake. Sydney rolled toward his clock radio. One o'clock, his plan to sleep ruined by the landlord's serenade. He kicked off the covers, hit the floor and peered out the window.

Old man Franklin revved the weed whacker along the edge of the driveway. Sydney had to decide what to do about his lisp. When he rented this place for Jose, the landlord would have noticed. He'd have to create Jose without a lisp. During the recent, hasty moves, he hadn't considered his speech defect.

The red roof of his new truck's canopy glistened in the afternoon sun. He smiled at how he'd been able to manipulate his mother. Her desire for his success made her susceptible to his ploys. The cartel story had a ring of truth. No doubt he left one angry Hispanic woman behind, but nobody would chase him around the world over a dumb little dog.

Sydney placed his lunch on the small kitchen bar beside his laptop. The off-shore server had no new messages from the newspaper. He ground his teeth, angry at the refusal of an editor and stupid cops to link his murders. On top of that, the family of his first kill jumped in front of news cameras and called him a "wanna be." A taunt, but he'd not play their silly game. Calmed by a heavy sigh, he browsed his favorite websites.

Theme music played on his phone. Mother. He regretted giving her the number, but during travel to and from Mexico he needed to be able to reach his money source in an emergency.

"Mother."

"Sydney, did you come back by the house last night?"

"No. Why?"

"Just wondering. I might've had a dream. Thought I heard a noise in the house."

"Anything mithing, Mother?"

"No. No, I don't think so. I found a couple bills on the floor in the kitchen, but I could've dropped those."

"Maybe we better thart locking the backdoor."

"Oh, I know. I'm not too good at that. I'll check," she said. "Sydney, the probation officer just called again. I told her you'd be back soon."

"Yeah. Okay. I'll give her a call."

"Do you remember the private detective I told you about? I think I'd seen him on TV before, but I'm not sure."

"Might be famous—I've got his card, I'll check up on him." He opened his picture folder to view his collection.

"Sydney, are you still there?"

A nod, "Oh … yeth. I've got to go, Mother." He tapped to end the call.

After his slide show, he grew curious. Sydney searched for information on Matt Kinler. Private Investigator, Salem address, he'd have to check this guy out.

Dressed, he gathered his phone and laptop, and headed for his truck.

"You must be my new renter." Franklin approached with the weed whacker hung from his shoulder.

Sydney nodded and waved his free hand as he struggled with the door and his load.

"Jose Garcia, your brother, told me."

Sydney tossed his gear on the seat and faced the man. He nodded as he mouthed words and gestured with his hands.

"Can't you talk?"

Sydney gave a vigorous shake of his head.

"Well, … I never … your brother didn't warn me."

Sydney shrugged.

"Don't make no difference, I guess. Thought I heard you talking to somebody in there." Franklin pointed to the trailer's open window.

Sydney shook his head.

"Radio maybe?"

Sydney nodded

"Guess we won't talk much."

Sydney tried an apologetic expression he didn't feel. Nosey old man had snuck around outside to eavesdrop. This guy reminded him too much of Barnes.

Chapter 28

"Where's Allen? Trudeau rolled the swivel chair closer to their work table.

Matt set his pencil down. "He wanted to stop and swap the memory card in the trail cam." The sight of the bags under his friend's bloodshot eyes troubled him. "You okay?"

"Haven't slept well last few nights."

"These cases do that." Vi placed a hand on Trudeau's forearm. "Take care of yourself. We need you."

"Don't understand ... why he's been so quiet." Trudeau's eyes went to the victims' photos on the wall. "Hope he hasn't killed another daughter—a sister."

"Could be in custody for some minor thing," Vi said. "That happens."

"That computer guy's out of town," Matt said. "If he's our killer, I'd think he could find a computer to use somewhere."

"Has Allen captured anything on the camera ... up at the falls?" Trudeau asked.

"Animals and hikers. That's about all." Matt sipped from his coffee. "Had a wireless set up to catch the action real time, but spotty reception ruined that plan. He's been swapping out the memory cards."

"Matt, I've been away and only heard bits of what the Bandon woman told you," Vi said. "Is that something we should take a look at?"

"I'm certainly not ready to dismiss what she said." Matt shared the details of Winter Vanderscoot's encounter near the Cape Blanco campground.

"As you tell her story, you've got them all. The lisp, the tires flattened by valve stem, the bad complexion, a hoody, and the old red truck," Vi said.

"Yes," Trudeau said. "But everything has been in the newspaper ... except the lisp and valve stems."

"Those are significant excepts," Vi said. "How about the DA or detectives—they following this?"

"Not really," Trudeau said. "Bigger fish to fry. They're zeroed in on the ... off-shore server and the State's email system. They won't talk Bandon—not yet."

"Priorities have to be set—no doubt." Vi propped her elbows on the table. "Matt, I may not remember all you learned when you accompanied the probation officer. Can you run that by me, again?"

"He's high on my list," Matt said. "Self-taught computer whiz. Trouble with "S" words, bad complexion, and had an old red truck. Neighbor said he's got a newer gray one." He leafed through his notes. "The guy's had that one arrest by the Feds for computer hacking. No violent crimes to speak of." He straightened his papers. "Oh, there is something else. His time in prison coincides with the seven years or so between our victims, Mari and Judith."

"Didn't you say he's just had plastic surgery?"

"Yeah. Makes you wonder why now?"

"Yes—does. This neighbor, have you talked to him?" Vi asked.

"No. He's the neighborhood snitch for the probation officer. When Smythe gets back in town, she may bust him for a violation. Might be a chance to interview him."

"That'd be good. Do you know if the neighbor said anything about this guy's behavior?" Vi asked.

Matt closed his eyes to search his memory. "Not much." He drank from his cup. "The old man thinks Smythe killed his dog. Apparently, the dog and Smythe had a mutual dislike."

"I've heard dogs are good judges of character," Trudeau said.

"Oh, another thing," Matt said. "The old man also believes that, before Smythe entered high school, he burned down the neighbor's chicken coop. There's no proof."

"Hope the chickens got out," Trudeau said.

"Think so," Matt said.

Vi left her chair and studied the wall of crime scene photos. "Something to think about—it's not uncommon to find arson and animal cruelty in a serial killer's past." She walked over to the restroom.

Matt grabbed his phone and called Fran in the probation office. While he talked, his eyes followed Allen, who had parked his truck in front of the office. Fran hadn't heard from Smythe. He asked her to call the house to see if Mrs. Smythe had heard from her son.

Allen entered. "Did I miss anything?"

"No," Matt said. "We've been waiting for your wildlife pictures."

"Give me a minute." Allen moved the folding chair and punched the power button on his desktop.

Fran called. "Is he back?" Matt asked.

"Yes, but he's not staying at home."

"What's that mean?"

"Wanda says he came in last night, packed his clothes and left."

"For where?"

"Mom thinks he has a girlfriend somewhere. I'm pretty sure she's not telling me everything. The neighbor said he'd keep me posted on any changes."

"This is Barnes?" Matt asked.

"You got it," Fran said.

"Do you mind if I call him?"

"Be my guest."

"Talk to you later." Matt ended his call.

"Hey, look at this." Allen studied the picture on his screen.

The team gathered behind him.

"What's he doing?" Trudeau asked.

"Hard to tell. These shots are stills at three second intervals—taken last night." Allen reversed the sequence and replayed.

"Well, he approached the cache and now he's kneeling." Matt returned the phone to his pocket.

"He may've put his face in his hands ... back up," Vi said.

"Think you're right," Allen said. "See, here he's dropped his hands."

"Freeze on the best frontal," Matt said.

All eyes studied the image.

"Buzz cut—complexion normal and no paunch." Trudeau straightened. "Not much like the Smythe guy." He shuffled back to the table.

"The picture's too grainy, but we haven't seen Smythe's new look." Vi touched the face on the screen. "Expression's almost like grief or anguish. Hard to tell."

"No hoody." Matt leaned closer to the screen. "Don't know what to think."

"Maybe he had more than a facelift," Allen said.

"Possible." Vi returned to her chair beside the old detective.

"Not enough for a warrant, but we need to find this guy," Matt said.

"Even if he lawyers up, we could get his DNA and a good set of finger and palm prints," Trudeau said

"Yeah. We've got partial male DNA from under Mari's fingernails and palm prints from the Lonerock victim's SUV," Matt said.

"Gentleman," Vi said. "More and more—I'm convinced Smythe is your guy."

"I don't think this big memorial thing's going to smoke him out." Allen brought the folding chair to the table. "I think he's gone to ground."

"Maybe another email from the paper—or do another presser," Matt said.

"Let's stick with the plan," Vi said. "We've got Mari's mom on board and everything in place for the memorial service at Shellburg. We've made the press releases. The geocache websites put the word out."

"Too bad it's not a birthday memorial—give a little more reason for the event," Allen said.

"Her birthday's a long way off," Trudeau said.

"Our guy probably doesn't know that," Matt said.

Vi nodded. "Wouldn't matter."

"I'll set the trail camera to shoot video instead of still shots," Allen said.

"We'll all be there with cameras on our phones," Matt said.

"Yeah. What am I thinking."

"I'll make another call to Linh," Trudeau said.

"We got a fifty-fifty chance this will work," Vi said. "The anniversary of her death is several months off."

"If that's him—" Allen aimed his finger at the image on his desktop. "—he did show up on his own without any invite. Maybe this will work."

"I'm in," Matt said.

Trudeau talked with Linh on the phone while the others planned how to cover the memorial.

"I'd like to make sure the DA still backs us on this," Matt said.

"Yeah, hope they don't cut us out," Allen said.

"We'll have to see," Matt said.

"She's still all for it." Trudeau slid his phone onto the table.

"We discussed the DA while you had the phone stuck to your ear," Matt said. "It'd be nice to know the task force won't pull the rug out from under us. Maybe call them again?"

"Yep."

"We're afraid they'll like our idea and take over," Matt said.

"Hmm." Trudeau rubbed his chin. "Suppose they could, but it's just a public memorial service. The most that could happen is we'd spot our guy and either grab him or get a fix on him. Then we'd give 'em a call."

Matt's phone vibrated. The screen displayed a familiar number. "Vanderscoot." He tapped to answer.

"Hi Eva," Matt said. "How's Winter?"

"Fine, she's fine. I'm not sure this is important. Probably nothing. But some gawker dropped by the restaurant." She paused. "One of the waitresses caught him—really interested in Winter."

"Tell me what happened," Matt said.

After she finished, Matt said, "So you didn't witness any of this?"

"No. I was outside with Winter and her boyfriend."

"I see." Matt studied his notes on the physical description she gave. "You called her later to find out what she meant by talking funny?"

"Yeah. What she said about funny started to bug me. So I called and when she said the guy had trouble with the "S" sound—Matt, that's what Winter said about the guy in the old red pickup. Thought I'd better call."

"Glad you did, Eva. He's still not around Bandon, is he?"

"No way. The troopers and the PD are on that. Not many places to hide down here."

"Good. Eva, just so you know—this isn't for public consumption, but we think we've got the guy identified. Just don't know where he is."

"That's not much comfort."

"No, it's not, but you've been a great help and I thought you should know where things stand."

"How's this going to end, Matt? Scary with a guy like that running around."

"We've got a plan to get him to show himself. When he does, we'll nab him."

"A trap?"

Matt explained the memorial service plan. "Figure we've got a fifty-fifty chance of success."

"We'd like to come."

"You'd be better to just lay low down there until he's hooked up."

"I need to do something to support your victim's mother—and the other mothers. Matt, it scares me to think of how close Winter came to being another one. This guy has to be stopped and we want to help."

Matt ended the call and tapped a pencil on his notes. "I think Smythe has been back in Bandon again. He's slimmer, has a buzz cut and his complexion has been smoothed out."

"Does he drive the same red truck?" Allen asked.

"Nobody in Bandon saw what the guy drove, but the neighbor up here says Smythe has a newer gray one. Still got the lisp."

"We could send my trail cam picture. See if it's the same guy," Allen said.

"Eva didn't get a look at him," Matt said.

"How 'bout her friend that did?" Allen asked.

"That's why I keep you around," Matt said. "Send her an email with the picture to her to show her friend."

"Think he wants another shot at her daughter?" Allen asked.

"Possible," Vi said. "But it'd be unusual for him to turn into a stalker now. Most serial killers I've studied, like the anonymity of random kills."

"Hard to believe his showing up was a coincidence," Matt said. "We don't even know if he knew where she lived."

"No, we don't," Vi said. "He may've been cruising the towns along the coast for another peek at her. She is an attractive lady."

"And got lucky? That what you're saying?" Allen asked.

"Exactly," Vi said.

"I don't buy coincidence or luck. The guy's up to something," Matt said.

"He may be, but serial killers have good and bad luck too—just like normal people," Vi said.

Trudeau re-entered the office, phone in one hand, cane in the other. He settled into his chair at the table. "The task force chief says go ahead with the memorial service. They don't want their fingerprints on it. He just wants us to let them know if the killer shows up."

"Right," Allen said. "I'll sit on his chest until they arrive on their white horses."

◆◆◆

Over a home-cooked dinner, Matt told Anna of the plans for the memorial service in the morning.

"Do you think she feels you're using her daughter's death?" Anna passed the salt and pepper.

"What do you mean? Instead of remembering her?" Matt seasoned his meatloaf.

"Yeah. She might think you guys only want to use this memorial to catch the killer."

"Well, that's true—kinda." A glance at his phone, "Allen—but Trudeau explained what we wanted to do. She's on board. At the press thing, she couldn't have been happier." He tapped, swiped and read the screen.

"No doubt she's waited a long time for the killer to be caught." Anna raised her voice as she went into the kitchen. "I talked to Phyllis. She and Herb can't come."

"Supposed to rain tomorrow. Hope not."

She returned with a basket of fresh rolls. "Maybe they got the forecast wrong."

He held a roll close to his nose and inhaled the fresh baked fragrance. "You remember Eva? She wanted to come and bring her daughter."

"That's quite a trip for someone they don't know."

"Yes, but Winter's close call gave 'em a scare. With all the murders, they want to support the victims' families. Eva plans to network with all of the mothers."

"Are they all coming too?"

"Oh, I don't think … maybe, I don't really know."

"What's Allen's message say?" She pointed with her fork.

"We sent Eva the trail picture. Big disappointment. Her friend couldn't say the guy at the falls was the one in the restaurant."

"She didn't say he wasn't."

"True."

"Beth has to work tomorrow."

"Allen's going to be busy anyway."

"What's he doing?

"He'll be catching the license plate numbers on all the vehicles, except for those he recognizes."

"Is your profiler coming?" Anna smiled.

"Vi—you're teasing, huh?"

Anna smiled. "I remembered how touchy she is."

"Don't you dare. She's a nice lady—been a big help—tomorrow she's Allen's helper."

"Pastor's got a portable rain shelter to bring," she said.

He nodded as he swallowed. "Some of Mari's geocache friends might come."

"Sounds like a decent turnout. Is there parking?"

"Not a lot. Got to get Trudeau and Linh close to the campground. He'd have a tough time going too far on any trail."

"Let's take my van," Anna said. "They can park here and I'll drive us."

"The task force may send someone, but Trudeau has doubts."

Sydney waited until the landlord's lights were out before he drove up to his trailer. He closed the shades. After a snack, he fired up his laptop to browse for information. One of his favorite geocache websites had a banner that caught his attention, "Mari Johnson Memorial, tomorrow at Shellburg Falls, follow the signs." He clicked the link for the video announcement.

The cripple, the mother and the family's mouthpiece invited geocachers to attend a memorial service for Mari Johnson. After all these years, why now? Why the short notice? Couldn't be the anniversary of her death, that's several months away. This smells like a trap.

Sydney checked the websites for local law enforcement. Not one mention of the memorial. The local newspaper had a small story.

A fighter, she had surprised him. With the refined methods learned in prison, now his victims never got a chance. Except for Blanco, but he didn't have everything ready for her. Thoughts of his first, again stirred an emptiness deep inside. He never understood why, but the failure had haunted him over the years. Urges tugged like an invisible force. He'd visited last night, but a memorial service—they'd talk about her. Something he'd never tried. Could rekindle his memories, but if he sensed danger, he'd flee. He must.

Chapter 29

Sydney parked on the shoulder of the road across from the small, empty lot. He didn't want to be penned in if he had to get out fast. Thick clouds hung low in the sky. He grabbed his tan, floppy, wide-brimmed rain hat. From under the back canopy, he chose the dark oversized rain shell he'd bought at the thrift store. The hem bounced against his thighs as he trotted across the pavement to the graveled access road.

Closed to traffic, the road led uphill into a stand of evergreen trees. He followed a path on the shoulder to bypass the cattle guard and a single, yellow iron rail installed as a gate. As the grade leveled, Sydney paused to catch his breath. Beyond a strip of forest, the road cut through pasture land. He hunched his shoulders to shift the weight of his pack and trudged up the hardpacked rock surface. The athletic shoes and jeans wouldn't handle rain well, but they'd have to do. The long jacket and hat served as his disguise. Most people would drive to the other side of the recreation area for the memorial service. Not Sydney, he needed to arrive early and avoid being connected with the event. He planned to blend in with other hikers who used the trails.

Cattle grazed without alarm as he passed. Entering the forest again, he remembered that someone told him or he had read, old timber surrounded Shellburg Falls. He didn't care. Never thought much about old growth, second growth or clear-cut. His trips into the wilds had been for one purpose, to stalk and kill.

He crossed the bridge over the lower falls and left the road for the trail to the upper falls. Plenty of time before the service began, but he needed to check the area before people arrived. The spray from the falls dampened his outerwear as he ducked under the basalt overhang. He picked his way along the slippery trail and passed under the falls. The roar of the water drowned out all other sound. On the other side, the low rock ceiling caused him to duck. The trail zigzagged up the steep climb to the top of the falls.

The trail leveled above the falls. Hands on his knees, Sydney gasped for air. Sweat rolled down his face. He used the floppy hat as a sweat rag and opened the front of his jacket. The trail followed the small river. With each step, the sound of rushing water faded to background noise.

He spotted two couples beside their tents in the campground. A lazy column of smoke swirled up from their campfire and disappeared into the low cloud cover. Sydney left the trail for the gravel road and searched the surroundings. He needed a vantage point, one with concealment. An ideal location would to be close enough to hear the speakers describe his first kill, to bring her to life in his mind. The failure had haunted him. He'd been robbed.

Both sets of campers secured flaps on their tents. One couple rode off on mountain bikes, the other donned daypacks and hiked away. Sydney waited to confirm their departure before he entered the campground. A slight wisp of smoke drifted up from the smoldering fire. He rushed to the edge of the clearing and grabbed a fistful of dead branches and twigs. The floppy hat worked as a fan and the flames jumped to life. He added scraps of scrounged wood.

Sydney grabbed a folding stool left beside one of the tents and perched beside the fire. Any passer-by wouldn't pay attention to a camper with a fire. At first, this site for the memorial puzzled him, made him suspicious. Then he recalled how the trail near the cache where he left her body wouldn't accommodate a crowd. This campground provided more space and easier access.

The sound of tires on the gravel road signaled the arrival of a small compact. A middle-aged couple climbed out of the car and opened the trunk. Sydney kept track of them with glances and peeks from under the brim of his hat. They set up an open-sided, pop-up canopy on the other side of the campground. The woman hauled an accordion from the back seat and carried it to a table under their shelter.

He cringed as she started to practice with religious sounding tunes. Ignorant, superstitious people rubbed him wrong. He stirred the coals and added a few branches. Someone cleared their throat nearby, but he kept his head down.

"Are you here for the service?" a man asked.

Sydney rolled the brim back to see the man and with his best raspy voice said, "No." The man carried a Bible under his arm.

"You been here long?"

Sydney made a cutting gesture at his throat. "Can't talk," he croaked.

"Not a good place to be with a sore throat. Take care of yourself." The man moved back to the canopy.

He kept his head down and squinted as the smoke swirled in his face. As long as the hikers and bikers stayed away, this campfire provided a place to hide in plain sight. The fanatic wouldn't make a return visit.

More people arrived in a minivan and parked behind the compact. He recognized three of the passengers from the news stories streamed on the Internet. How could he forget the man who called him a "Wanna be?" His face flushed with anger behind his hat brim. The Asian mother stayed beside the short, crippled man with a cane.

The driver, a woman he didn't recognize, opened the back of the van and let two fuzzy little dogs out. Tethered on leashes, the dogs danced around her feet. He'd had his fill of dogs and dog troubles.

The driver of a pickup parked in the middle of the road, jumped out and left the door open. The engine rumbled. Sydney eyed the large man. After hurried words with the one who'd hurled insults at Sydney, the big man drove off. He remembered the pickup as one parked at the private investigator's office. A few more people trickled into the campground to gather around the canopy.

The musician warmed up on the accordion and a few folks sang along. Sydney stared at the coals as he jabbed his poker. Police he hated, but religious people maybe more.

The fanatic spoke first and introduced the mother. Sydney read somewhere the mother came from Vietnam, but he didn't care. The soft accented voice didn't carry to his ears. Others spoke of his first kill, her beauty, athleticism, the brown belt she'd earned. Sydney stared at the flames, mesmerized by the memories. She'd fought hard.

Music and singing broke the spell. The fanatic held a small white cross over his head. He invited the group to follow him to where Mari had been found. The campground grew quiet as the small cluster of people hiked away. Sydney glanced over at the shelter. The man with the cane remained.

"This is our campsite." The biker dismounted. "What are you doing here?" he asked. "Hey, that's my stool."

Sydney rose to face the couple. "Got cold. Didn't mean nothing."

"You with them?" The woman nodded toward the shelter.

"N—no." He snatched his daypack and headed for the road. One last glance, his eyes met those of the lone cripple. Paranoia flared, maybe he'd fallen into a trap. He swiped a hand across his forehead. Sydney fought an impulse to bolt and run.

On the trail to the upper falls, out of sight, he broke into a headlong rush. He slipped and stumbled on exposed roots in the muddy manmade trail and clung to the handrails along the wooden steps.

Panic, haste and the steep downhill carried him faster and faster. He fought to control his momentum as he reached the basalt overhang where the path led under the falls. Misjudgment and a stumble tossed him forward. His head struck the underside of the rock ceiling.

Sydney tumbled onto the inside edge of the rocky cavern and rolled to a stop, face first, on the outside edge of the trail. He clawed to keep his body from sliding over the edge. Frozen by fear, he clung to the narrow trail as he passed out.

"You okay?" the hiker asked. "Mister, you awake?"

Sydney groaned as he felt a hand on his back. "Ohhh." He tried to raise his face from the muddy path.

"Are you okay?" A hand shook his shoulder. "You were out cold."

Sydney gathered his strength and forced his body to all fours. "I think tho." His head throbbed. He had to move, to run.

"Can I help you?" The stranger tugged on Sydney's coat. "You're awful close to the cliff—long ways down."

Sydney twisted away from the trail's edge and sat closer to the inside wall of the overhang. He shook his head to clear his vision. "Ohooo." Sharp pain ricocheted behind his eyes.

"You got quite a cut on the side of your head." The man handed him a bandana.

Sydney pressed the cloth above his ear.

"You whacked yourself good. Better get some cold on the forehead too."

With his free hand, Sydney tested the size of the swollen knot centered above his eyes.

"Can I help you get out of here?" the hiker asked. "I don't know how long you were unconscious before I found you."

"N—no. I'll be okay. Need a minute."

"If you're sure, I gotta go. I'm late for a memorial service," he said.

After the man left, Sydney assessed his condition. Wet, muddy muck covered his front from head to toe. He had to get to his truck.

Unsteady legs carried him down the trail to where he rejoined the gravel road. His head felt woozy as he staggered across the bridge. Will power kept him upright. The road led down for almost a mile before he'd reach his truck.

On the graveled road, he picked up the pace. Wobbly, he had to concentrate to stay on his feet. His head throbbed.

He rounded the last turn and spotted the single, yellow iron bar across the road. Exhausted, on unconditioned legs, he stumbled and regained balance as he closed the distance. Ahead, a woman hiker with two young children blocked the path bypassing the cattle guard and gate.

Impatient to reach his truck, Sydney lurched for the cattle guard. As he crossed and prepared to duck under the gate, his left foot slipped down and caught between two rails on the guard. Sydney cursed as he sprawled forward onto the gravel surface. Pain shot from his left ankle. He rolled and gripped his new injury. Through gritted teeth, he fumed as he waited for the pain to subside.

"Stop," the woman said to the giggly boys. "You need help, Mister?"

"Ahh—loth my thoe." He groaned.

"Stop now," she said again to the youngsters. The woman knelt by the cattle guard and fished his shoe from between the rails.

Seated on the gravel, Sydney grimaced as he reached. "Thank you." He worked the shoe on his foot and struggled to stand. Ahead, he focused on how to reach his truck. He reeled as he gauged the distance to the intersection at the bottom of the grade and the paved road he must cross.

"Do you need help?" she asked.

He waved her off as he limped away.

Inside the cab, he struggled to remove his oversized shell. He'd escaped. Now he had to flee, but where?

Chapter 30

Snarled traffic, long gas line, and a wrong turn ruined her early start. Vi faced being late for the memorial service. She punched the gas and blew the speed limit to regain the time lost. The plan called for her to be positioned in the parking lot several hours before the memorial. Now, she'd be lucky to be positioned an hour before they began.

Vi turned off the highway and drove up the windy road to a small, graveled, day-use lot. She backed into a space where she could observe arrivals and departures.

On a note pad, she recorded the description and license plate numbers of the vehicles in the lot. On foot, she captured the numbers not visible from her car. A light drizzle chased her back inside.

A black subcompact arrived, turned around in the graveled lot, drove across the paved road and parked on the shoulder in front of a red pickup. Screened by the strip of trees and brush between the parking lot and road, VI watched as two hikers jumped out, trotted back across the pavement, and followed the signs for the trailhead. She didn't get the tag number nor had she noticed the red truck until now. A rookie mistake, she'd correct.

She jumped out and jogged across the paved road. On the back of the canopy, the pickup had a dealer's temporary tag taped on the inside of the glass.

She wrote the information and listed the plate number from the subcompact.

Back in the car, she ran the engine and defroster to clear the windshield. Hikers and bikers left and others arrived. She deleted and added to her list as the morning crept toward noon. The phone played a favorite tune. The screen identified the caller as Allen.

"Hey," she said. Many years ago, she'd worked on a surveillance team. Today awoke those memories.

"Any activity?" Allen asked.

"Some. Nothing suspicious. Several cars and trucks were here when I arrived. I've got the numbers and descriptions."

"Good. I drove by and checked with Matt. Nothing up there. The service is about over."

"You got many vehicles up there?"

"Not a lot, but when this is over we'll meet at the office and sort through the owners we have on our lists."

"Let me know when you want me to pull out."

She ended the call and stuck the phone in a cup holder. The sun peeked through the clouds. She lowered the window a few inches and cut the engine.

A short time later, the sound of voices drew her attention to the trail entrance. An embankment and trees blocked her view of the gravel road used by hikers. She watched the unpaved apron where the gravel met the paved road.

Soiled and wet, a man stumbled down to the pavement and hobbled across the road to the red pickup. A floppy hat drooped crooked on his head. He fumbled with keys and climbed inside the cab. Vi studied the man as he appeared to struggle with his pack and clothing. Moments later the red pickup sped away. She guessed there'd be a story behind the muddy mess.

A woman, who Vi figured to be a mother, entered the lot with two boys, grade school age. They approached the small SUV parked beside her. The children jabbered, laughed and giggled as they crossed the lot.

"Oh—I loth my thoe." The boys laughed. "Loth my thoe." More giggles.

"Boys, stop. That's enough." Mother bent down and wagged her finger. "We don't make fun of people who talk different. That man couldn't help it. Now, get in the car."

The boys continued their misbehavior in the back seat behind closed doors, while mother stowed the daypacks inside the back hatch.

Vi slipped out from behind the wheel and met the woman at the rear of the SUV. "Hi. Excuse me. I couldn't help but overhear." She nodded at the children.

"I'm sorry. They can be so bratty sometimes. Hope you're not offended." The mother removed the sweat band and fluffed her hair with her fingers.

"No. I'm working on a case with the Sheriff's Office. We've been searching for a man who talks a little different. Your children said something that caught my ear. Did the man ahead of you say something to you?"

"Well, not to us. He tripped on the cattle guard—lost his shoe and said a few choice words."

"That's what the kids were laughing at?"

"No. they teased him because he spoke with a lisp. Really upset me. They know better."

Vi rushed to her car and grabbed the phone. When Allen answered, she described the soiled man, the pickup, and the lisp.

"What's the plate number?

"Only got a temporary dealer's plate." She read the number.

"Shucks. Those are tougher to do a quick check on."

"This one, maybe not. The dealership stamped their name and address on the bottom."

"Give it."

Chills shot down his back. Sydney's fingers trembled as he reached for the temperature control. Nauseous, he grabbed the hat as a precaution. At the highway intersection, traffic passed left and right. He had to get home, but puzzled over which way to turn. The throbbing in his head pummeled his memory.

Sydney flinched at the blast of a truck's horn behind him. He punched the gas into a right turn. More horns sounded. He squinted and blinked his eyes to focus on the road. Pressure from the bandana enflamed the swollen knot on his forehead. He fingered the bump and the wound near his temple. Blood showed on his fingertips. He grimaced at the pain as he wiped the blood on his trousers. *Where am I?*

Sydney slowed as he overtook a string of cars slowed by a semi-truck and trailer loaded with bales of hay. He struggled to remember the way home.

The two-lane highway split into four lanes. Cars in front of him broke to the fast lane to pass. Sydney remained behind the truck. With his thoughts scrambled, the back of the trailer helped him stay inside the lane markers. Sleep, he wanted to sleep. He worked his eyes to clear the blurred vision.

Ten, twenty, thirty minutes ... he lost all sense of time. The truck signaled for an exit off the highway. Sydney followed. He'd find a place to stop and get his bearings. Plenty of daylight ... he had to get home.

As the hay truck gained speed, Sydney panicked—he had to find a turnoff, to stop, to get his head straight. He gripped the wheel. The truck passed a paved road to the left. Sydney punched the gas and shot across the oncoming lane. A horn blared, but he ignored it. He drove until he found a dirt lane to the right into a stand of trees. He pressed the brake and cranked the wheel. His foot slipped to the gas pedal. *What'd I do?* The truck flew off the end of the culvert, plowed through a barbed wire fence and crashed into a large fir tree. The airbags deployed and battered his head. Sydney passed out.

◆◆◆

Earlier that afternoon, Matt followed Anna, who walked arm and arm with Linh. They'd placed a wreath at the small wooden cross planted near the spot Mari had died. The clouds had thinned and allowed the sun to peek down. Mari's geocache friends had left them behind on the hike back to the campground.

"Matt." Anna spoke back over her shoulder. "Did you know Linh comes up here every year?"

"I did. Didn't you tell me, Linh?" He spotted Allen ahead under the shelter with Trudeau.

Linh nodded.

"I'm going to start coming with you," Anna said. "If you like?"

Linh looked up and smiled.

"Almost everybody's gone." Matt hurried to Anna's side. "Allen waved for me to come. Better see what he wants." He jogged the short distance.

"We might've caught a break." Allen briefed him of the incident Vi witnessed, and the dealer's tag, name and address.

"We need to check this guy out," Trudeau said.

"Vi had the address," Allen said. "I told her to head for the dealer. We can call her off if we need to."

"Shouldn't we call the detectives?" Matt asked.

Trudeau leaned on his cane. "Let's check this out first. They didn't send anyone up here. May be nothing."

"Hoped you'd say that," Allen said.

"I'll ride with you." Matt bumped Allen's arm with a fist. "Let me tell Anna what's up."

"Wait," Trudeau said. "I'm going too. Tell Linh to stay with your wife … until we're back."

"You sure?" Matt asked. "What if something happens?"

"You better take me. I'm on the task force. Besides, I got two hands and one good leg." The detective smiled as he brushed his jacket open to display his badge and holstered gun.

"Okay." Matt grinned and shook his head. He believed the Sheriff had allowed the legendary detective to say a long farewell with this cold case after his stroke. He didn't want to jump in the middle of their business.

Matt briefed Anna before he climbed into the front passenger seat. With Trudeau buckled in the backseat, Allen headed out of the Santiam Forest for Salem.

On the highway, Matt tapped out a text message to inform Vi they would meet her at the office when she finished with the dealer.

Two hours later, Vi briefed them on what she'd learned.

Matt crossed his arms on the work table. "This isn't what I expected. Sydney Smythe has to be our killer. Everything pointed to him. Now you—" he nodded at Vi "—bring us this Jose Garcia with a red truck—not gray—and he lives south of town."

"He's had plastic surgery," Trudeau said. "Isn't that what his mom told you … and the probation officer?"

"Yep," Matt said.

"The kid's mother definitely told me this driver had a lisp," Vi said. "But, he didn't look anything like I'd expected—not as heavy."

"Vi, could you tell if this guy was Hispanic?" Allen asked.

"No way—covered with mud, head to foot. Besides, a floppy hat hung down over his face."

"Light colored hat?" Trudeau asked.

"Yes," Vi said.

"I'd bet he's the same guy who had the fire over in front of the tents," Trudeau said. "Right after everyone left to put out the cross, he had words with a couple of mountain bikers and left in a hurry—nervous like."

"So, maybe he did come," Allen said.

"And you say the task force has an op going at the address for Garcia and the red truck?" Matt asked.

"Yes. But we're going too," Trudeau said. "I'll ride with Vi—you guys follow in Allen's truck."

Chapter 31

"Can I find the eggs all by myself tonight? Please, Sissy." The towheaded boy shouted from the booster seat in back.

"We'll have to see, Bubby. You always break too many."

"I'll be careful."

"That's what you said last night."

"Please, Sissy."

"Quit begging."

Sissy glanced at her five-year-old brother in the rearview mirror. His pout brought a smile to her lips. Every night for the past week, Bubby had accompanied her to the neighbor's farm. They'd put out feed and water for a few sheep, and gathered eggs from a couple of laying hens. Two more days and the neighbors would be back.

"Somebody crashed, Sissy."

"Where?" She gauged her brother's seriousness in the mirror.

"In the trees—back there." Bubby strained against the seat harness to point behind them.

"Did you see a driver or anybody?"

"No."

"We'll take a look on our way home—if it's not too dark."

After chores and five eggs in a sack, Sissy drove for home. "We're getting closer. Show me where you saw the wreck." She slowed.

"There."

She hit the brake and studied the damaged fence and the back of a red truck. Puzzled over how she'd overlooked the accident when they'd passed earlier. "Good eye, Bubby." She parked in the entrance of the dirt lane near the damaged fence.

"I'll take a look. Stay in your seat." She eased out of the car and approached the truck.

Wedged between two saplings, the truck had smashed into a large fir tree. Condensation clouded the glass on the passenger side. She shaded her eyes as she got close to peer inside. "Oh." She gasped and ran back to the car.

"There's a man in the truck, Bubby."

"Is he dead?"

"I don't know. He's not moving."

"Mama has Band-Aids."

"Yes, she does." Behind the wheel, she wrestled with her choices. She drew a deep breath and sighed. "I better go see if he's alive." She'd better find out before she called anyone.

Through the window, she studied the man. The position of his body hadn't changed. She tapped the glass with her cell phone.

The man stirred. "Ooh."

She flinched and shouted, "Mister, are you okay?"

With slow and deliberate movements, he inched himself upright behind the wheel. Blood stained the bandana tied around his head. He rolled his head and squinted.

"Do you need an ambulance?" She slipped the phone in a front pocket and stuffed her car keys in the usual back pocket with the pink fob out to dangle. Hands free, she grabbed the door handle. Jammed and bent, the passenger door didn't budge.

The man released the seatbelt, cleared the airbag residue and tried the driver's side door. He threw his shoulder against the door. The metal groaned as the door creaked open. The man held his head as he leaned against the seat back. He grabbed a long jacket, a pack, and a hat from the floor and pushed through the open door.

She couldn't leave an injured man, but Sissy moved back to her car. "Bubby, you stay inside," she said.

The man steadied himself with one hand on the truck as he limped around to the back and opened the lid on the canopy.

Something about the man made her want to keep her distance. "Can I call someone?"

He hoisted the backpack into the back of the truck and pulled out a small duffle. "Yeth—but I can't find my phone. Let me use yours. I'll call a friend to help me."

Hesitant, Sissy approached, but stopped. "I'll call 9-1-1."

Before the operator answered, the man rushed her and grabbed the phone.

Shocked, frozen in place, she couldn't move.

He spun away and limped back to the truck as he fumbled with the phone and his bag.

Her instincts signaled danger. As she back-peddled, her heel caught on something, she stumbled, and landed on her rump. Jarred, she scrambled back to the car.

She grabbed for the fob on her keyring, which she always let dangle outside her back pocket. Gone—after a frantic glance, she spotted the round, cherry-sized, hot pink fob in the middle of the dirt lane where she had fallen.

"No," she gasped.

She rushed to the rear passenger door. "Unbuckle," she whispered and put a finger to her lips. "Get out."

"Where we going?" Bubby whispered.

"We have to run and hide. Quiet."

The man had talked to someone on her phone before he turned back. "They're not home. Could you give me a ride? Hey—"

She grabbed her brother's hand.

"What're you doing?" The man yelled and clutched his head in pain. In one hand, he held a knife.

Sissy scooped Bubby from his feet and ran. When she reached the pavement, she crossed the road and rushed to hide in the field of Christmas trees. She clutched Bubby to protect him as the boughs scratched and clawed as she plunged between trees.

Several rows deep, gasping for air, she tumbled forward. Before impact, Sissy rolled onto her shoulder to protect Bubby. Between breaths she checked on her brother, who sat in the grass, eyes the size of olives.

She listened. "I don't think he's coming," she whispered.

"What if he does?" Bubby asked.

"He's crippled or injured. Don't think he will."

Tears formed in his eyes. "I want to go home."

"We will, Bubby." She scooted close and put an arm around him. "We will." The man needed to have a way of escape. Her keys and car gave him one. She hoped he'd take it.

"How will Daddy find us?" Bubby whispered.

"It's getting dark—when we're not home he'll come for us."

She heard the sounds of a car racing away. "I think he just left. In a little bit, we'll go down to the road and wait for Dad."

◆◆◆

In Salem, Sydney waited in the stolen car for his mother. Wanda said she'd bring him some pain pills. She had plenty. Throbbing had stopped, but his headache remained profound. The pain spiked with any sudden movement. He despised his mother's dependence on drugs, another weakness he had avoided. But tonight, he'd relent and accept her offer. He needed relief.

Sydney lifted the brim of his hat to search for Wanda's car. Parked on the far edge of the parking lot, she'd be able to find him. Concern over his injuries distracted her from the news of another truck totaled. He'd always been able to play on her sympathy.

Customers flowed in and out of the big box store. The traffic in the parking lot made this a good place to hide and wait. After his mother arrived, he'd wipe the car down before he left. The call to his mother in front of the girl had been a mistake. Wanda had him repeat the location several times. He hoped the girl hadn't heard his directions.

Sydney stuffed the girl's sweat shirt in his bag. Wouldn't be good to leave it behind after wiping the blood and soil from his head, face and hands. He'd removed the bloody bandana from his painful goose egg.

The old maroon sedan approached.

Sydney tossed his belongings in the backseat and grabbed a rag from his mother's car to wipe down the stolen car. Finished, he slid in beside his mother. His head throbbed.

"What'd you do all that for?" Wanda asked.

"Look at me, Mother. I'm filthy. Didn't want to leave her car dirty—never loan it to me again."

"You look terrible, Son." She handed him a pill bottle. "You're going to have bruises."

"Jutht get me home."

"I wish you'd tell me what's going on." She drove out of the lot.

"There'th thomeone after me, Mother. I told you." He leaned back in the seat and closed his eyes.

"Shouldn't you go to the police?"

"No."

"I don't like you gone all the time. I bought myself some pepper spray."

"Won't do much good if thome bad guy hath a gun."

"I don't like guns."

"What? Afraid you'll thoot yourthelf?"

"Doesn't matter." She glanced at him. "I had a visitor, Sydney. You'll be mad."

"Why?"

"Same man who came with your probation officer."

"The one that left the card?"

"Yes. Kinler—he's a private investigator."

"What'd he want this time?" His alarm soared.

"Told me you might be involved in a murder."

He rolled his head to gauge her intensity. "I couldn't do anything like that, Mother."

"That's what I told him. He said it happened about ten years ago."

"I wath probably at Lompoc." Time to shore up his defenses with the enemy at the gate.

"I told him that too."

◆◆◆

In an empty field on the southern outskirts of town, Allen's blue pickup parked beside the white sedan driven by Vi. They tracked the parade of vehicles allowed to pass the roadblock manned by deputies.

"The swat team's been down there awhile," Matt said. "Hope they caught him in his trailer."

"This unmarked probably has another load of detectives," Allen said.

"I wonder if they got him without a fight?" Matt asked. "Holler over at Trudeau—find out what's going on down there."

"He's on the phone."

An ambulance with flashers sped past the deputy. "Maybe he didn't surrender," Matt said.

"Trudeau's off his phone—here he comes."

The short detective's chin cleared the bottom of Allen's open window. "He's not there."

"What's with the ambulance?" Matt asked.

"They think the landlord might've had a slight heart attack. They're going to check him out."

"No Smythe or Jose Garcia?" Matt asked.

"Nope. No red truck either. He hasn't lived there very long. Not much in his trailer," Trudeau said.

"Do they have any leads?" Matt asked.

"I think just the APB on the red truck," Trudeau said. "Why don't you reach out to his probation officer, see if she has any ideas."

"I'll call her. Surely, some officer will spot his truck somewhere. I'm actually surprised you didn't spot him on the way in, Vi—you weren't too far behind."

◆◆◆

In a tree line two hundred yards from Matt, el Término pressed binoculars to his eyes. The vantage point gave him a clear view across pasture land. His wait for Smythe had become quite a spectacle. Roadblocks, swat team, forced entry on the travel trailer and then the ambulance.

Disappointed, he stuck the binoculars back in the case, slung the strap over his shoulder, and left his brushy stand. If they'd snagged Smythe and put him in lock-up, Vaquero could easily find someone to do the job without help from a hitman. After all, he worried about his luck running out as much as Vaquero did.

Thanks to the cops, his search had narrowed to one address. He climbed in behind the wheel of his wife's SUV and headed into town. After midnight, he'd make another visit to the disabled mother's house.

Chapter 32

Sydney trudged up the stairs. His mother's bedtime news blared from the television in the front room. After a shower and nap, hunger pangs had replaced nausea.

"I need to eat, Mother." He grabbed the pill bottle from the kitchen table for another round.

Wanda arrived on her scooter. "I could use a sandwich and a little wine before bed."

He piled cold cuts, cheese and condiments on the table. She rode around to gather bread, plates, utensils and wine.

"Mother, you've got the TV too loud." He held his head.

"I wanted to hear the ten o'clock news."

"Maketh my head hurt. You got the remote?"

"In by my chair."

"I'll turn it down. They'll repeat at eleven." He entered the living room. The sight of the red truck made his blood run cold. He pressed mute and punched closed captions. Yellow crime scene tape had been strung around his truck and the tree. A reporter interviewed the father about his daughter and her stolen car. *Should've killed her.* The whack on his head had scrambled his thoughts and now he had a mess on his hands.

The shirt clung to his sweaty back as the scene changed to a police roadblock near a rural property.

Sydney choked back a gasp as the camera panned the lot where he had rented the trailer. A nauseous knot formed in the pit of his stomach as a reporter interviewed his landlord. "Manhunt" the caption read.

"Sydney," she whined.

He jabbed the off button and stuffed the remote down between the armrest and the seat cushion. Until he had a plan, she didn't need to hear this newscast.

"Why are you sweating?"

Sydney winced as he wiped his forehead with a napkin. "The pain pillth." He had to do something and fast. To report his truck stolen now might draw attention at the wrong time. He'd deal with that later.

He refilled her wine glass. "I took two more pillth—I'm having a reaction."

"They don't do that to me." She gulped from her glass. "Make me drowsy."

He topped off her glass. She needed to be more than drowsy tonight.

With his mother in the bathroom, Sydney tuned the bedroom television to her favorite rerun channel and slipped the remote into the drawer of the nightstand. He hoped to buy some time before he had to explain away the news stories.

Impatient to cover his tracks, Sydney paced outside his mother's door. He peeked and listened until she drifted off to sleep. Downstairs, he gathered his laptop and other belongings to hide from the cops. The headache flared with his hurried pace. He downed more pain pills. With his gear loaded in Wanda's car, he headed for the storage unit.

◆◆◆

In Matt's office across town, Vi swiveled the chair and stood. "I'm sorry—I can't do an all-nighter here. I've got to be on the coast in the morning."

"I'm staying until they've wrapped up the manhunt for the night," Trudeau said.

"Before you go, remind me of what to expect from my last visit with this guy's mother," Matt said.

She slipped into her jacket. "Hard to predict how a mother's love will express itself."

"As I said before, when I suggested her son might be a murderer—she didn't have much of a reaction."

Vi reached back to free her hair from under the jacket's collar. "Her muted reaction could mean she was shocked—or she had her own suspicions and you merely confirmed them."

"What are the odds she'll give us a call?" Matt asked.

"I don't do odds," Vi said. "That's what I told the task force when I suggested you pay her a visit. I've known mothers who'd walk the plank for a son like this. There's other mothers who'd turn him in without a second thought."

"I'd sure like to know ... what she knows," Trudeau said.

"It's possible she doesn't have any idea what he's been up to," Vi said. "On the other hand, she might be in denial—or an enabler."

"I could see her not knowing," Allen said. "He leads a double life and Mama's only part of one."

"Well, she's on notice and has my number. Just wait and see which she is," Matt said.

"You got the neighbor as a backup," Allen said.

"I do," Matt said. "He'll call if Sydney shows."

Trudeau answered his cell phone as Vi left for home.

"Hope she doesn't fall asleep behind the wheel. It'll be after midnight by the time she reaches the coast," Matt said.

"She chose to live off the beaten path— probably an old hand at nighttime trips," Allen said.

Matt smiled. "You're probably right." He listened to Trudeau's side of the conversation.

"We better call our wives to let them know we're going to be a lot later." Allen held up his phone.

"Good time for that." Matt grabbed his phone and waited for Anna to answer.

"About time you called," she said.

"Yeah, well, sorry. You in bed?"

"No. I wanted to wait until I heard from you. I've seen lots on the news. How much longer?"

"Hmm. Not sure—Trudeau's on the phone getting an update now. Did you get Linh home okay?"

"Yes, I did. She's a sweet lady. I hope you guys can get justice for her."

"She's waited a long time. I want to hang around until the detectives have closed out all of the immediate leads. I'm halfway waiting for our guy's neighbor to call—don't have my hopes up."

"Sounds like you'll be up all night."

"Hope not."

"Me too, but we've been down this road before."

"Guess we have."

"Beth called earlier. She's worried. Maybe us girls will have a slumber party."

"Allen's on the phone with her now."

"Matt, please be careful. You don't need to be out front on this."

"Told you, I've been benched."

"Yeah, but you have a habit of jumping in the middle of things."

"I'm too tired to jump, but I need to stick around."

"For Trudeau?"

"You got it."

"I'm going to call Beth. Love you," Anna said.

"Ditto."

Across the table, Trudeau waited as Matt finished his call.

"They catch him?" Matt asked.

"Not yet." Trudeau stroked his forehead. "They've wrapped up the crime scene where he crashed his truck. They've also finished with the girl and took her home."

"Get any pings off her phone?" Allen asked.

"No. Dead, but they're serving a warrant to get the last number he called."

"That can be slow going sometimes," Matt said. "Depends on the carrier."

"They're about done at the trailer house he rented. Didn't find much."

"Doubt he'll go back there with all the news coverage," Matt said.

"They'll leave a couple of deputies ... just in case." Trudeau said. "As far as we know ... he hasn't seen any news ... running around in that stolen car."

"True. I heard you say something about emergency rooms," Matt said.

"Ah huh." Trudeau glanced at his phone. "They've got 'em watching ... for anyone with a head injury." He tapped and swiped at the screen. "Ha. They've located the girl's car at the mall."

"How long ago?" Allen asked. "If he's got a gimpy leg, he won't walk far."

"No new stolen cars reported." Trudeau scrolled through his text messages. "They've already hauled the girl's car off to the impound lot."

"So, that's old news," Allen said.

"Yeah—and the detectives are scaling back for the night."

"It's almost two—maybe we should knock off," Matt said. "Gave Barnes my number—told him Smythe didn't have the truck anymore."

"If he's an insomniac, like he says—he'll keep an eye on the house," Allen said.

"You're about to fall asleep." Matt smiled at Trudeau. "We can drop you off at your house. Anna and I can bring your truck to town tomorrow."

"Not yet." Trudeau rubbed his eyes. "Just a little longer."

"Do we have time for a snack?" Allen asked.

"You're driving," Matt said.

Near the freeway, they found a coffee shop. Drained and tired after the long day, the threesome waited for their order. Matt yawned. "We're so close. I thought he'd get scooped up today."

"Me too," Trudeau said.

"Yesterday, you mean," Allen said.

"Yeah," Matt said. "Maybe today. But I'll probably be asleep and miss it."

The phone vibrated beside his coffee cup. Matt glanced at the screen. "Barnes. I'll go outside." He left his friends in the booth and pressed the phone to his ear. "Mr. Barnes. Standby."

Under the entrance portico, he asked, "Okay, what's up?"

"I ah … sorry to call you, but I'm not sure what's going on next door."

"What do you mean? Is he back?"

"No—that's what I don't know. Wanda—his mother went out earlier and then returned."

"Anybody with her?"

"Not that I could see—but her outdoor lights have quit working."

"Is she there now?"

"No—ah, I'm not sure. She left again in her car before midnight and she's not back. Well … I think it was her ... must've been."

"Does she go out this late very often?"

"Never."

"I'm glad you called. If we decide to check this out, will you be up?"

"Yeah."

Matt rejoined his partners inside. "Not sure what this means, but Barnes says Mrs. Smythe left a little before midnight and hasn't returned." He gave the details.

"I'd suggest we stake out the house … talk to whoever returns in the car," Trudeau said.

"Shouldn't we call the detectives?" Matt asked.

"They've got a bunch tied up canvassing the neighborhood around the mall. The rest have quit for the night. Besides, she may have just gone out … for some antacid tablets."

"True. But I'd worry about you if this goes sideways," Matt said.

"Don't worry 'bout me. I'll stay with the truck," Trudeau said.

Chapter 33

El Término had arrived after midnight. With his SUV parked blocks away, he'd eased into the neighborhood on foot. Clad in black, dead still, he surveilled the neighborhood from the shadows. Except for the unmarked police car an hour ago, there'd been no traffic. Up the street, a couple of cats sparred. A dog barked in the distance.

The scene around the house hadn't changed since his last visit. As before, the corner bedroom had a light on behind closed curtains. No doubt, he'd find the disabled woman asleep in the room, but would her son be inside? El Término had to know.

Again, the man next door stood in the window and appeared to study the house el Término had targeted. He pressed a small spyglass to his eye and studied the neighbor. Not made for nighttime use, el Término spewed a silent curse at the poor quality of the image. The man appeared to be holding a phone to his ear.

He'd invested a couple hours to ensure the cops didn't have the house staked out. The nosey neighbor made the approach risky, but not impossible. After the cops raided the trailer, Smythe had to hide somewhere. El Término had combed the nearby streets for the red truck, but he had to check inside the house.

When the neighbor moved away from the window, el Término broke for the house. He kept a low profile as he sprinted up the driveway and ducked into the darkness between the house and garage. The motion light on the front of the garage remained off. His luck held.

He peeked inside the garage through the side door—no car. El Término crept to the back entrance. Again unlocked, he eased the door open. From the laundry room, he slipped through the kitchen and down the hall. The only sound in the house came from the bedroom. Door ajar, the woman appeared to be asleep with the television on, but muted.

In the basement, he shined his light on an unmade bed and spotted soiled clothing strewn on the floor. His man had been here since the last time he'd prowled. With the woman in bed and this guy gone would explain no car in the garage. El Término decided to wait.

Upstairs in the living room, he stationed himself beside the front window with a view of the driveway entrance.

When the dark sedan arrived with the headlights off, he drew his pistol and tightened the suppressor.

◆◆◆

A few blocks away, Allen switched off the headlights and slowed before they entered the neighborhood. "My taillights might tip someone when I stop in front of Barnes' house."

"The Smythe house will be ahead of us, let's take the chance," Matt said.

"We'll have to make ourselves small if her car comes down the street," Allen said.

"That'll be hard for you, partner."

"You'd be surprised."

"There's Barnes. Out front," Matt said. He lowered the window as the truck stopped.

Barnes approached and whispered, "Her car's back in the garage."

"Did you see the driver?" Matt asked.

"No—too dark."

"How long ago?"

"Only a minute or so."

Matt asked back over his shoulder. "Will you stay with the truck?"

"I'll leave the keys in the ignition," Allen said.

Without another word, Matt led Allen along the edge of the street to the Smythe driveway.

◆◆◆

Moments earlier, in the Smythe house, after el Término spotted the car, he went to the front door to ensure an escape route. The loud clunk of the deadbolt pierced the quiet in the house. Startled, he froze—to listen. Maybe the sound didn't carry to the back bedroom. Too close to stop now, he left the front door ajar.

El Término fixed a bandana below his eyes to conceal his face and hid on the basement stairs.

"Sydney, is that you?" the woman yelled from the bedroom.

The storm door rattled at the back entrance. El Término hunkered.

"Sydney?" Light streamed from the hallway and filtered into the kitchen. The woman rode into the room.

A man clattered through the backdoor and said in a loud whisper, "Turn out the lightth, Mother— they're after me."

El Término sprang from the stairs to face the man.

"Out of my house!" the woman screamed.

El Término glanced at her and caught a burst of pepper spray in his eyes. "Ahh—" He spun to face the taller man, who thrust a long knife into his gut. El Término dropped his gun as he doubled over and grabbed at the pain.

The woman erupted with hysterical screams.

Survival instinct drove el Término to grapple with his assailant. Weakened by the wound, he dropped to his knees in front of the attacker. *Is this it—has my luck run out?*

The man yelled as he grabbed the gun. "Thut up, Mother."

El Término gasped for air as he clutched at the wound to staunch the blood—the pain.

"No, Sydney. What've you done? Stop." The scooter brushed el Término as she moved between them.

"Go to your room, Mother," he yelled. "I thaw more men outhide. They're after me." The son grabbed at the scooter and shoved her back. "Go!" he shouted. "Don't open your door until I come back."

Again, the scooter bumped el Término as she rammed her son. "Enough, Sydney!" she screeched.

The son stumbled back cursing in rage. Mother and son battled to gain control of the power scooter.

"Stop, Sydney!" she shouted.

El Término seized the moment, gathered his strength and lunged for the front door.

Chaos and curses continued as he stumbled out of the house.

◆◆◆

Seconds before, Matt heard a woman scream and loud voices erupt inside the house. He drew his gun as he rushed up the driveway to the back entrance. Hysterical shrieks streamed through the open door.

Matt crouched and dove across the laundry room to grab cover along the wall. Allen's flashlight shot a beam around the kitchen. Alone, Mother pressed misshapen hands to her face as she rocked back and forth. Frantic, hysterical sounds spilled from her muffled lips.

Allen swept past to clear the back of the house while Matt focused on Wanda and the front of the house. With the all clear from his partner, Matt approached and eased the pepper spray can from under her arm. "Ma'am? What happened?"

She didn't answer but reverted to a soft moan.

Allen shined his light on a dark puddle near the top of the basement stairs. "Blood." A few feet away a pistol. "Is this your gun, Ma'am?"

She shook her head.

"Mrs. Smythe, we're here to help. What happened? Is your son here?"

She pointed to the stairs, "Down there," she bawled.

Allen sought cover and shined his light into the basement.

"Is that what I think?" Matt asked.

"Yep." Allen flipped the stairwell light switch and headed down the steps.

Sydney Smythe lay quiet in a still, unnatural heap on the basement floor.

Wanda groaned in anguish and backed her scooter away from the scene.

"Mrs. Smythe, please—what happened?"

With danger defused, Matt took his time and drew the painful details from her. The dark clad intruder, the pepper spray and her son's fight with the stranger. She couldn't explain Sydney's fall. When the wounded man scrambled toward the front door, she thought Sydney might have lunged in pursuit, but tripped and tumbled headfirst into the basement.

"Do you know what he tripped over?" Matt asked.

She avoided eye contact. "Scooter maybe—but he might've slipped."

Matt studied the puddle of blood—no smears or skid marks.

Trudeau entered the front door and leaned on his cane. "I called this in. You'd be proud of me. Caught the guy who ran out of the house."

"Who? Where?" Matt asked, as Allen joined them.

"Used the truck. Caught up with him in the street—right out front." Trudeau smiled as he pointed with his cane. "Actually … I spotted him when he stumbled across the yard. He got as far as the street and collapsed."

"Who's got him?"

"Don't need watching. He's dead." Trudeau glanced at the mother and queried Matt with his eyes.

Matt motioned and led his partners out onto the front porch. "Sydney's dead." He kept his voice low. "Mom's taking it pretty hard."

"How'd he die?" Trudeau asked.

"Fell down the stairs. We think he broke his neck." Matt said. "How—or why he fell? Don't know."

"I'm not sure," Allen said. "Yellow stuff all over his face—think he got pepper sprayed."

Epilogue

"Heard you on the phone out here. Who was it?" Anna came out onto the porch and set her coffee mug on the table between their chairs.

Matt opened his eyes. "Vi—she gave me a rundown on her talk with the mother."

"Oh—how'd that go?"

"Good, I think. They're going to talk some more." Matt gazed out across the canyon. A resident eagle soared above the distant ridge. "She said Mrs. Smythe still has mixed emotions—but is reconciled with her situation."

"Maybe Vi can help her work things out."

"If talk can help—yes. But Vi's doing research. She's collaborating with some behavioral scientists. They're interviewing members of families who have produced other serial killers. Trying to answer the age-old question, what leads to the development of a Sydney, nature or nurture?"

"What do you think they'll find?"

"More questions."

"I'd guess nature would win that argument— knowing what the Bible says about creation and our sin nature," she said.

"I agree. We're born slaves to sin and offered a way of escape through our belief in Christ—by God's mercy He's our only hope for rescue. Not sure how many behavioral scientists have the same starting point as we do."

"Does Vi?"

"Not yet—someone to add in our prayers."

"Does she think Wanda meant to knock her son down the stairs?"

"No. An accident—in the heat of the moment. Wanda said she didn't realize what her son had become until she saw the look in his eyes after he stabbed that guy in front of her. She just wanted him to stop—couldn't remember the pepper spray in the face or the fall down the stairs—blanked out."

"Probably good. Can you imagine—living with the realization you killed your own child?"

"Happens more often than we might think."

"Oh, Matt. How long will God withhold His judgement on this evil world?" Anna rose from her chair. "I need a refill. Want some?" She grabbed her handmade mug and headed inside.

"Sure." Matt leaned back and looked up through openings in the boughs at the blue sky. Beauty and evil all part of the same creation. Not many people stop to consider such things. Too busy chasing the soap bubbles of life instead of the essence.

"Here you go." Anna placed the carafe on the table and returned to her chair. "Have you talked to Trudeau since the Vietnamese feed Linh put on for the task force?"

"No. I haven't. That was quite a shindig."

"Did I tell you? I got her recipe for those fried pork spring rolls. She had a name for them, but I didn't write it down."

"Good. I liked those, especially with the dip she had. Didn't care much for that salad with cold noodles," he said.

Anna smiled. "I could tell. But you picked through the greens and noodles for all the pork and shrimp."

"I tried not to offend her. She was so proud of putting on a feed for everyone who worked on her daughter's case. I'm glad she didn't have any of that bird's nest soup Allen kept teasing about."

"Too bad Allen missed out," she said. "Talked to Beth after they got home. She said Misty and Yoda hit it off right away."

"I still have a hard time picturing Allen on a horse. Can't wait to see him."

"Dusty and Sarah were delighted to sell Yoda to someone who helped clear Timmy.

I get that," she said. "Just think—how many lives were affected by Sydney Smythe?"

"Yeah, people all over the state," he said. "Trudeau sunk his teeth in that case from the start. Now, after ten years he can let it go—the geocache killer is dead."

THE END